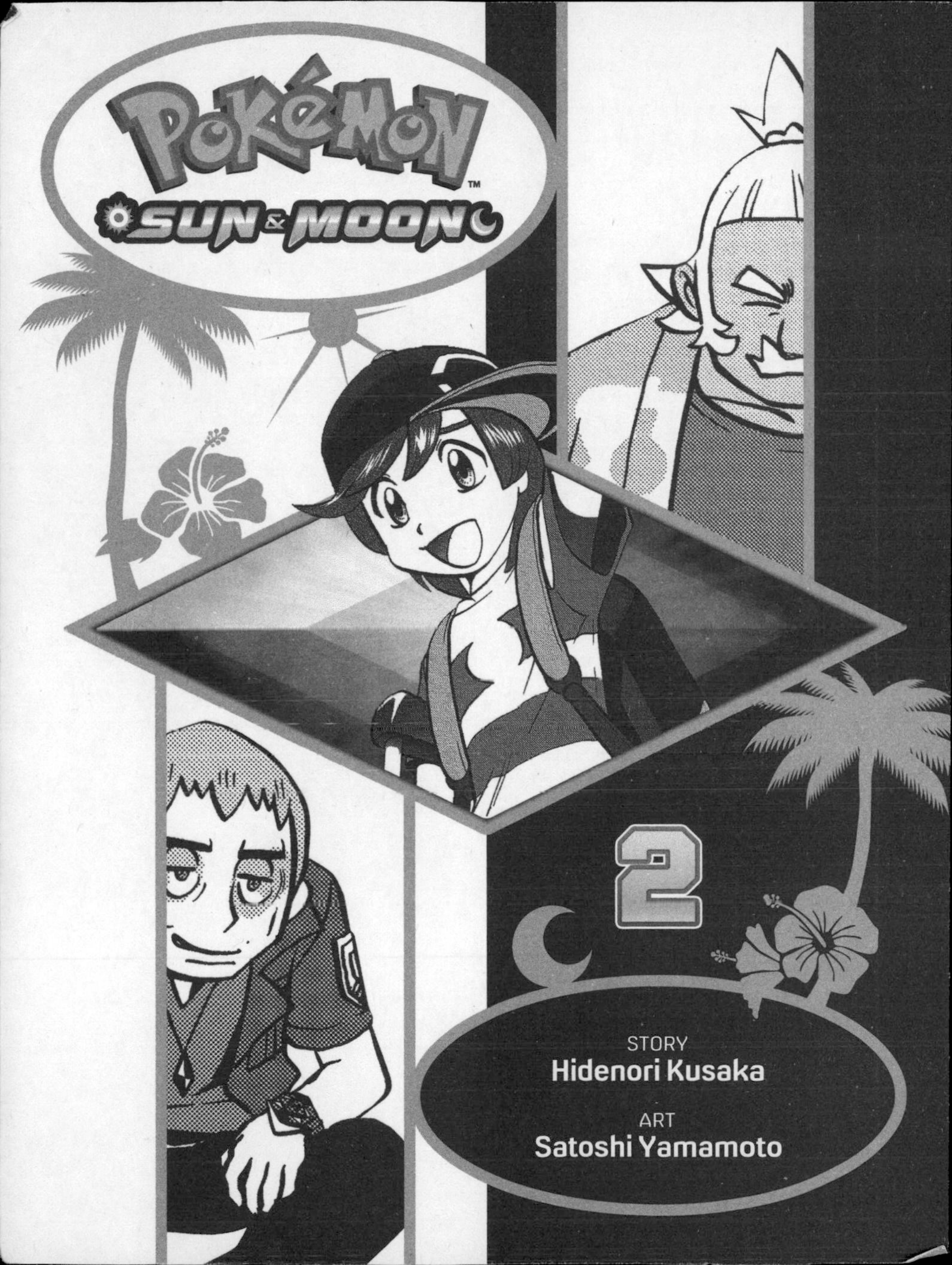
Pokémon™
Sun & Moon
2
STORY
Hidenori Kusaka
ART
Satoshi Yamamoto

Introduction

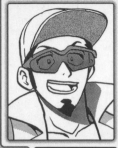

Professor Kukui

A Pokémon researcher with a laboratory on Melemele Island. An expert on Pokémon moves who likes to experience them used against himself!

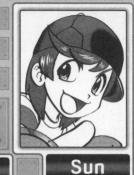

Sun

One of the main characters of this tale. A young Pokémon Trainer who makes a living doing all sorts of odd jobs, including working as a delivery boy. His dream is to save up a hundred million dollars!

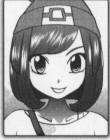

Moon

One of the main characters of this tale. A pharmacist who has traveled to Alola from a faraway region. She is a self-confident original thinker. She is also an excellent archer.

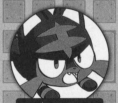

Dollar (Litten)

Cent (Alolan Meowth)

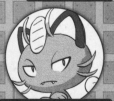

Character

Lillie

A timid girl found washed up on the beach. She carries a strange Pokémon whom she calls Nebby.

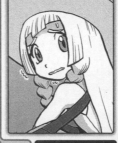

Gladion

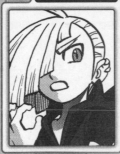

A mysterious loner.

Hala

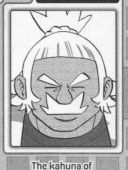

The kahuna of Melemele Island. Realizing that the Legendary Tapu Pokémon of the islands are angry about something, he begins working with the other kahunas to find out why.

Tapu Koko

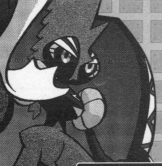

CONTENTS

ADVENTURE 4   The Decision and the ······ 07
Tournament of Six

ADVENTURE 5   The Announcement ········ 33
and the Prize

ADVENTURE 6   The Party Crasher and ····· 59
Guzma the Destroyer

ADVENTURE 7   The Final Match and ········ 85
a Surprising Finale!

Zzt zzt...♫

Adventure 4
The Decision and the Tournament of Six

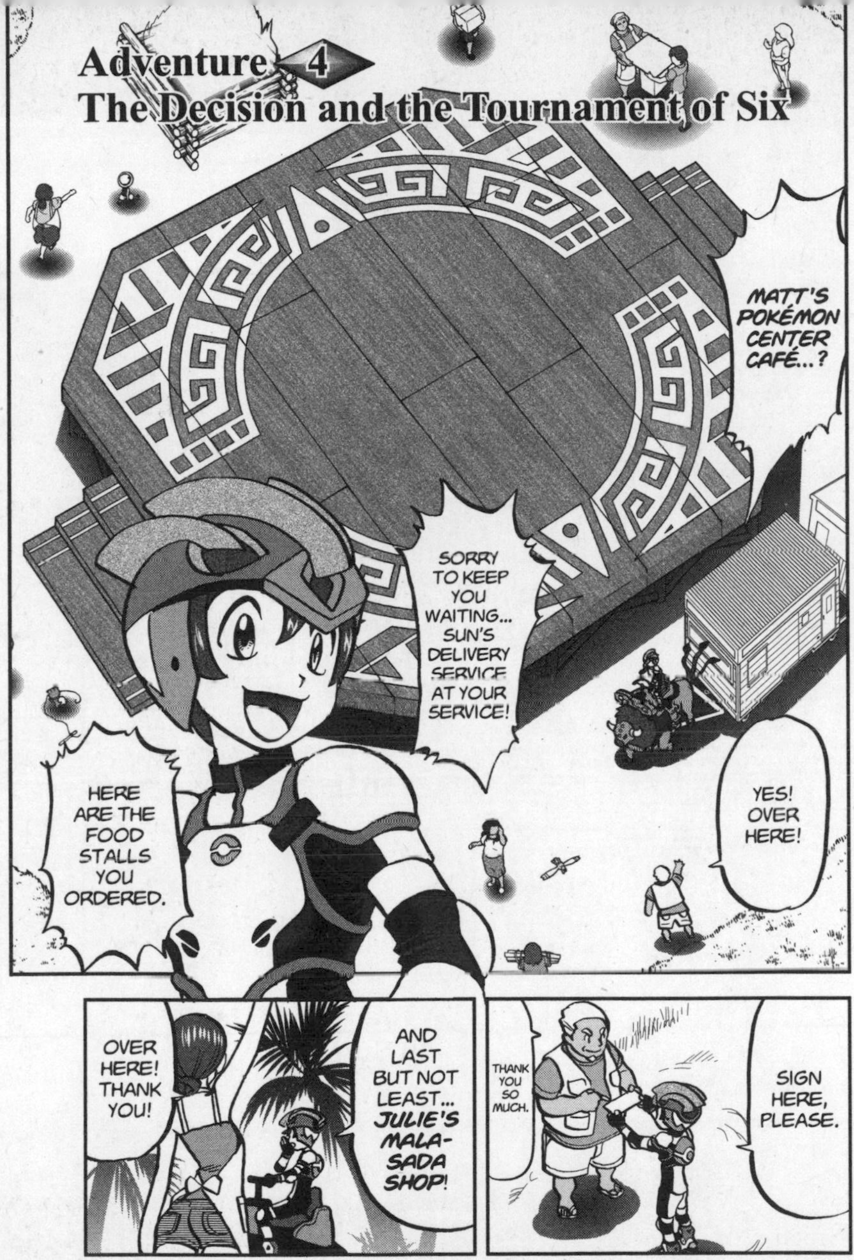

MATT'S POKÉMON CENTER CAFÉ...?
SORRY TO KEEP YOU WAITING... SUN'S DELIVERY SERVICE AT YOUR SERVICE!
YES! OVER HERE!
HERE ARE THE FOOD STALLS YOU ORDERED.
SIGN HERE, PLEASE.
THANK YOU SO MUCH.
AND LAST BUT NOT LEAST... JULIE'S MALA-SADA SHOP!
OVER HERE! THANK YOU!

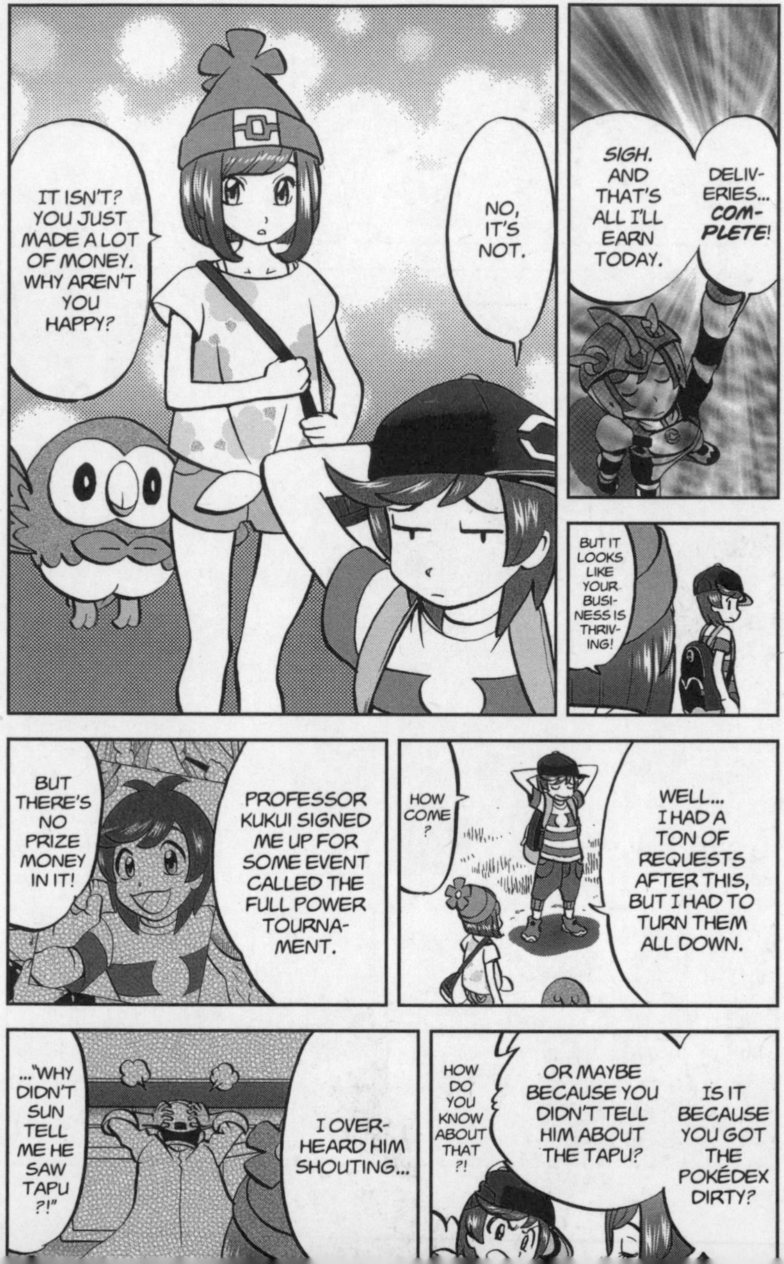
DELIVERIES... COMPLETE!
SIGH. AND THAT'S ALL I'LL EARN TODAY.
BUT IT LOOKS LIKE YOUR BUSINESS IS THRIVING!
NO, IT'S NOT.
IT ISN'T? YOU JUST MADE A LOT OF MONEY. WHY AREN'T YOU HAPPY?
WELL... I HAD A TON OF REQUESTS AFTER THIS, BUT I HAD TO TURN THEM ALL DOWN.
HOW COME?
PROFESSOR KUKUI SIGNED ME UP FOR SOME EVENT CALLED THE FULL POWER TOURNAMENT.
BUT THERE'S NO PRIZE MONEY IN IT!
IS IT BECAUSE YOU GOT THE POKÉDEX DIRTY?
OR MAYBE BECAUSE YOU DIDN'T TELL HIM ABOUT THE TAPU?
HOW DO YOU KNOW ABOUT THAT?!
I OVERHEARD HIM SHOUTING...
..."WHY DIDN'T SUN TELL ME HE SAW TAPU?!"

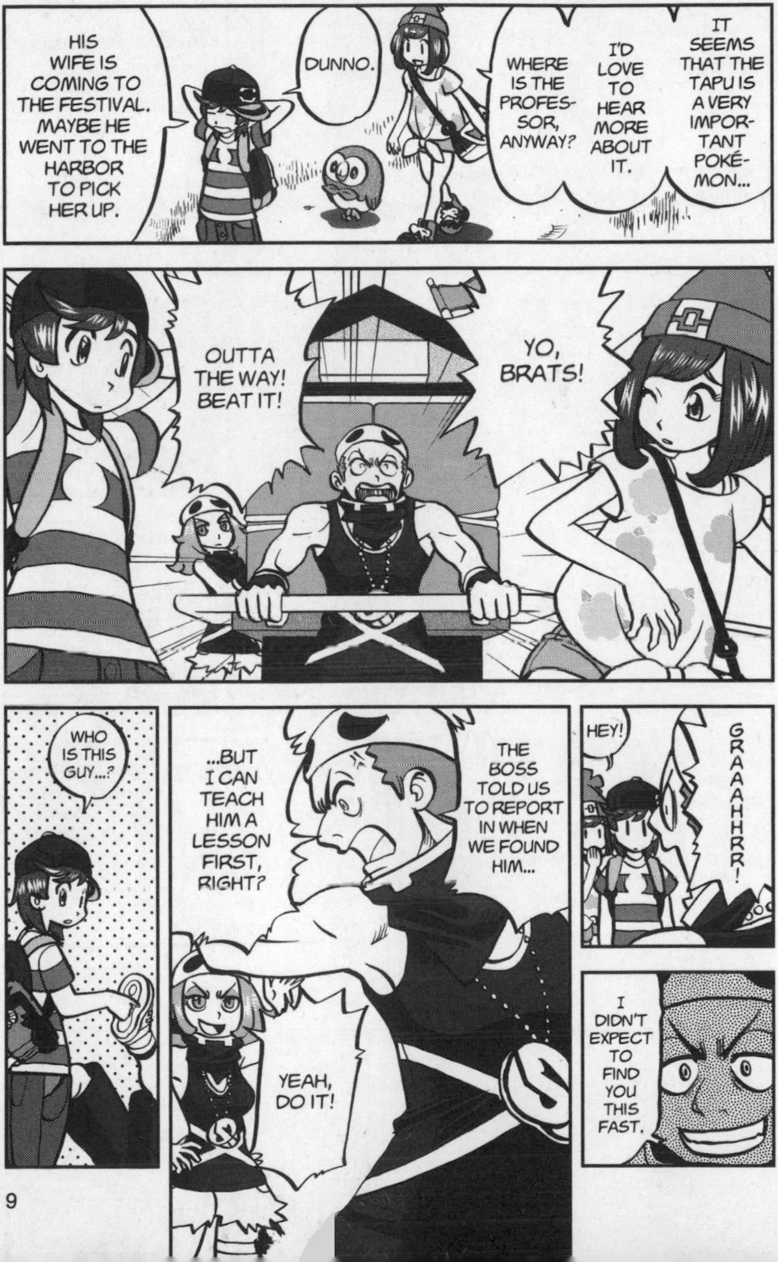
IT SEEMS THAT THE TAPU IS A VERY IMPORTANT POKÉMON...
I'D LOVE TO HEAR MORE ABOUT IT.
WHERE IS THE PROFESSOR, ANYWAY?
DUNNO.
HIS WIFE IS COMING TO THE FESTIVAL. MAYBE HE WENT TO THE HARBOR TO PICK HER UP.
YO, BRATS!
OUTTA THE WAY! BEAT IT!
GRAAAHHRR!
HEY!
I DIDN'T EXPECT TO FIND YOU THIS FAST.
THE BOSS TOLD US TO REPORT IN WHEN WE FOUND HIM...
...BUT I CAN TEACH HIM A LESSON FIRST, RIGHT?
YEAH, DO IT!
WHO IS THIS GUY...?

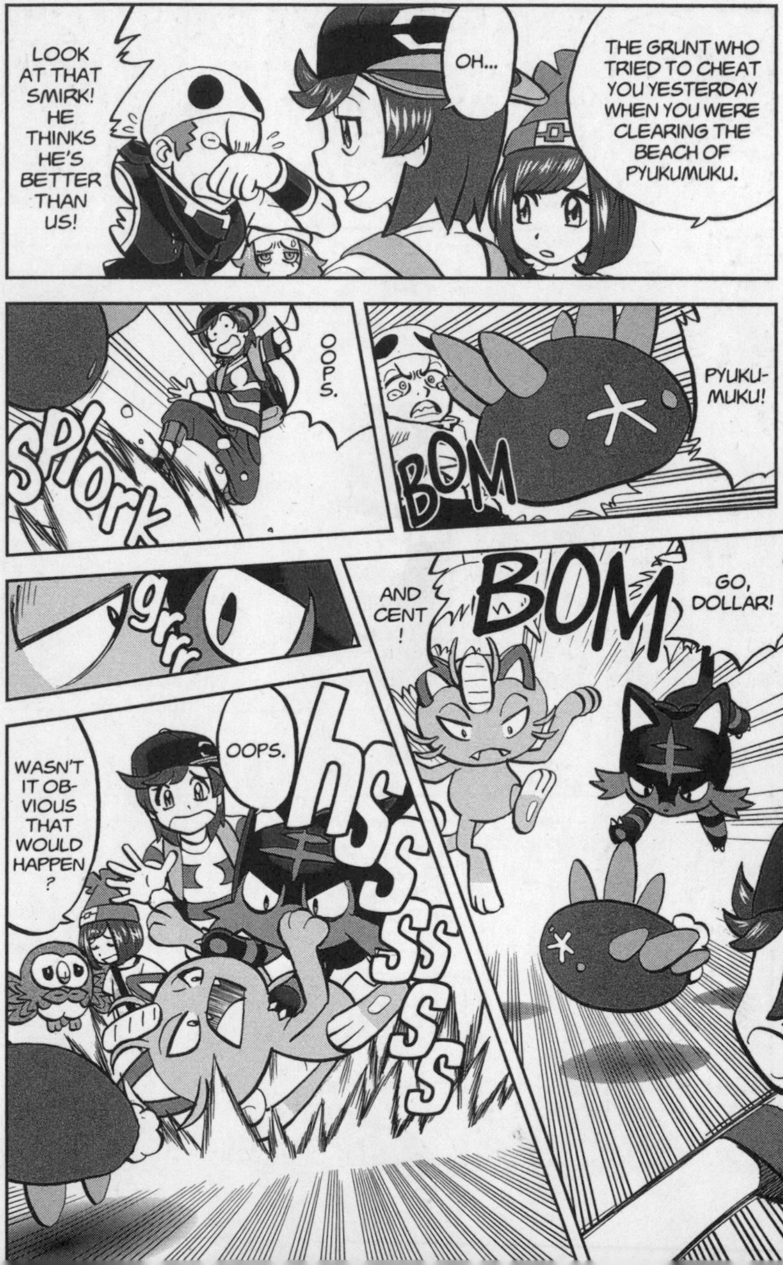
THE GRUNT WHO TRIED TO CHEAT YOU YESTERDAY WHEN YOU WERE CLEARING THE BEACH OF PYUKUMUKU.
OH...
LOOK AT THAT SMIRK! HE THINKS HE'S BETTER THAN US!
PYUKU-MUKU!
BOM
OOPS.
Splork
GO, DOLLAR!
BOM
AND CENT!
grrr
OOPS.
WASN'T IT OB-VIOUS THAT WOULD HAPPEN?
hSSSSSSS

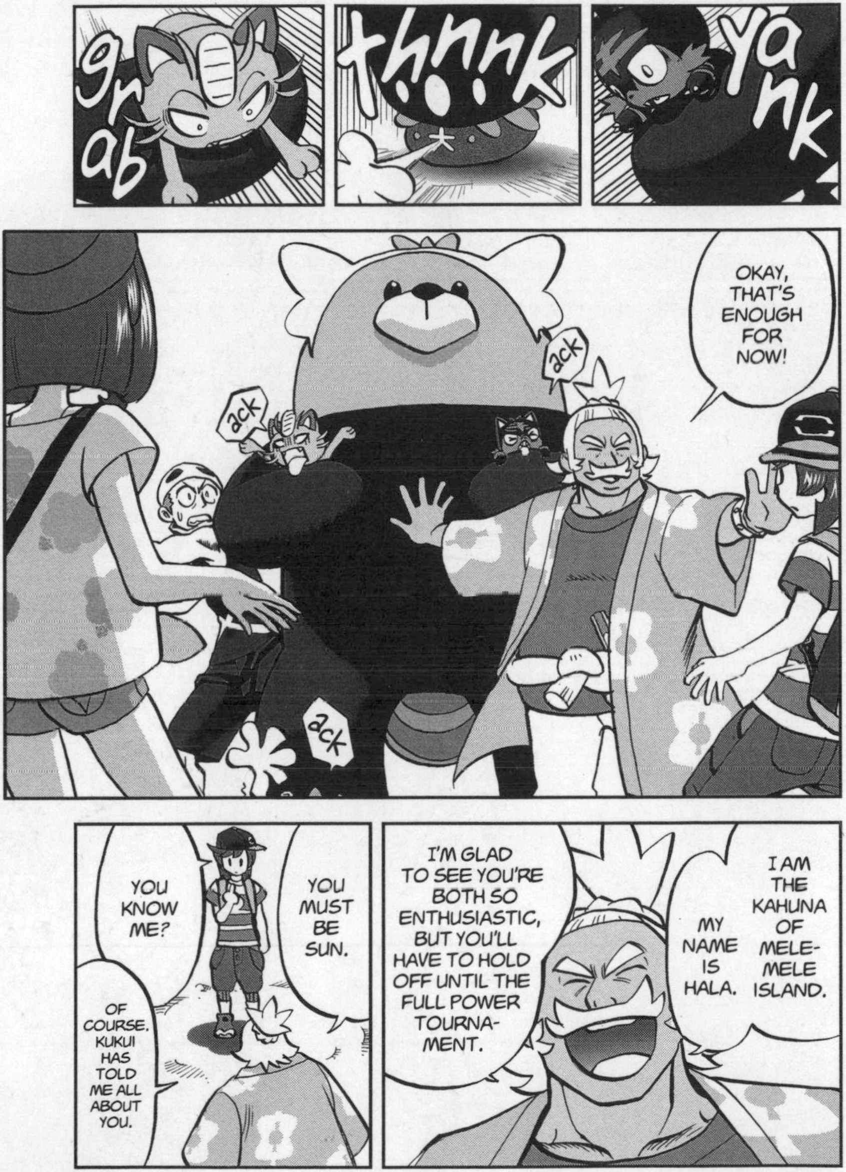
yank
thnnk
grab
OKAY, THAT'S ENOUGH FOR NOW!
ack
ack
ack
I AM THE KAHUNA OF MELE-MELE ISLAND.
MY NAME IS HALA.
I'M GLAD TO SEE YOU'RE BOTH SO ENTHUSIASTIC, BUT YOU'LL HAVE TO HOLD OFF UNTIL THE FULL POWER TOURNA-MENT.
YOU MUST BE SUN.
YOU KNOW ME?
OF COURSE. KUKUI HAS TOLD ME ALL ABOUT YOU.

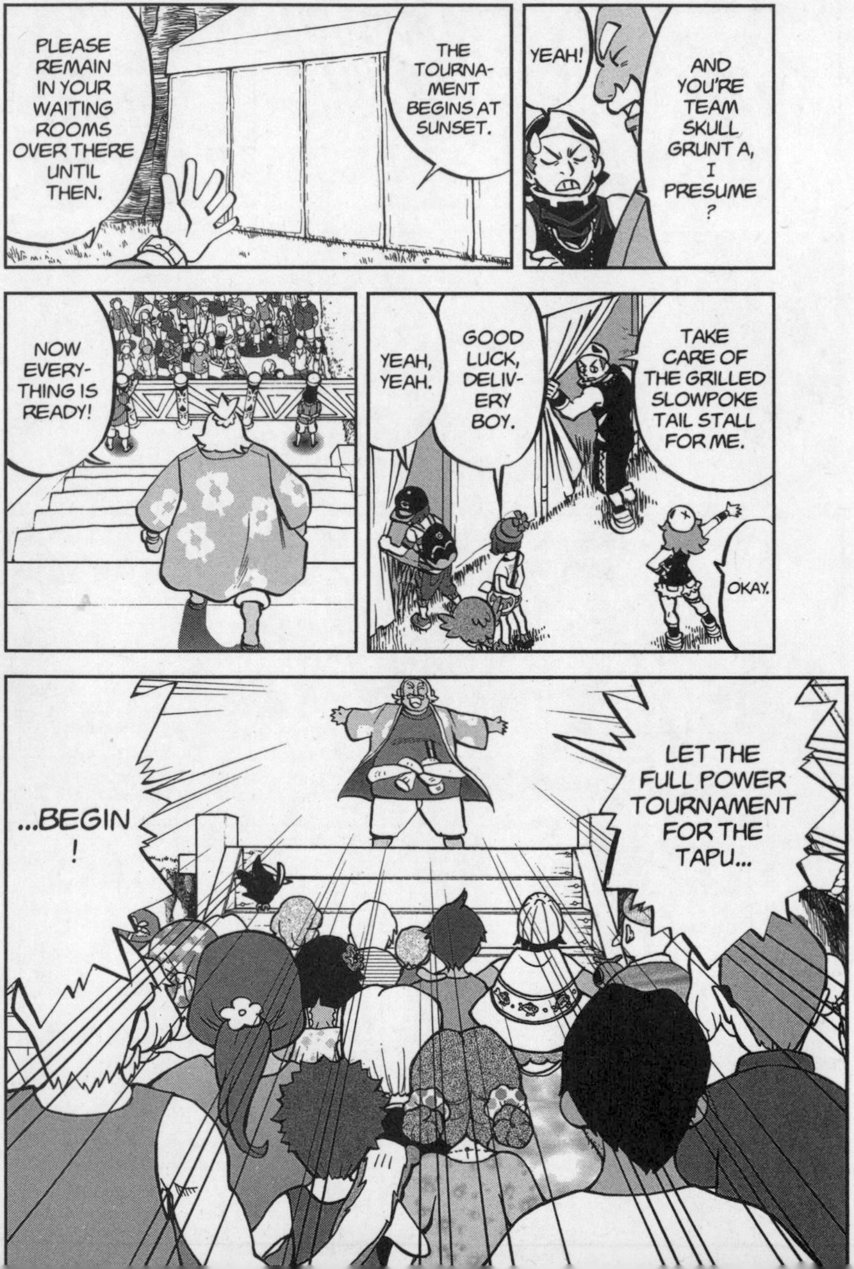
AND YOU'RE TEAM SKULL GRUNT A, I PRESUME?
YEAH!
THE TOURNAMENT BEGINS AT SUNSET.
PLEASE REMAIN IN YOUR WAITING ROOMS OVER THERE UNTIL THEN.
TAKE CARE OF THE GRILLED SLOWPOKE TAIL STALL FOR ME.
GOOD LUCK, DELIVERY BOY.
YEAH, YEAH.
OKAY.
NOW EVERYTHING IS READY!
LET THE FULL POWER TOURNAMENT FOR THE TAPU...
...BEGIN!

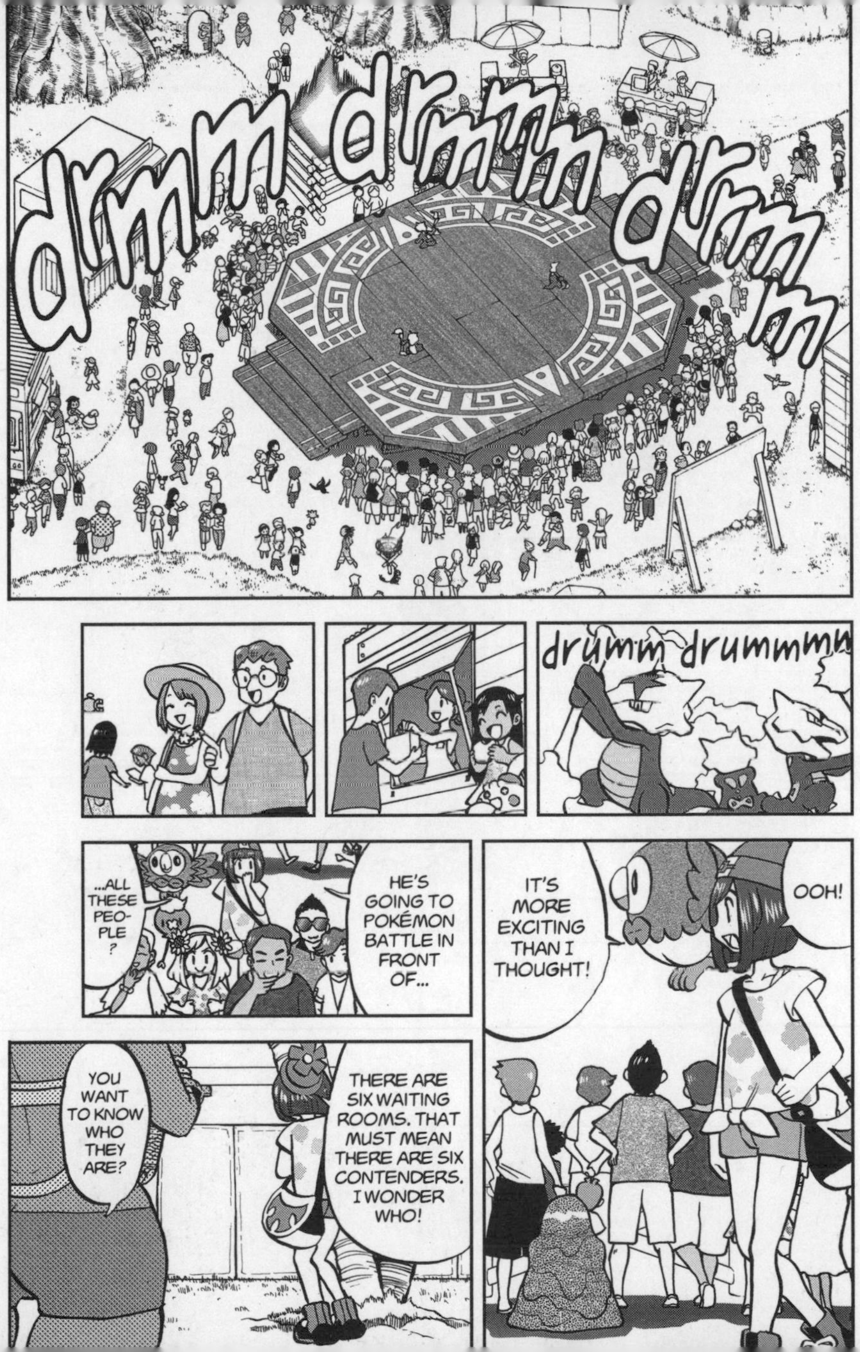
drmm drmm drmm
drumm drummmm
OOH!
IT'S MORE EXCITING THAN I THOUGHT!
HE'S GOING TO POKÉMON BATTLE IN FRONT OF...
...ALL THESE PEO- PLE?
THERE ARE SIX WAITING ROOMS. THAT MUST MEAN THERE ARE SIX CONTENDERS. I WONDER WHO!
YOU WANT TO KNOW WHO THEY ARE?

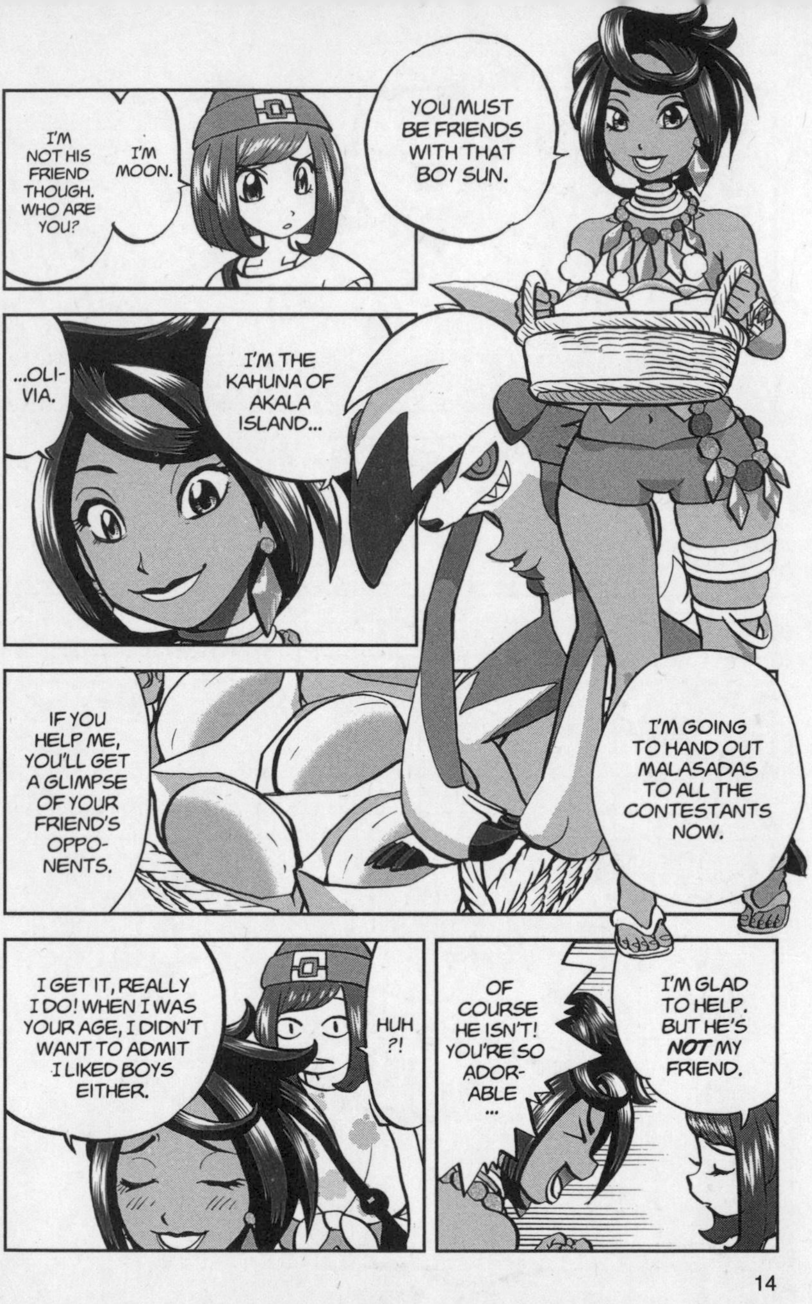
YOU MUST BE FRIENDS WITH THAT BOY SUN.
I'M MOON.
I'M NOT HIS FRIEND THOUGH. WHO ARE YOU?
I'M THE KAHUNA OF AKALA ISLAND...
...OLIVIA.
I'M GOING TO HAND OUT MALASADAS TO ALL THE CONTESTANTS NOW.
IF YOU HELP ME, YOU'LL GET A GLIMPSE OF YOUR FRIEND'S OPPONENTS.
I'M GLAD TO HELP. BUT HE'S *NOT* MY FRIEND.
OF COURSE HE ISN'T! YOU'RE SO ADORABLE...
HUH?!
I GET IT, REALLY I DO! WHEN I WAS YOUR AGE, I DIDN'T WANT TO ADMIT I LIKED BOYS EITHER.

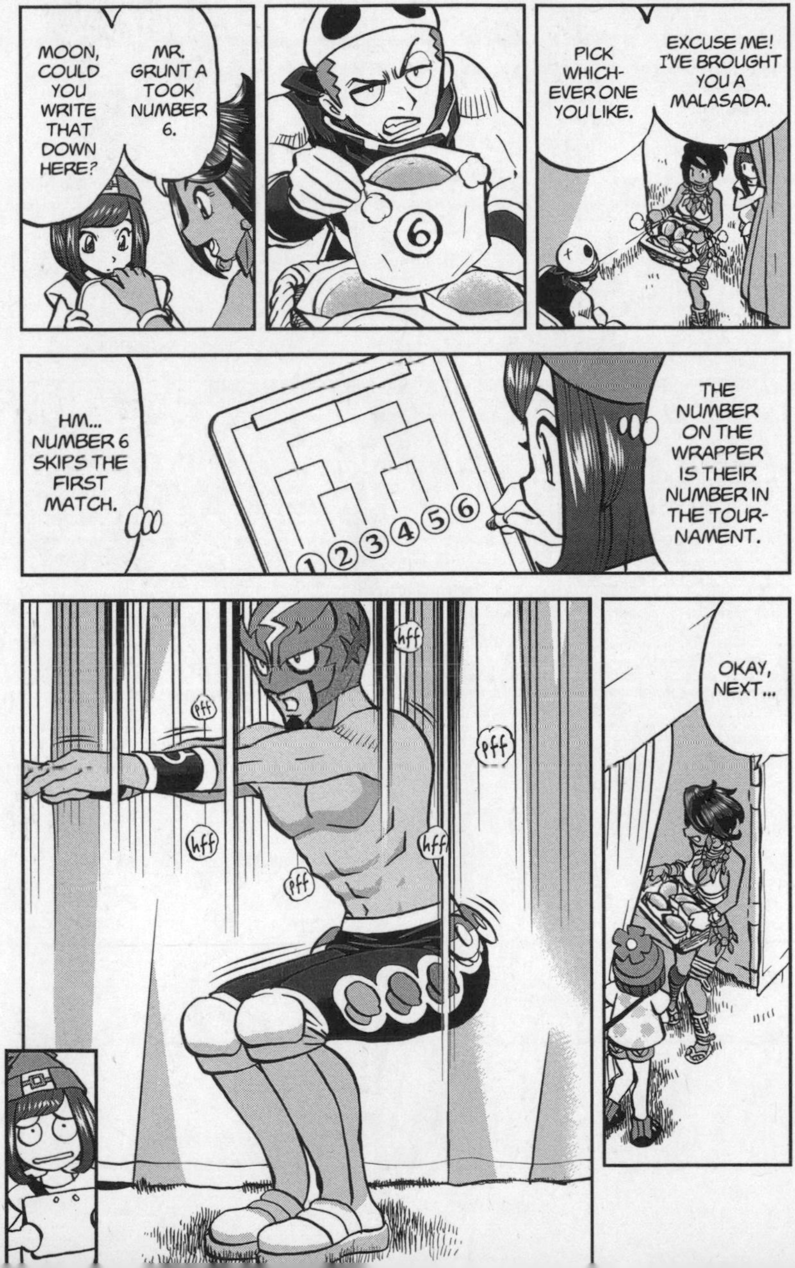

EXCUSE ME! I'VE BROUGHT YOU A MALASADA.
PICK WHICH-EVER ONE YOU LIKE.
6
MR. GRUNT A TOOK NUMBER 6.
MOON, COULD YOU WRITE THAT DOWN HERE?
THE NUMBER ON THE WRAPPER IS THEIR NUMBER IN THE TOUR-NAMENT.
1 2 3 4 5 6
HM... NUMBER 6 SKIPS THE FIRST MATCH.
OKAY, NEXT...
hff
pff
pff
hff
hff
pff

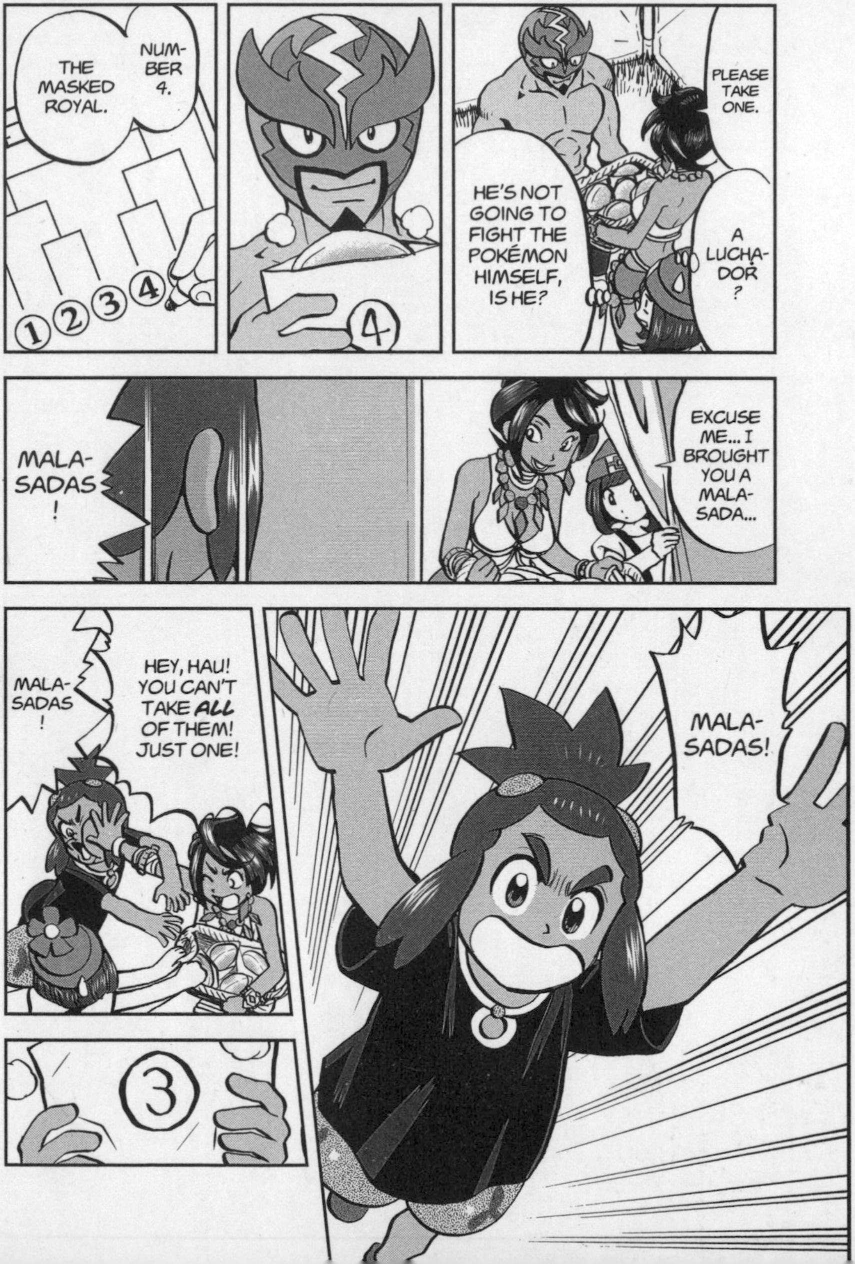
PLEASE TAKE ONE.
A LUCHADOR?
HE'S NOT GOING TO FIGHT THE POKÉMON HIMSELF, IS HE?
NUMBER 4.
THE MASKED ROYAL.
EXCUSE ME... I BROUGHT YOU A MALASADA...
MALASADAS!
MALASADAS!
HEY, HAU! YOU CAN'T TAKE **ALL** OF THEM! JUST ONE!
MALASADAS!

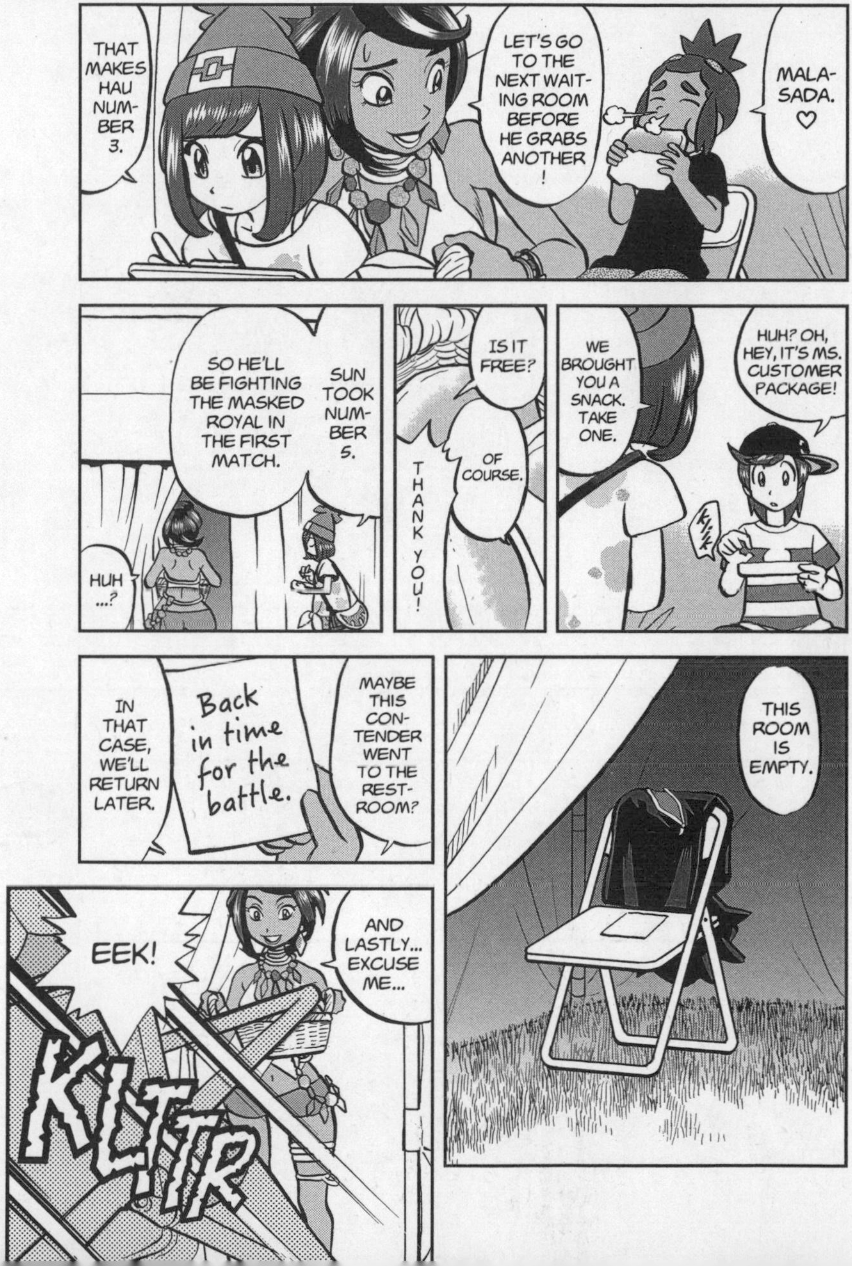
MALA-SADA. ♡
LET'S GO TO THE NEXT WAITING ROOM BEFORE HE GRABS ANOTHER!
THAT MAKES HAU NUMBER 3.
HUH? OH, HEY, IT'S MS. CUSTOMER PACKAGE!
WE BROUGHT YOU A SNACK. TAKE ONE.
IS IT FREE?
OF COURSE.
THANK YOU!
SUN TOOK NUMBER 5.
SO HE'LL BE FIGHTING THE MASKED ROYAL IN THE FIRST MATCH.
HUH ...?
THIS ROOM IS EMPTY.
MAYBE THIS CONTENDER WENT TO THE RESTROOM?
Back in time for the battle.
IN THAT CASE, WE'LL RETURN LATER.
AND LASTLY... EXCUSE ME...
EEK!
KLTTR

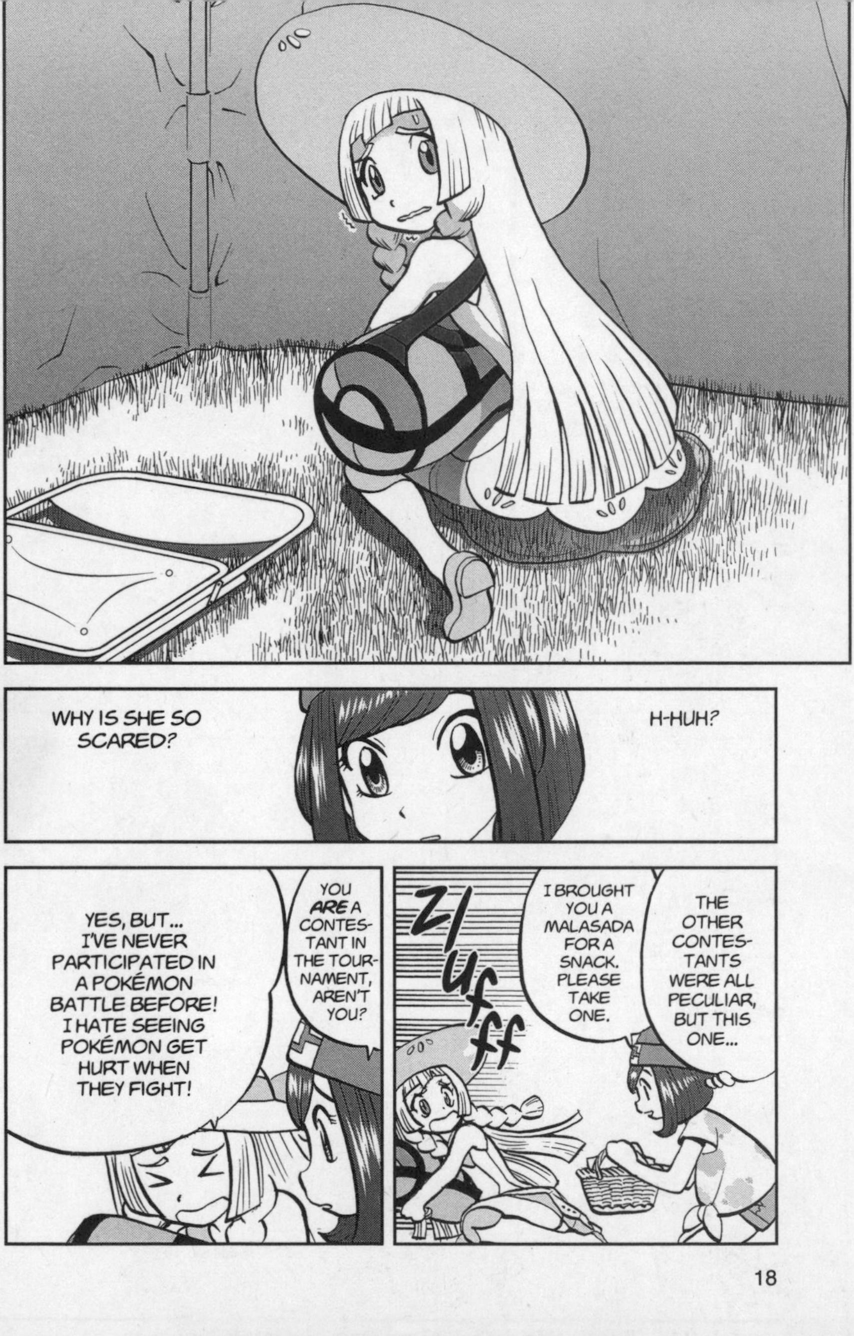
H-HUH?
WHY IS SHE SO SCARED?
THE OTHER CONTESTANTS WERE ALL PECULIAR, BUT THIS ONE...
I BROUGHT YOU A MALASADA FOR A SNACK. PLEASE TAKE ONE.
ZLUFFF
YOU *ARE* A CONTESTANT IN THE TOURNAMENT, AREN'T YOU?
YES, BUT... I'VE NEVER PARTICIPATED IN A POKÉMON BATTLE BEFORE! I HATE SEEING POKÉMON GET HURT WHEN THEY FIGHT!

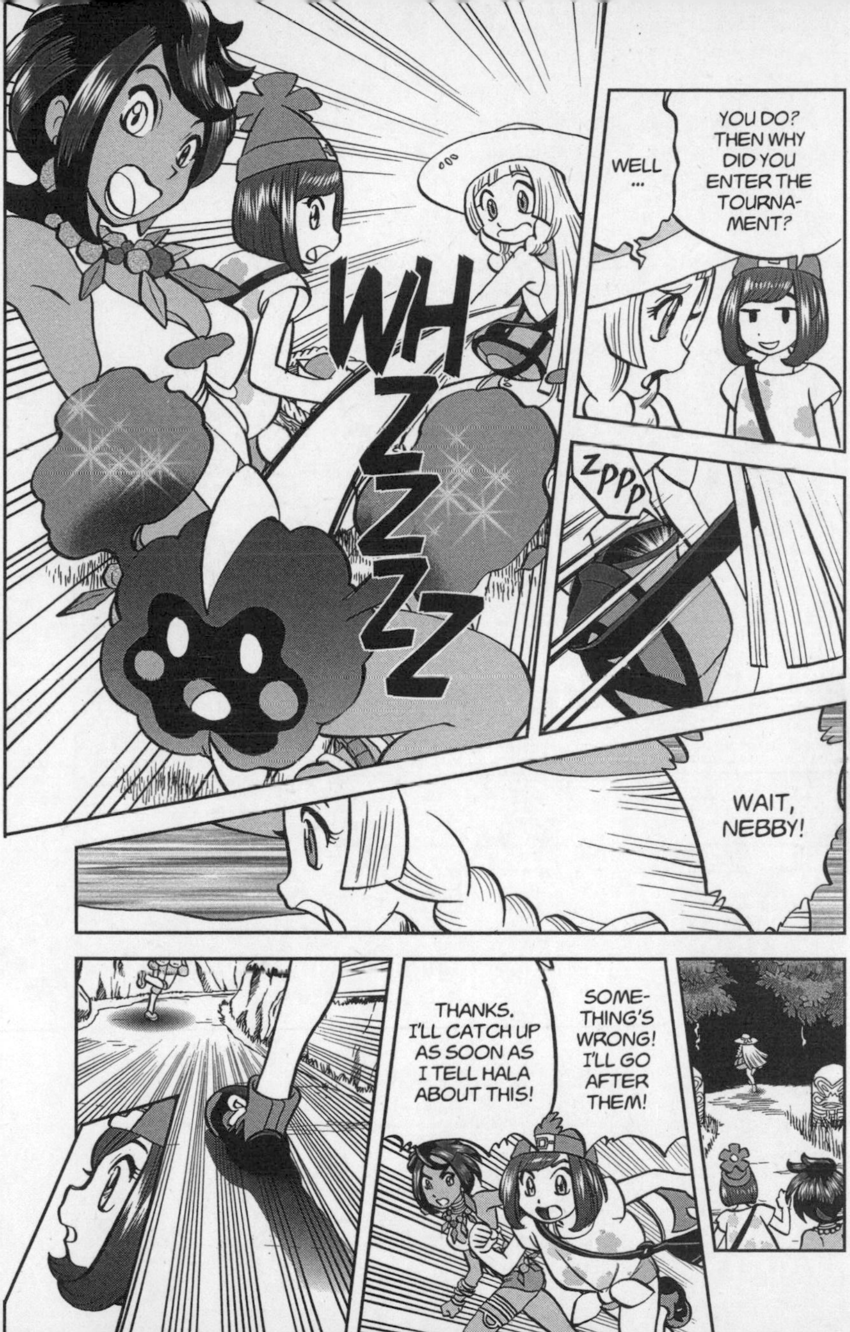
YOU DO? THEN WHY DID YOU ENTER THE TOURNAMENT?
WELL...
ZPPP
WHZZZZ
WAIT, NEBBY!
SOMETHING'S WRONG! I'LL GO AFTER THEM!
THANKS. I'LL CATCH UP AS SOON AS I TELL HALA ABOUT THIS!

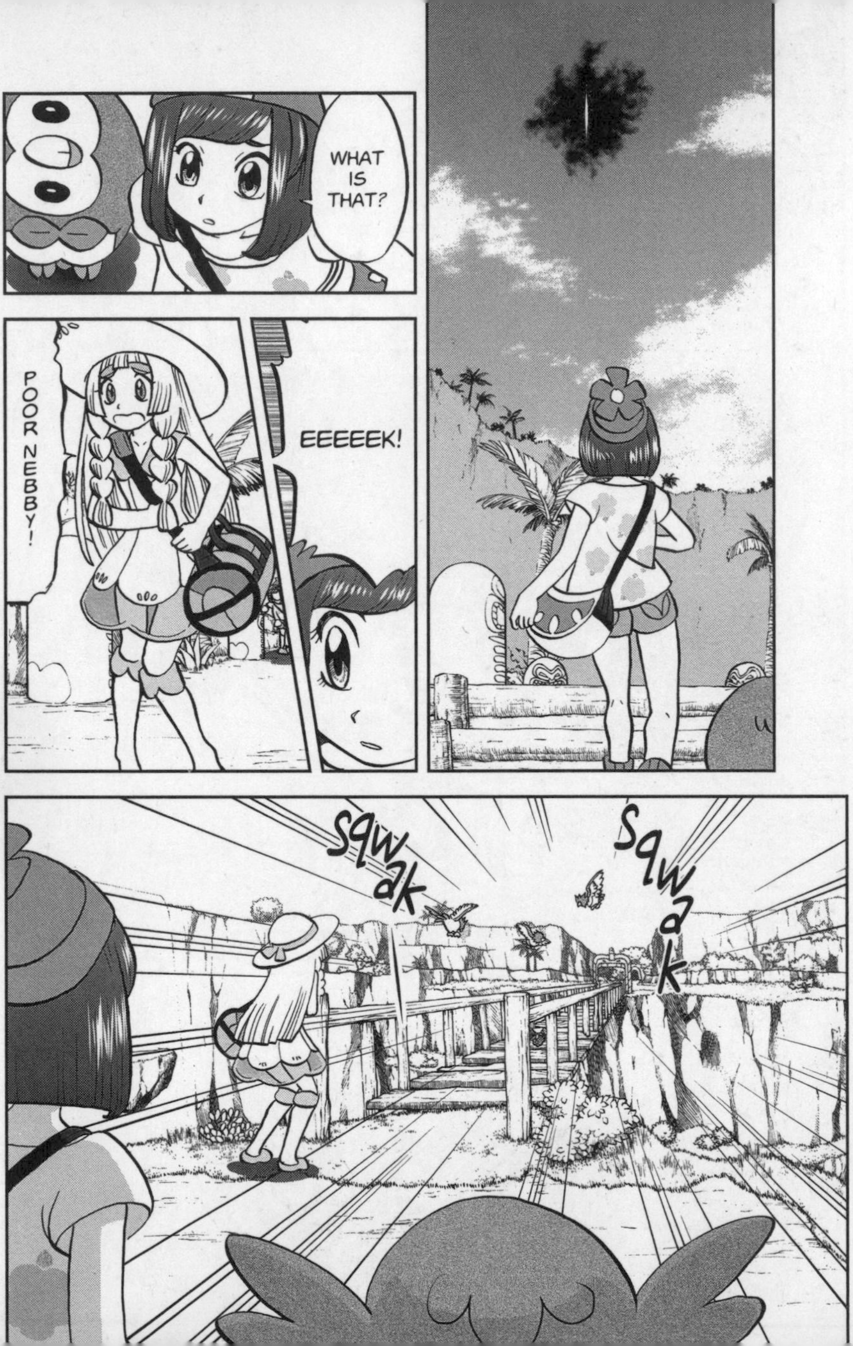
WHAT IS THAT?
EEEEEK!
POOR NEBBY!
SQWAK
SQWAK

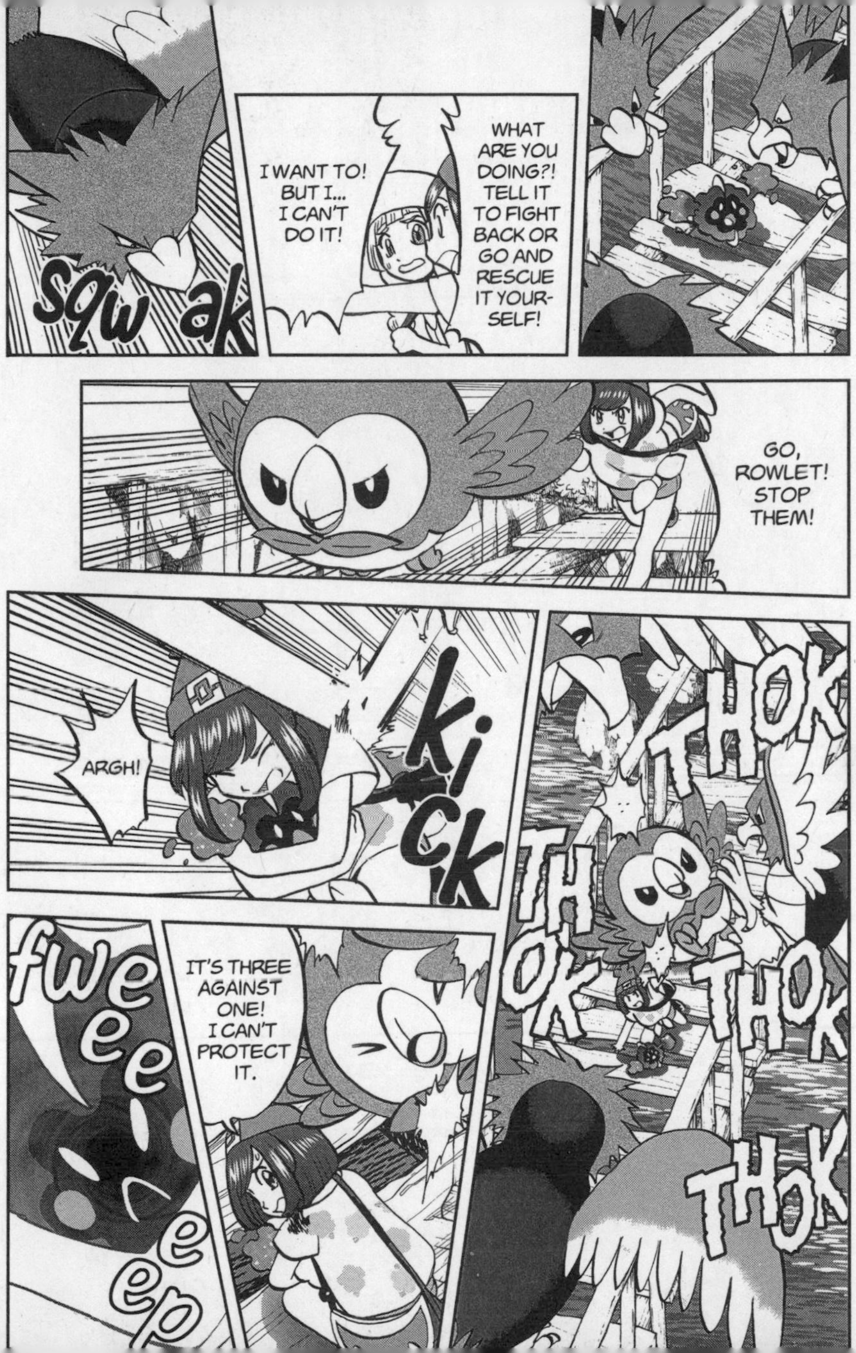
WHAT ARE YOU DOING?! TELL IT TO FIGHT BACK OR GO AND RESCUE IT YOURSELF!
I WANT TO! BUT I... I CAN'T DO IT!
sqwak
GO, ROWLET! STOP THEM!
THOK
THOK
THOK
THOK
kick
ARGH!
IT'S THREE AGAINST ONE! I CAN'T PROTECT IT.
fweeeeeep

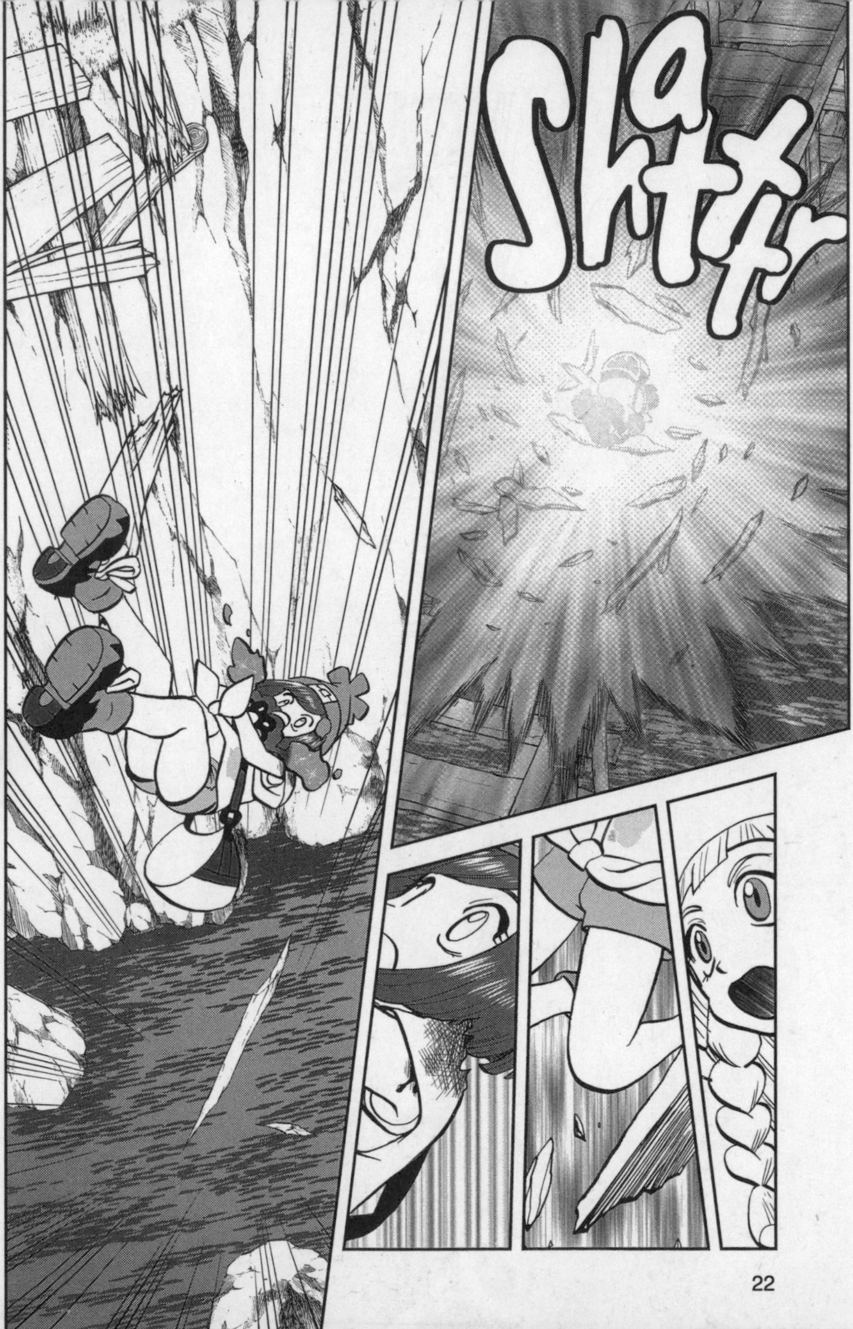
Slash

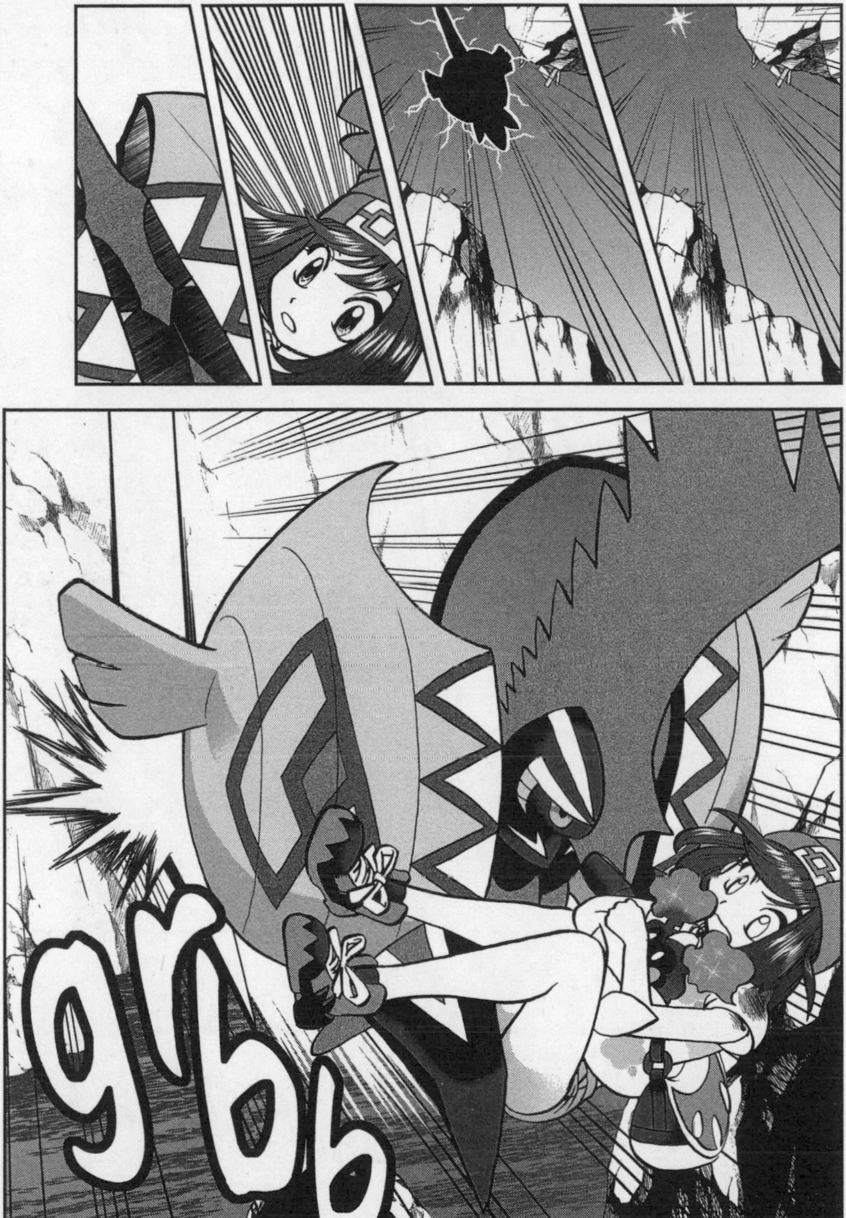
grab

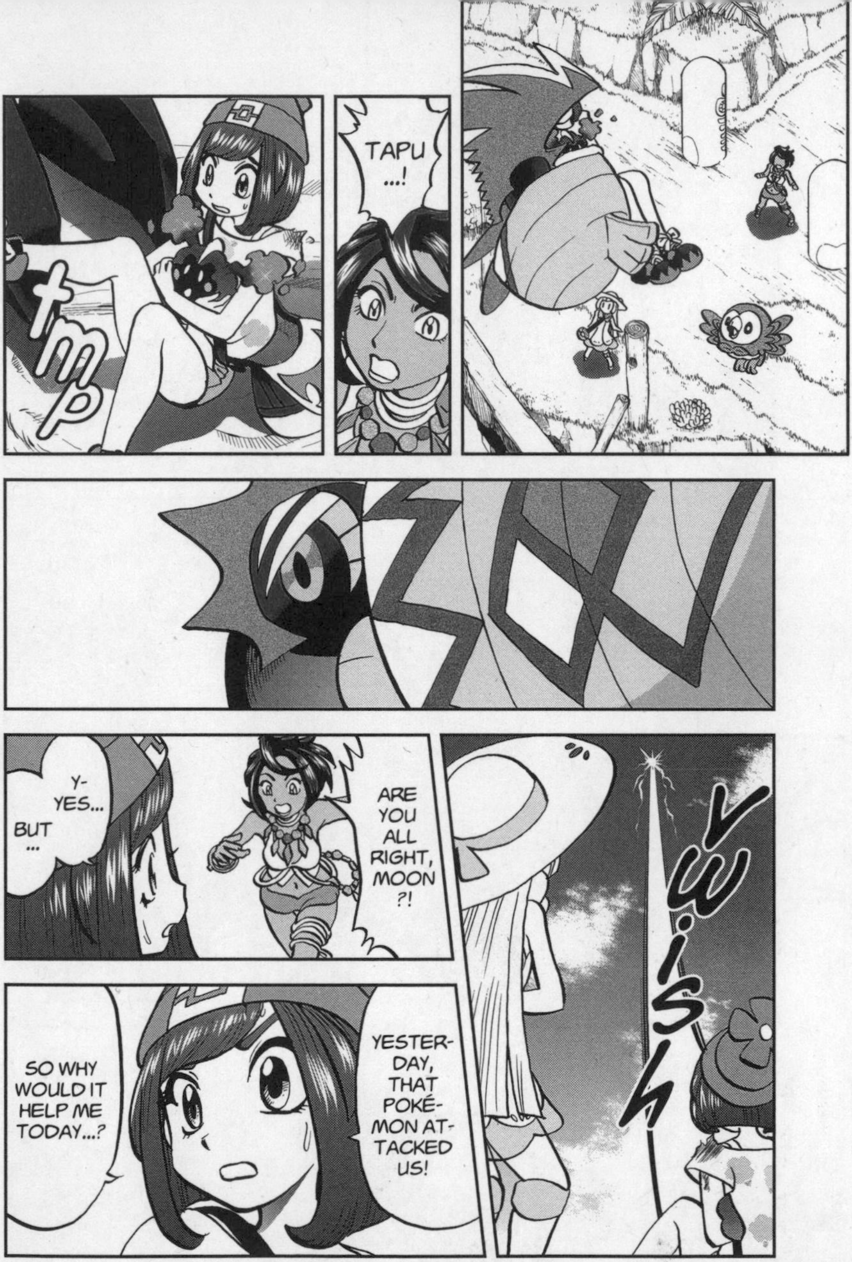
TAPU ...!
tmp
VWISH
ARE YOU ALL RIGHT, MOON ?!
Y- YES... BUT ...
YESTER-DAY, THAT POKÉ-MON AT-TACKED US!
SO WHY WOULD IT HELP ME TODAY...?

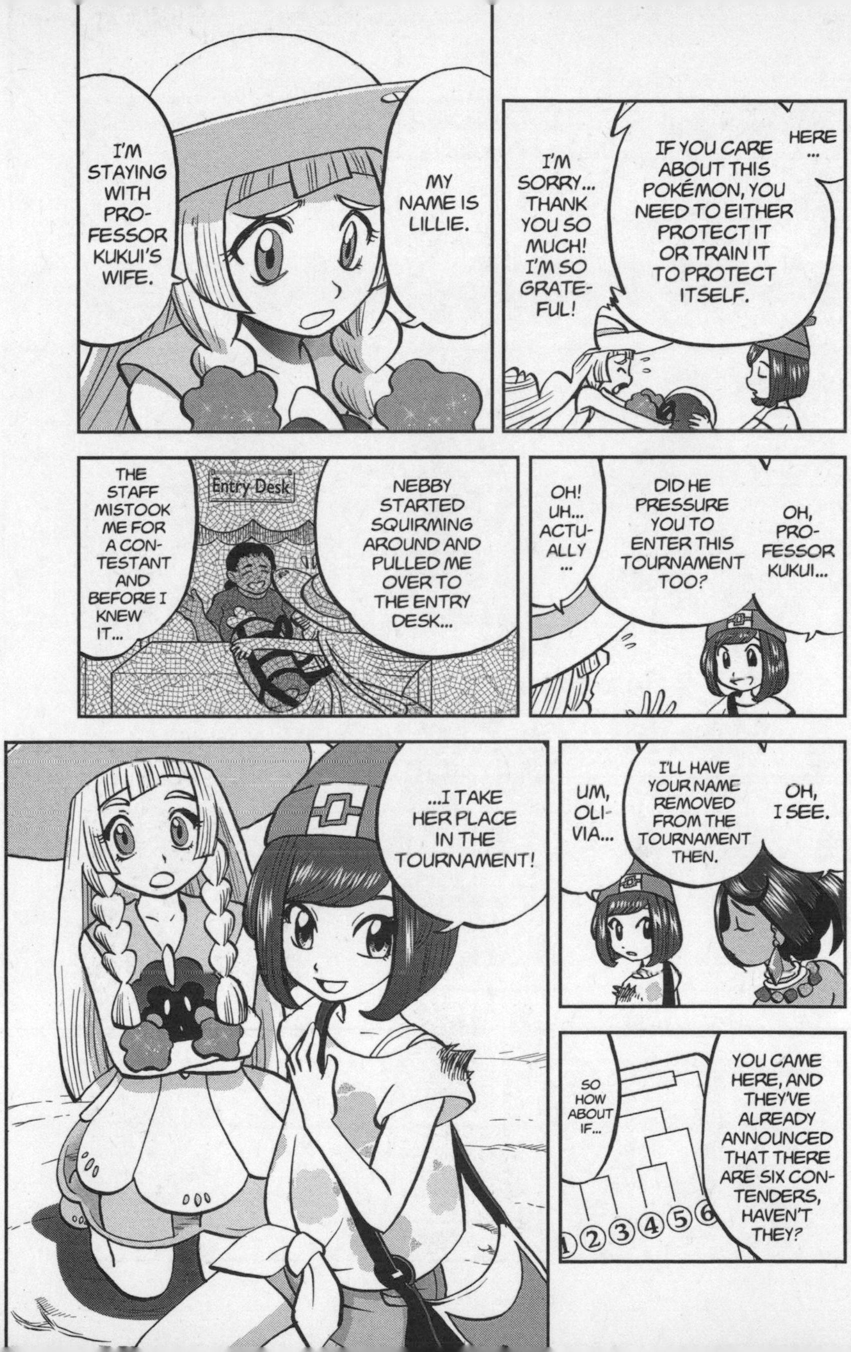
HERE...
IF YOU CARE ABOUT THIS POKÉMON, YOU NEED TO EITHER PROTECT IT OR TRAIN IT TO PROTECT ITSELF.
I'M SORRY... THANK YOU SO MUCH! I'M SO GRATEFUL!
MY NAME IS LILLIE.
I'M STAYING WITH PROFESSOR KUKUI'S WIFE.
OH, PROFESSOR KUKUI...
DID HE PRESSURE YOU TO ENTER THIS TOURNAMENT TOO?
OH! UH... ACTUALLY...
NEBBY STARTED SQUIRMING AROUND AND PULLED ME OVER TO THE ENTRY DESK...
Entry Desk
THE STAFF MISTOOK ME FOR A CONTESTANT AND BEFORE I KNEW IT...
OH, I SEE.
I'LL HAVE YOUR NAME REMOVED FROM THE TOURNAMENT THEN.
UM, OLIVIA...
YOU CAME HERE, AND THEY'VE ALREADY ANNOUNCED THAT THERE ARE SIX CONTENDERS, HAVEN'T THEY?
SO HOW ABOUT IF...
①②③④⑤⑥
...I TAKE HER PLACE IN THE TOURNAMENT!

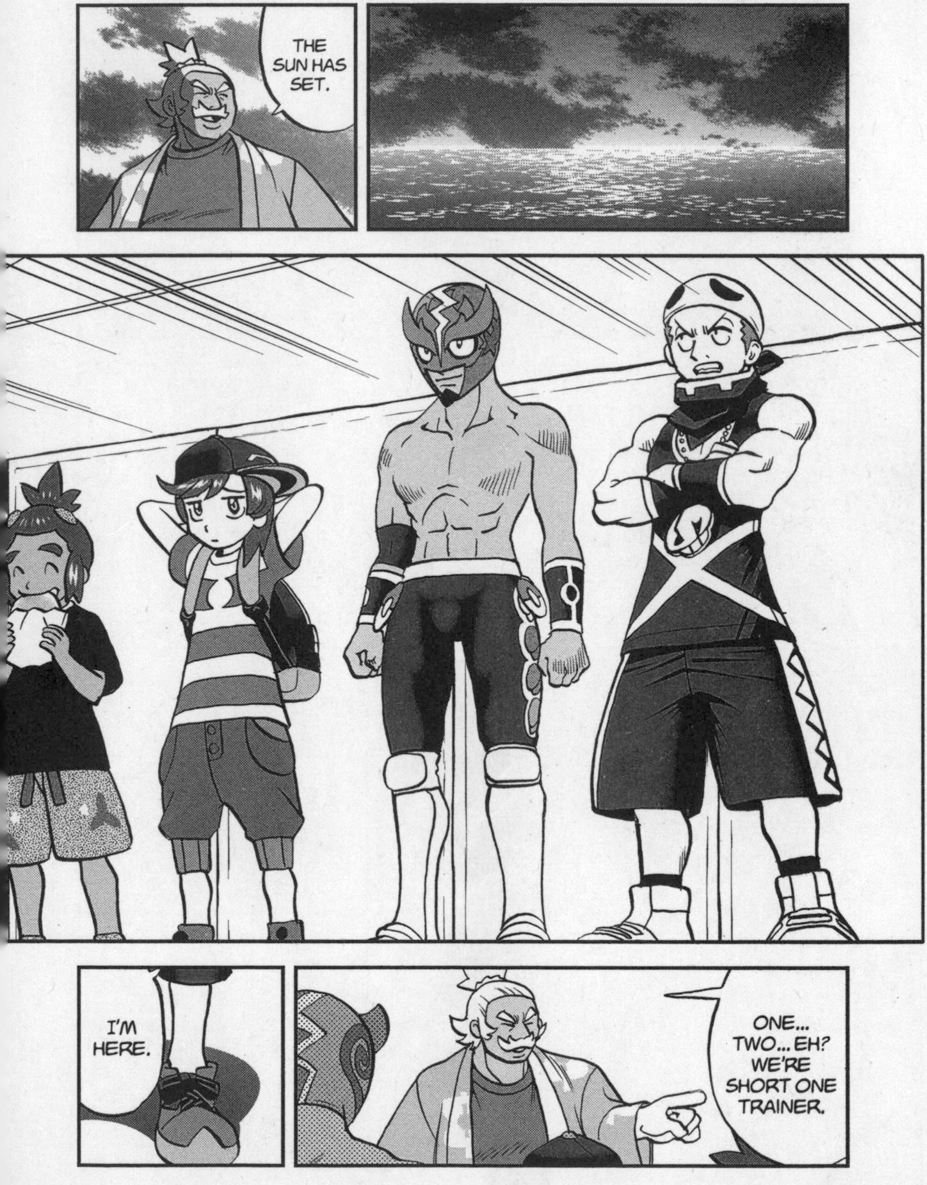
THE SUN HAS SET.
ONE... TWO... EH? WE'RE SHORT ONE TRAINER.
I'M HERE.

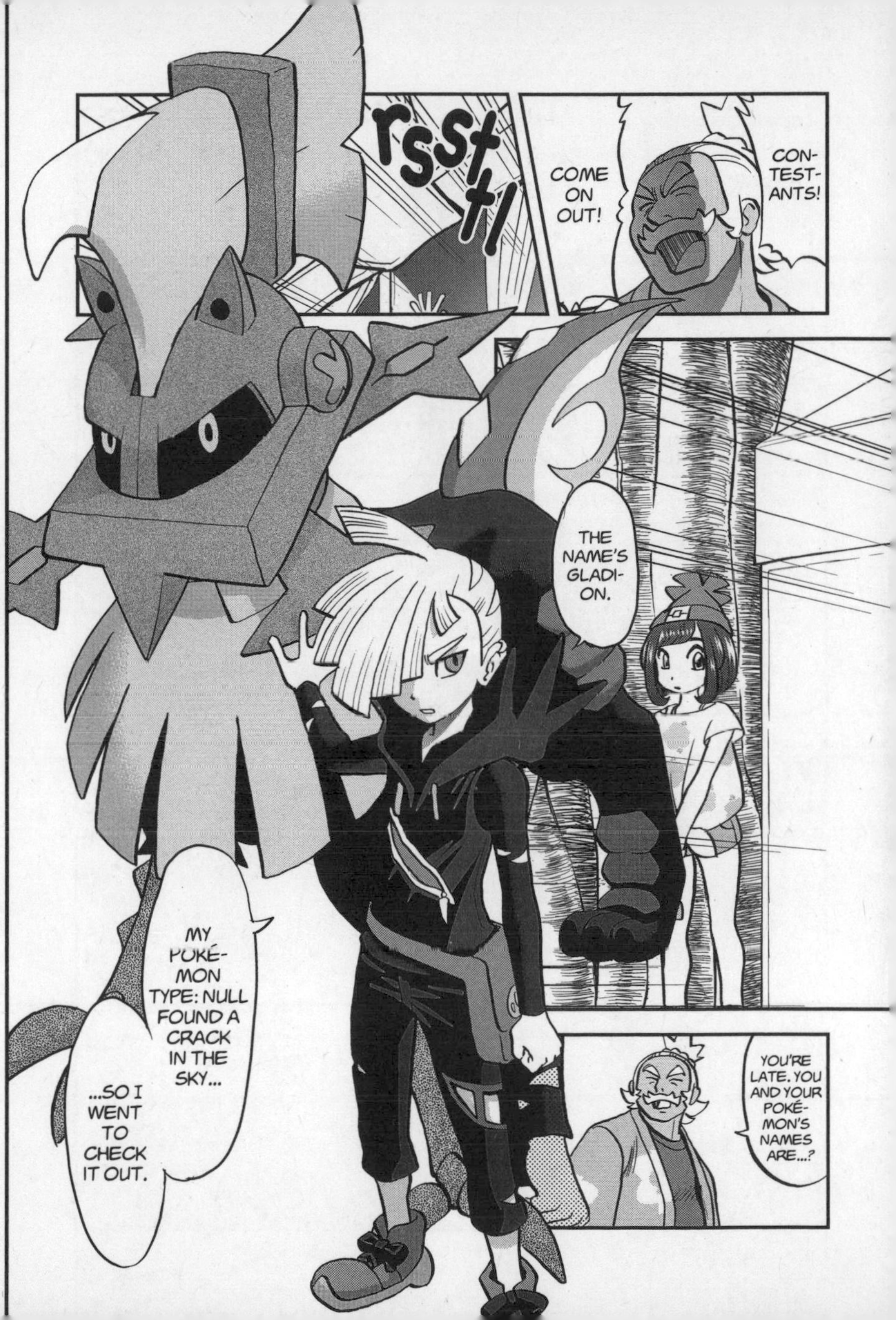
CON-TEST-ANTS!
COME ON OUT!
rsst!
YOU'RE LATE. YOU AND YOUR POKÉ-MON'S NAMES ARE...?
THE NAME'S GLADI-ON.
MY POKÉ-MON TYPE: NULL FOUND A CRACK IN THE SKY...
...SO I WENT TO CHECK IT OUT.

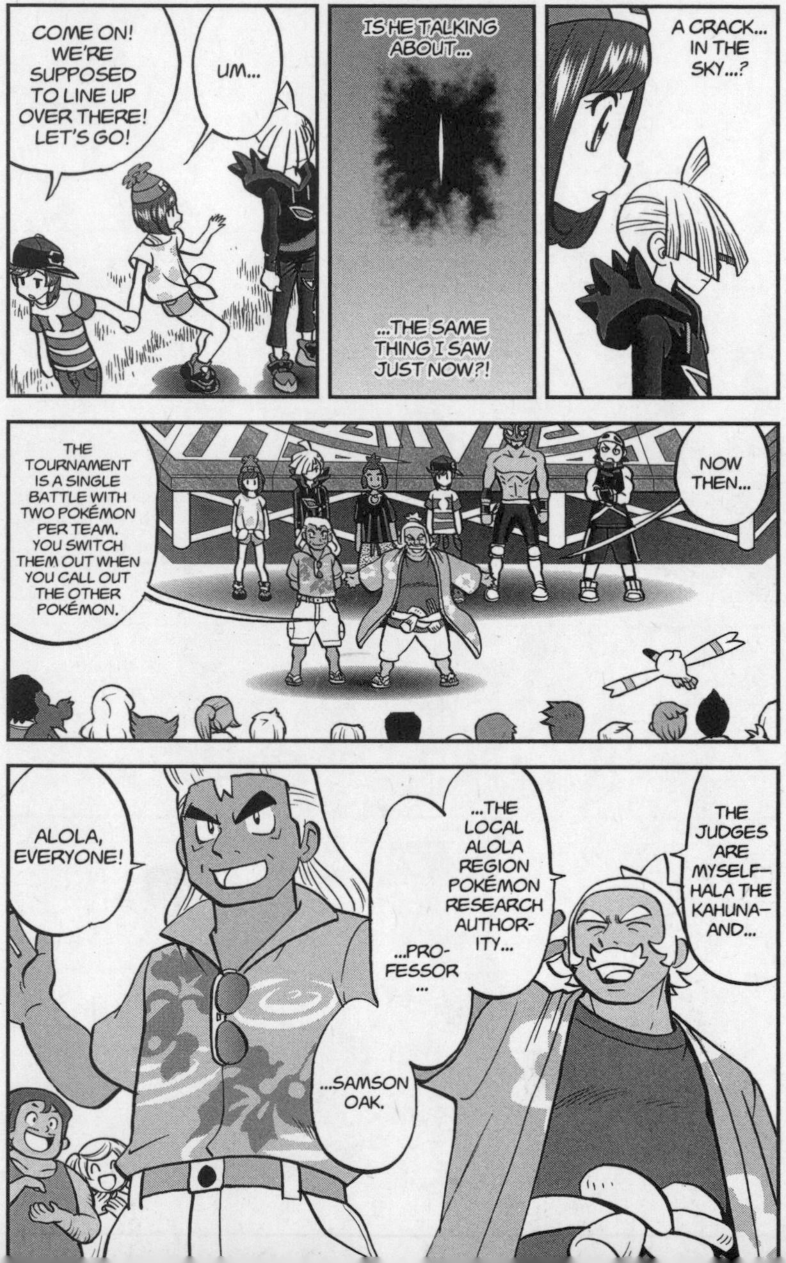
A CRACK... IN THE SKY...?
IS HE TALKING ABOUT...
...THE SAME THING I SAW JUST NOW?!
UM...
COME ON! WE'RE SUPPOSED TO LINE UP OVER THERE! LET'S GO!
NOW THEN...
THE TOURNAMENT IS A SINGLE BATTLE WITH TWO POKÉMON PER TEAM. YOU SWITCH THEM OUT WHEN YOU CALL OUT THE OTHER POKÉMON.
THE JUDGES ARE MYSELF—HALA THE KAHUNA—AND...
...THE LOCAL ALOLA REGION POKÉMON RESEARCH AUTHORITY...
...PROFESSOR...
...SAMSON OAK.
ALOLA, EVERYONE!

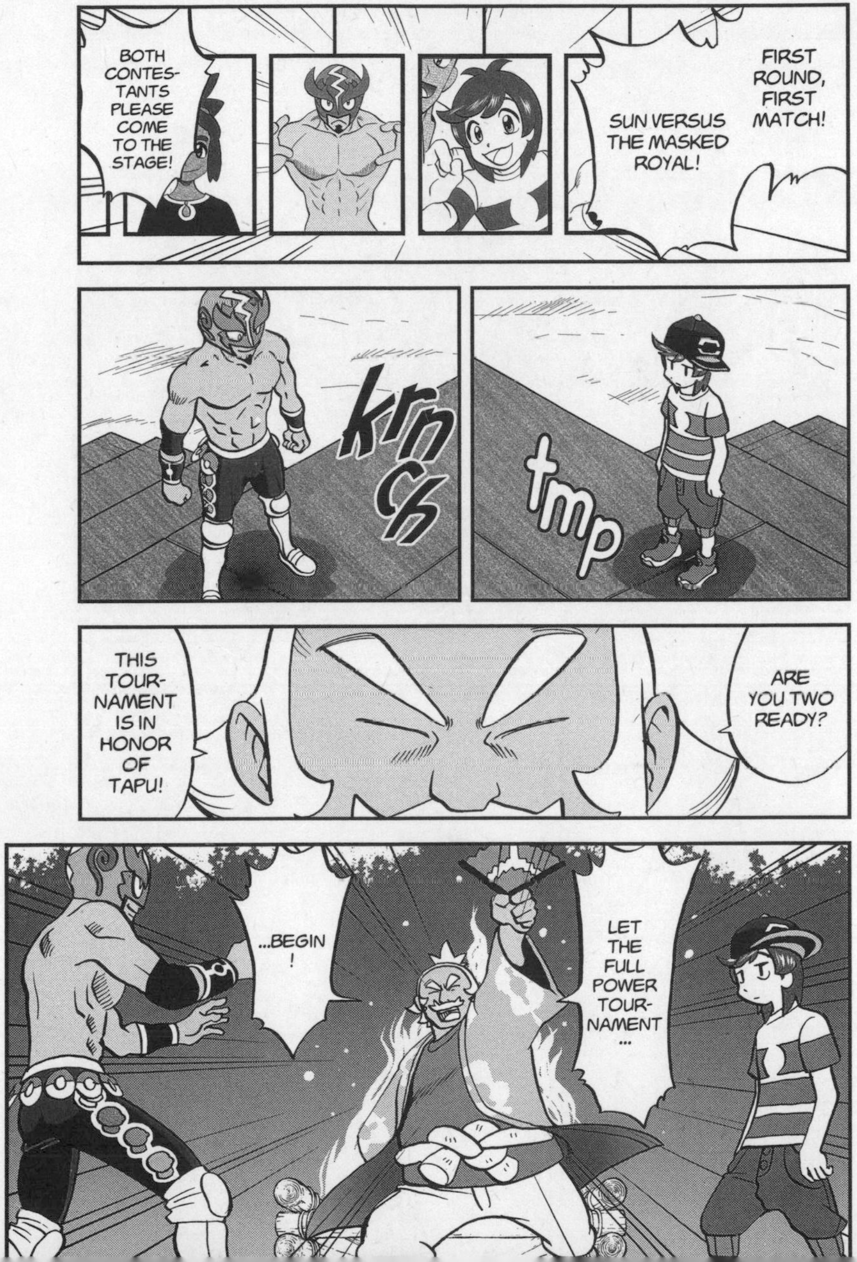
FIRST ROUND, FIRST MATCH!
SUN VERSUS THE MASKED ROYAL!
BOTH CONTES-TANTS PLEASE COME TO THE STAGE!
tmp
krnch
ARE YOU TWO READY?
THIS TOUR-NAMENT IS IN HONOR OF TAPU!
LET THE FULL POWER TOUR-NAMENT...
...BEGIN!

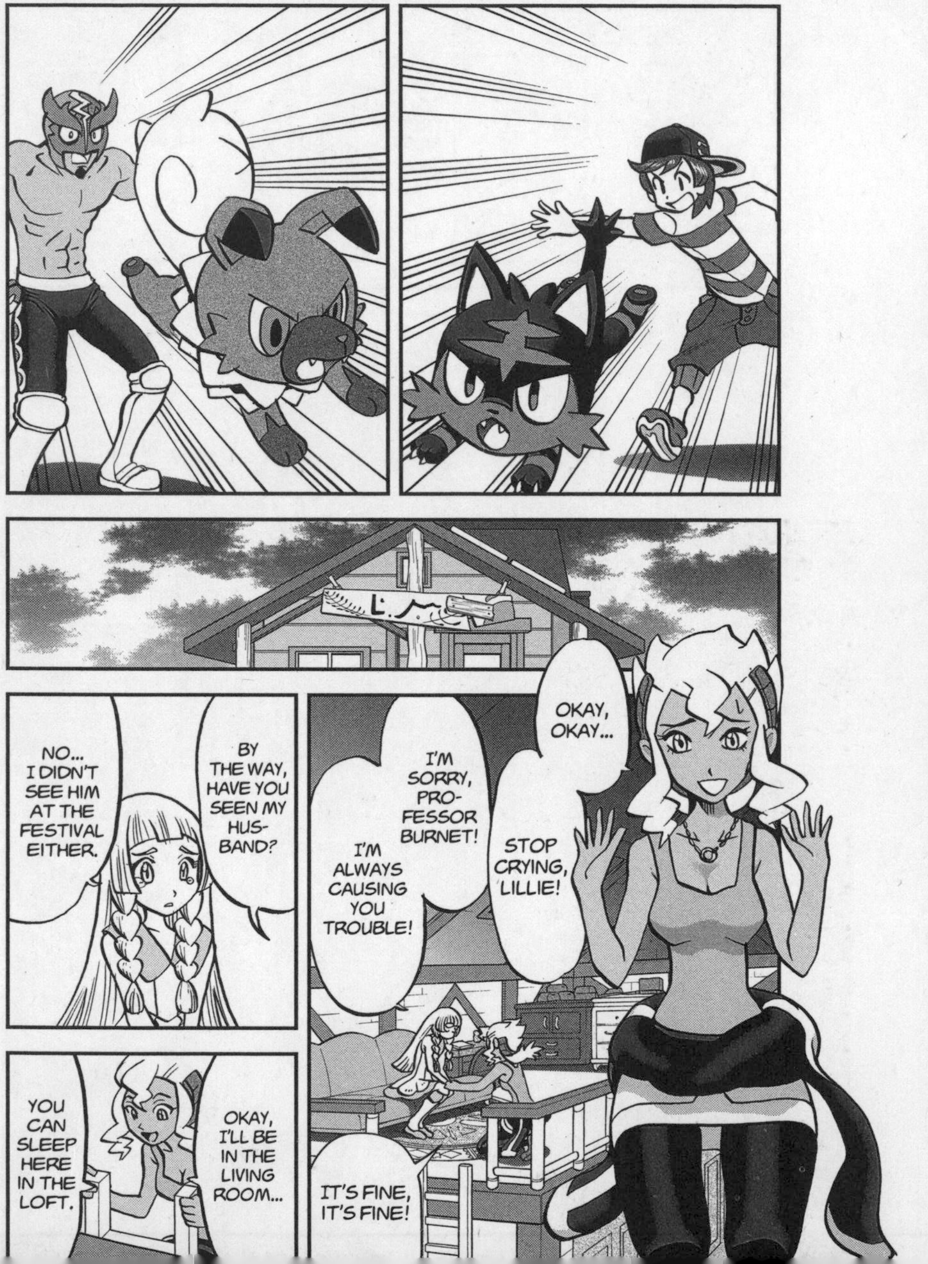
OKAY, OKAY...
STOP CRYING, LILLIE!
I'M SORRY, PRO-FESSOR BURNET!
I'M ALWAYS CAUSING YOU TROUBLE!
IT'S FINE, IT'S FINE!
BY THE WAY, HAVE YOU SEEN MY HUS-BAND?
NO... I DIDN'T SEE HIM AT THE FESTIVAL EITHER.
OKAY, I'LL BE IN THE LIVING ROOM...
YOU CAN SLEEP HERE IN THE LOFT.

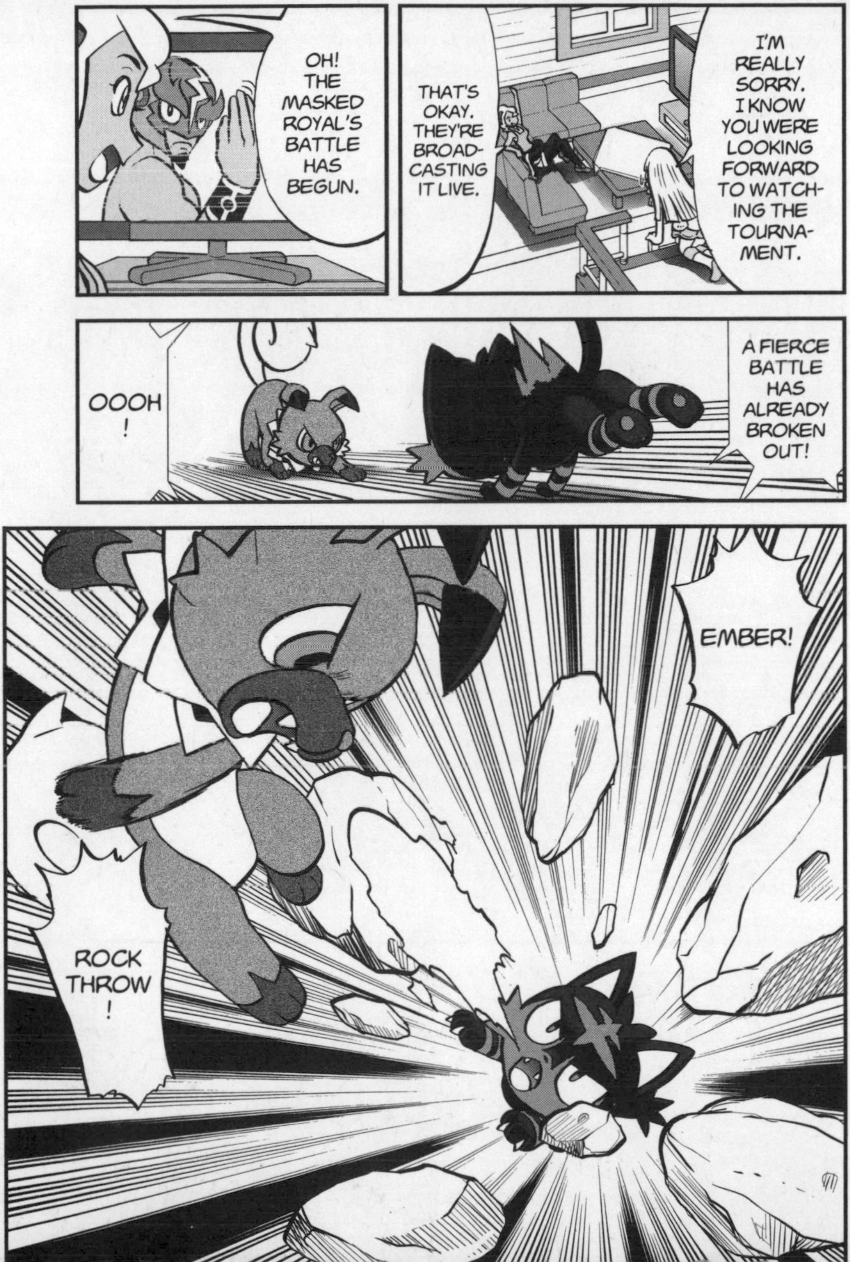
I'M REALLY SORRY. I KNOW YOU WERE LOOKING FORWARD TO WATCHING THE TOURNAMENT.
THAT'S OKAY. THEY'RE BROADCASTING IT LIVE.
OH! THE MASKED ROYAL'S BATTLE HAS BEGUN.
A FIERCE BATTLE HAS ALREADY BROKEN OUT!
OOOH!
EMBER!
ROCK THROW!

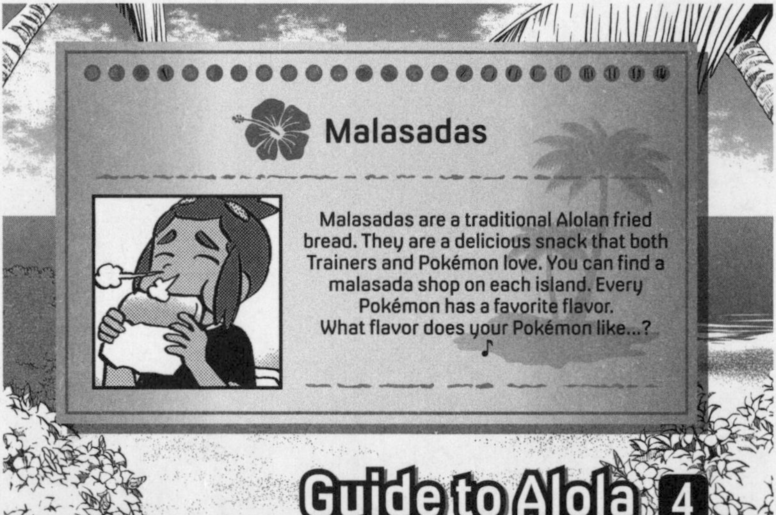

🌺 Malasadas

Malasadas are a traditional Alolan fried bread. They are a delicious snack that both Trainers and Pokémon love. You can find a malasada shop on each island. Every Pokémon has a favorite flavor. What flavor does your Pokémon like...? ♪

Guide to Alola 4

Adventure 5
The Announcement and the Prize

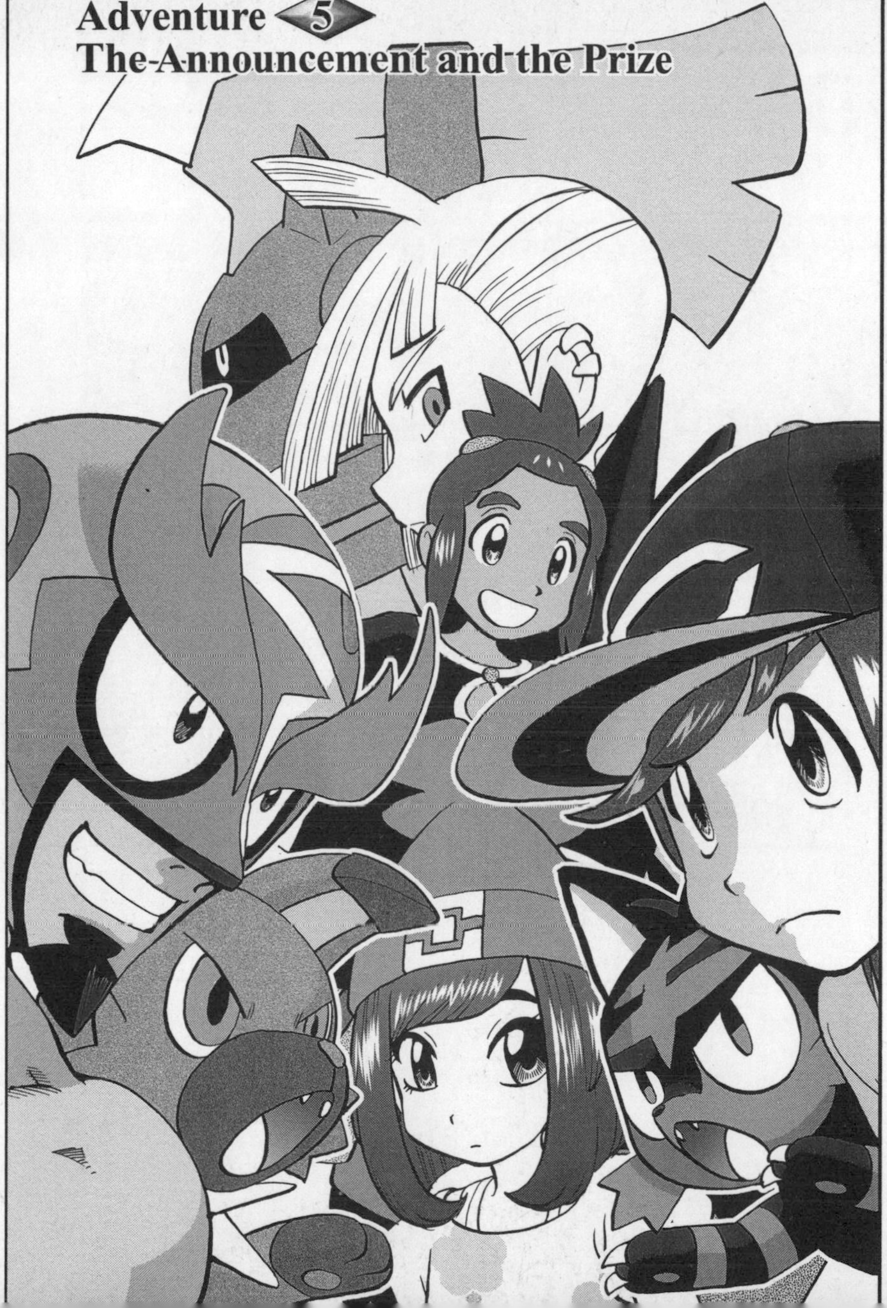

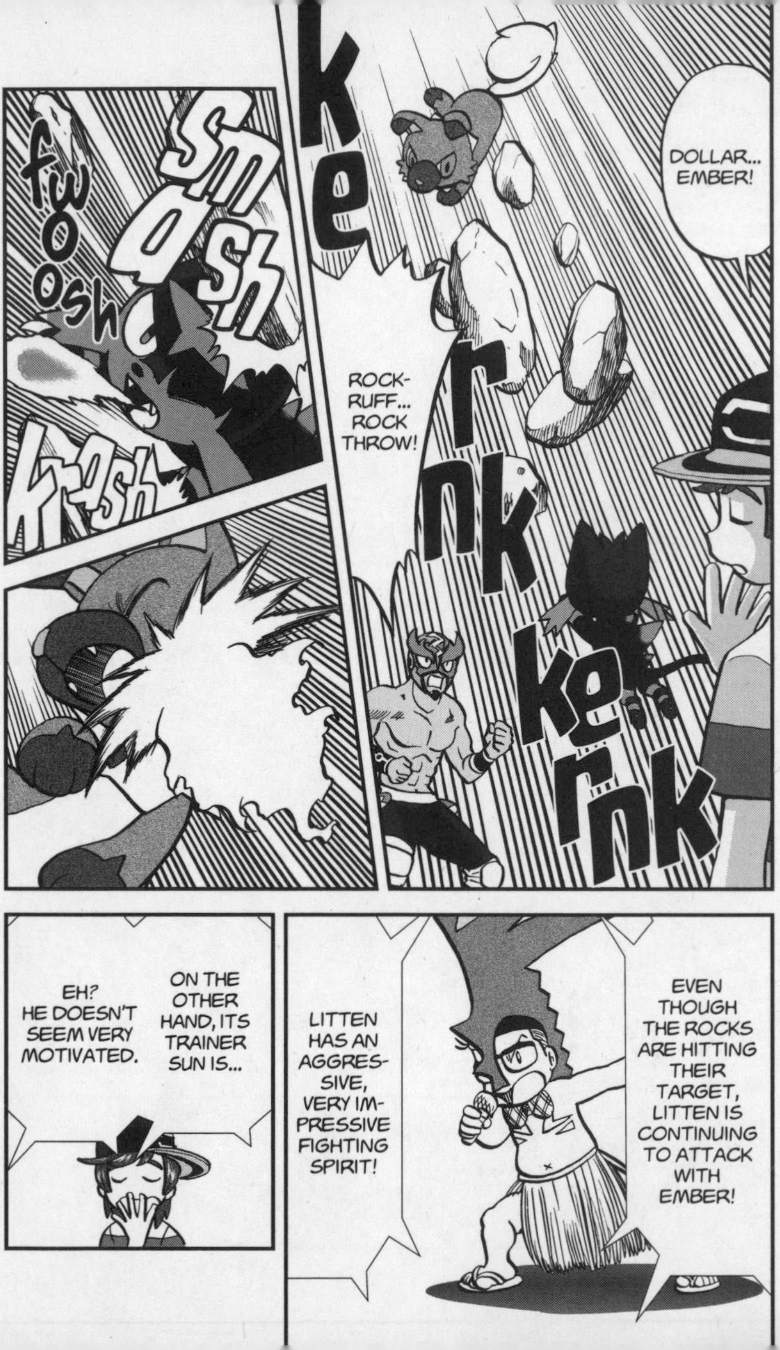
DOLLAR... EMBER!
ROCK-RUFF... ROCK THROW!
kernk
kernk
smash
fwooosh
krash
EVEN THOUGH THE ROCKS ARE HITTING THEIR TARGET, LITTEN IS CONTINUING TO ATTACK WITH EMBER!
LITTEN HAS AN AGGRES-SIVE, VERY IM-PRESSIVE FIGHTING SPIRIT!
ON THE OTHER HAND, ITS TRAINER SUN IS...
EH? HE DOESN'T SEEM VERY MOTIVATED.

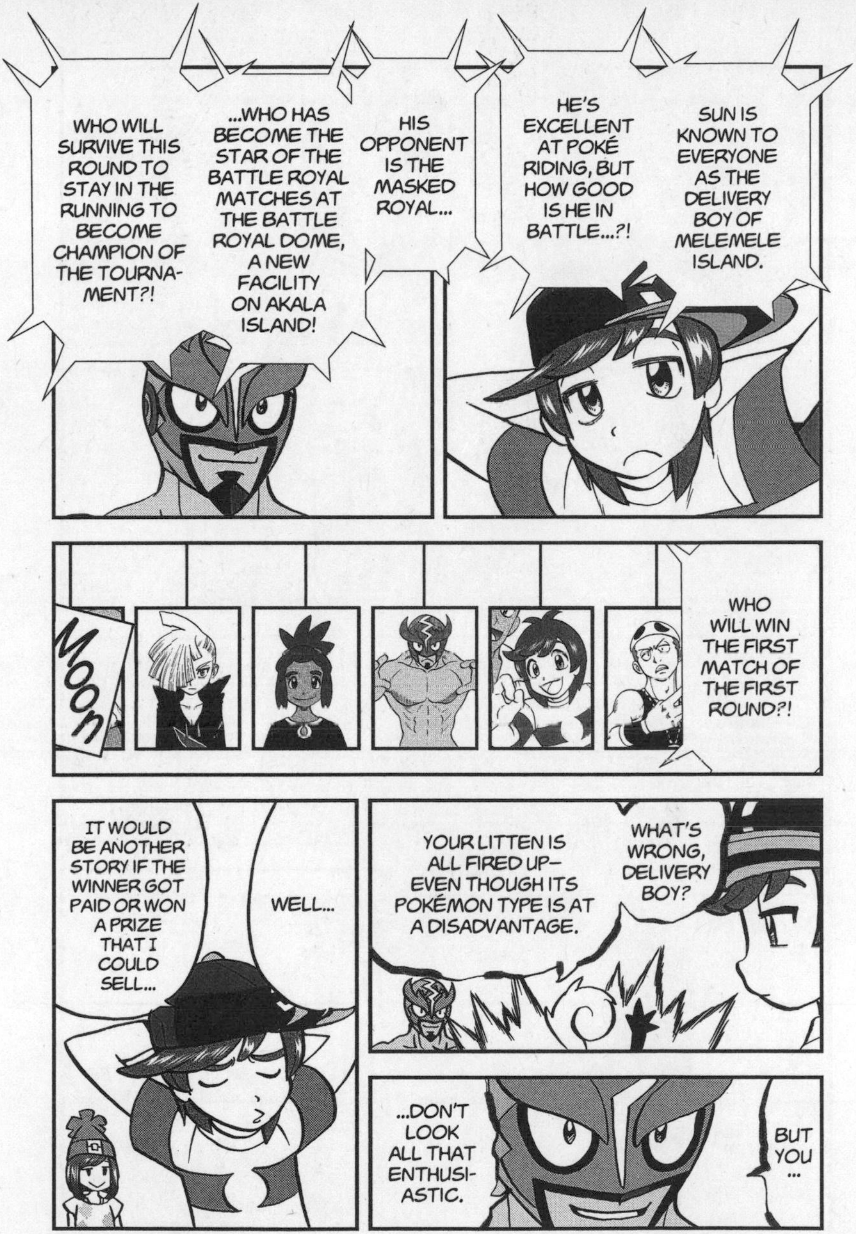
SUN IS KNOWN TO EVERYONE AS THE DELIVERY BOY OF MELEMELE ISLAND.
HE'S EXCELLENT AT POKÉ RIDING, BUT HOW GOOD IS HE IN BATTLE...?!
HIS OPPONENT IS THE MASKED ROYAL...
...WHO HAS BECOME THE STAR OF THE BATTLE ROYAL MATCHES AT THE BATTLE ROYAL DOME, A NEW FACILITY ON AKALA ISLAND!
WHO WILL SURVIVE THIS ROUND TO STAY IN THE RUNNING TO BECOME CHAMPION OF THE TOURNA-MENT?!
WHO WILL WIN THE FIRST MATCH OF THE FIRST ROUND?!
Moon
WHAT'S WRONG, DELIVERY BOY?
YOUR LITTEN IS ALL FIRED UP—EVEN THOUGH ITS POKÉMON TYPE IS AT A DISADVANTAGE.
BUT YOU...
...DON'T LOOK ALL THAT ENTHUSI-ASTIC.
WELL...
IT WOULD BE ANOTHER STORY IF THE WINNER GOT PAID OR WON A PRIZE THAT I COULD SELL...

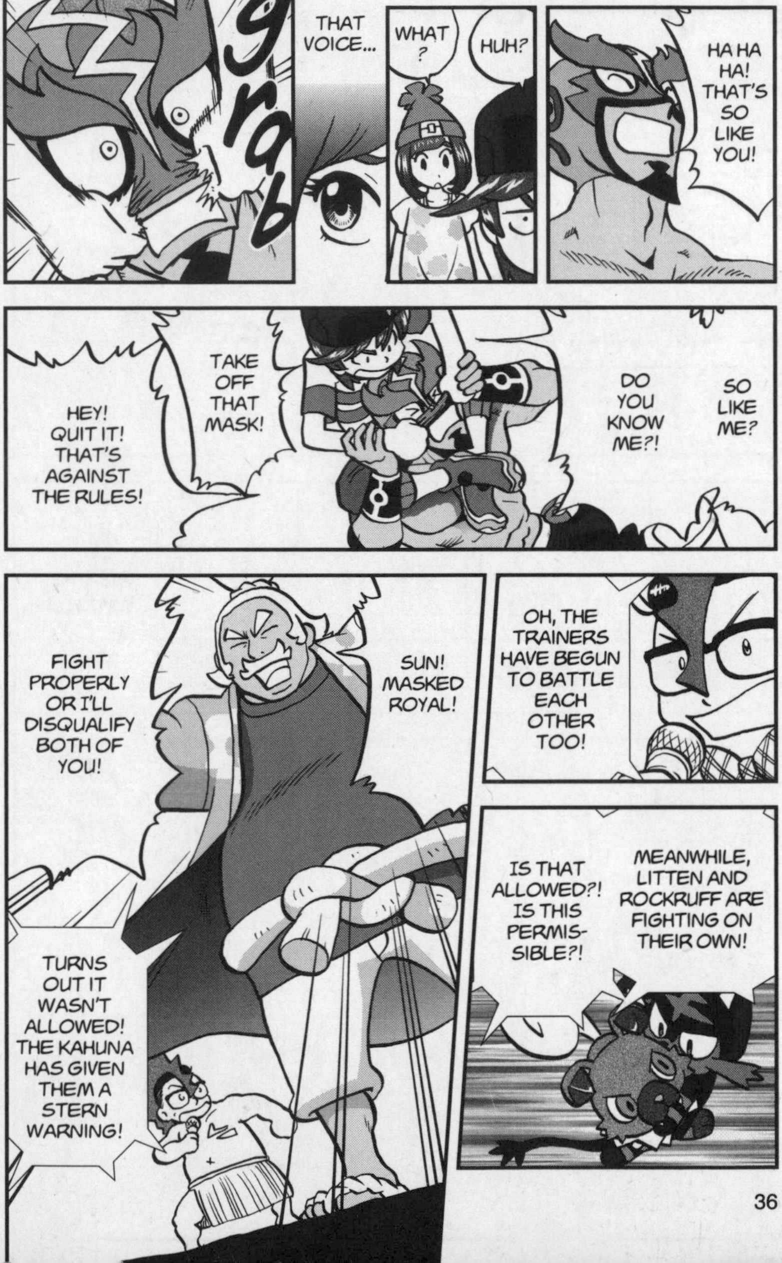
HA HA HA! THAT'S SO LIKE YOU!
HUH?
WHAT?
grab
THAT VOICE...
SO LIKE ME?
DO YOU KNOW ME?!
TAKE OFF THAT MASK!
HEY! QUIT IT! THAT'S AGAINST THE RULES!
OH, THE TRAINERS HAVE BEGUN TO BATTLE EACH OTHER TOO!
MEANWHILE, LITTEN AND ROCKRUFF ARE FIGHTING ON THEIR OWN!
IS THAT ALLOWED?! IS THIS PERMIS-SIBLE?!
SUN! MASKED ROYAL!
FIGHT PROPERLY OR I'LL DISQUALIFY BOTH OF YOU!
TURNS OUT IT WASN'T ALLOWED! THE KAHUNA HAS GIVEN THEM A STERN WARNING!

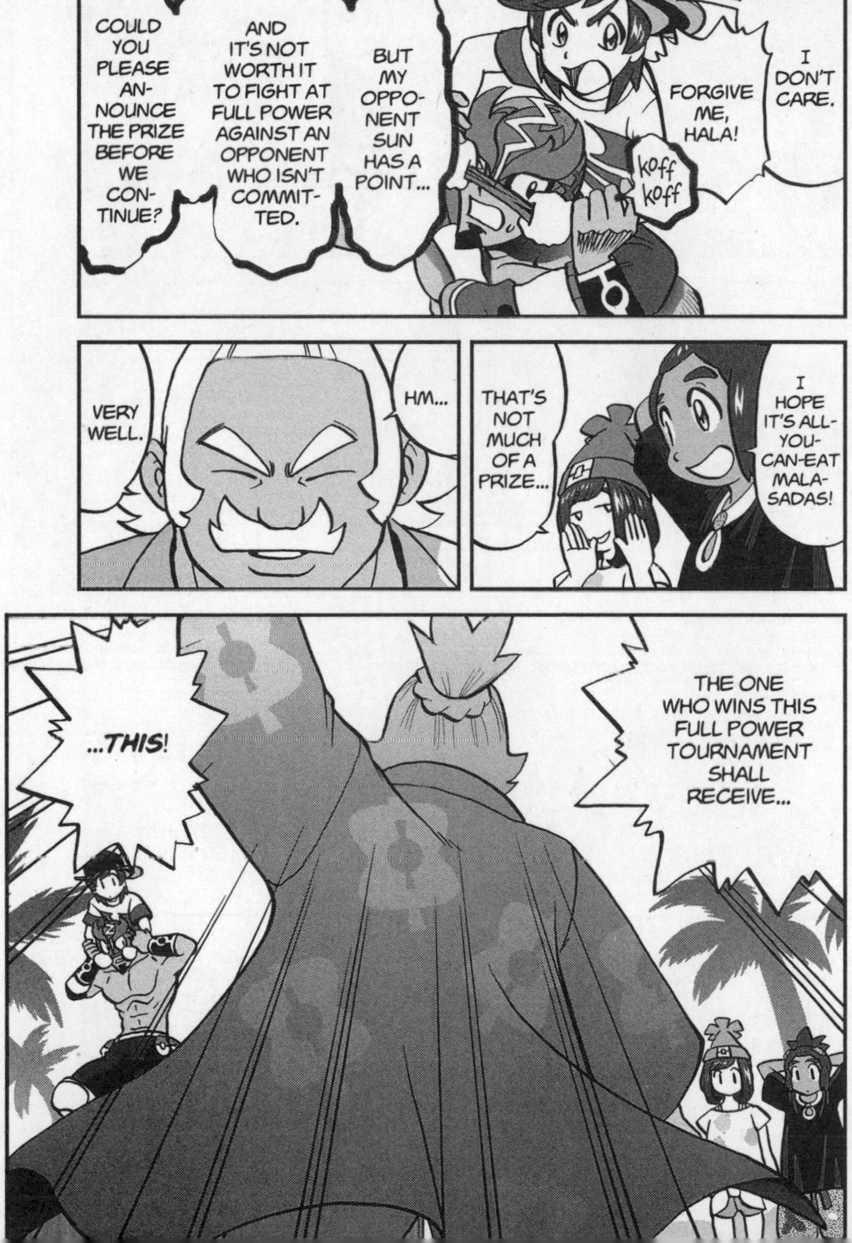
I DON'T CARE.
FORGIVE ME, HALA!
koff koff
BUT MY OPPONENT SUN HAS A POINT...
AND IT'S NOT WORTH IT TO FIGHT AT FULL POWER AGAINST AN OPPONENT WHO ISN'T COMMITTED.
COULD YOU PLEASE ANNOUNCE THE PRIZE BEFORE WE CONTINUE?
I HOPE IT'S ALL-YOU-CAN-EAT MALASADAS!
THAT'S NOT MUCH OF A PRIZE...
HM...
VERY WELL.
THE ONE WHO WINS THIS FULL POWER TOURNAMENT SHALL RECEIVE...
...THIS!

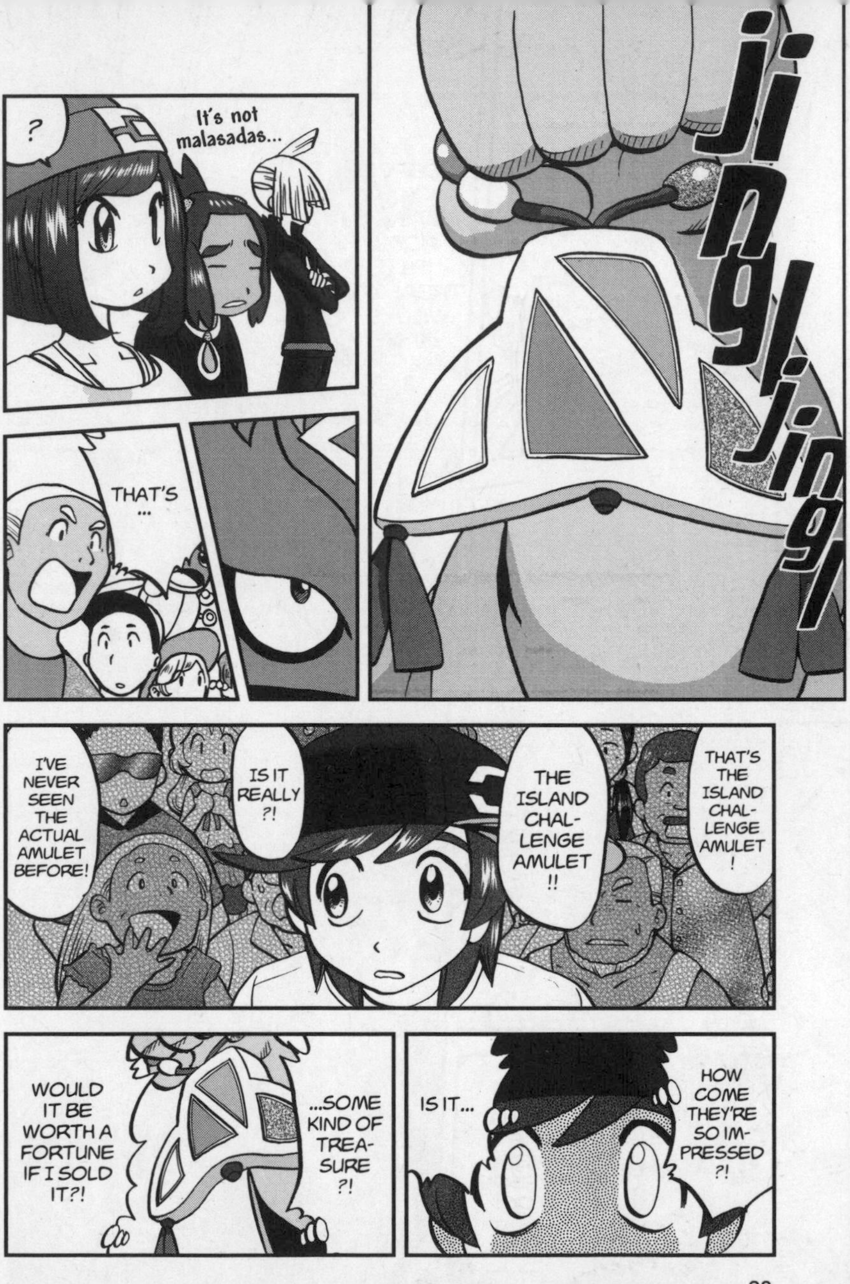
jingljingl
It's not malasadas...
?
THAT'S...
THAT'S THE ISLAND CHAL-LENGE AMULET!
THE ISLAND CHAL-LENGE AMULET!!
IS IT REALLY?!
I'VE NEVER SEEN THE ACTUAL AMULET BEFORE!
HOW COME THEY'RE SO IM-PRESSED?!
IS IT...
...SOME KIND OF TREA-SURE?!
WOULD IT BE WORTH A FORTUNE IF I SOLD IT?!

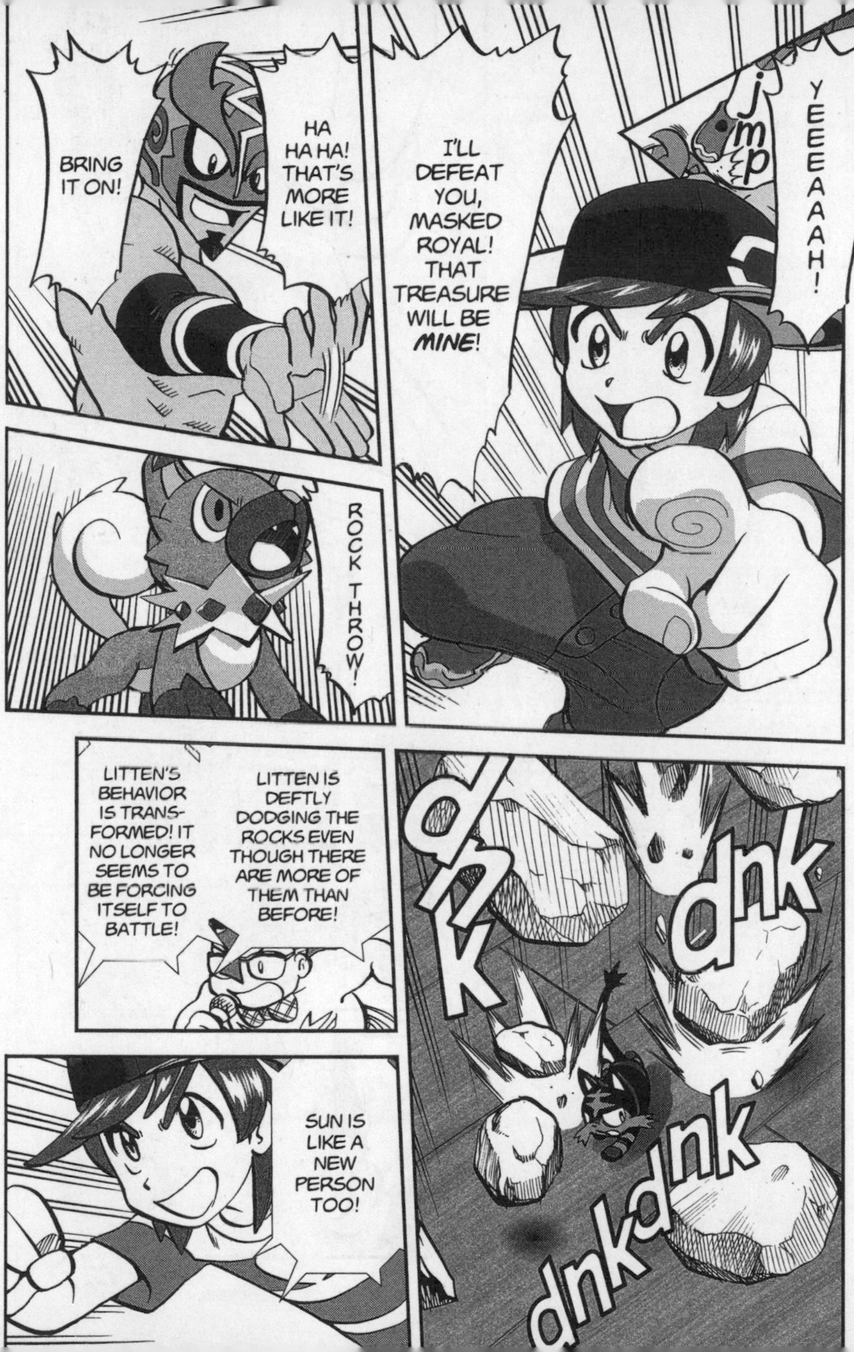
jmp
YEEEAAAH!
I'LL DEFEAT YOU, MASKED ROYAL! THAT TREASURE WILL BE *MINE*!
HA HA HA! THAT'S MORE LIKE IT!
BRING IT ON!
ROCK THROW!
dnk
dnk
dnkdnk
dnk
LITTEN IS DEFTLY DODGING THE ROCKS EVEN THOUGH THERE ARE MORE OF THEM THAN BEFORE!
LITTEN'S BEHAVIOR IS TRANS-FORMED! IT NO LONGER SEEMS TO BE FORCING ITSELF TO BATTLE!
SUN IS LIKE A NEW PERSON TOO!

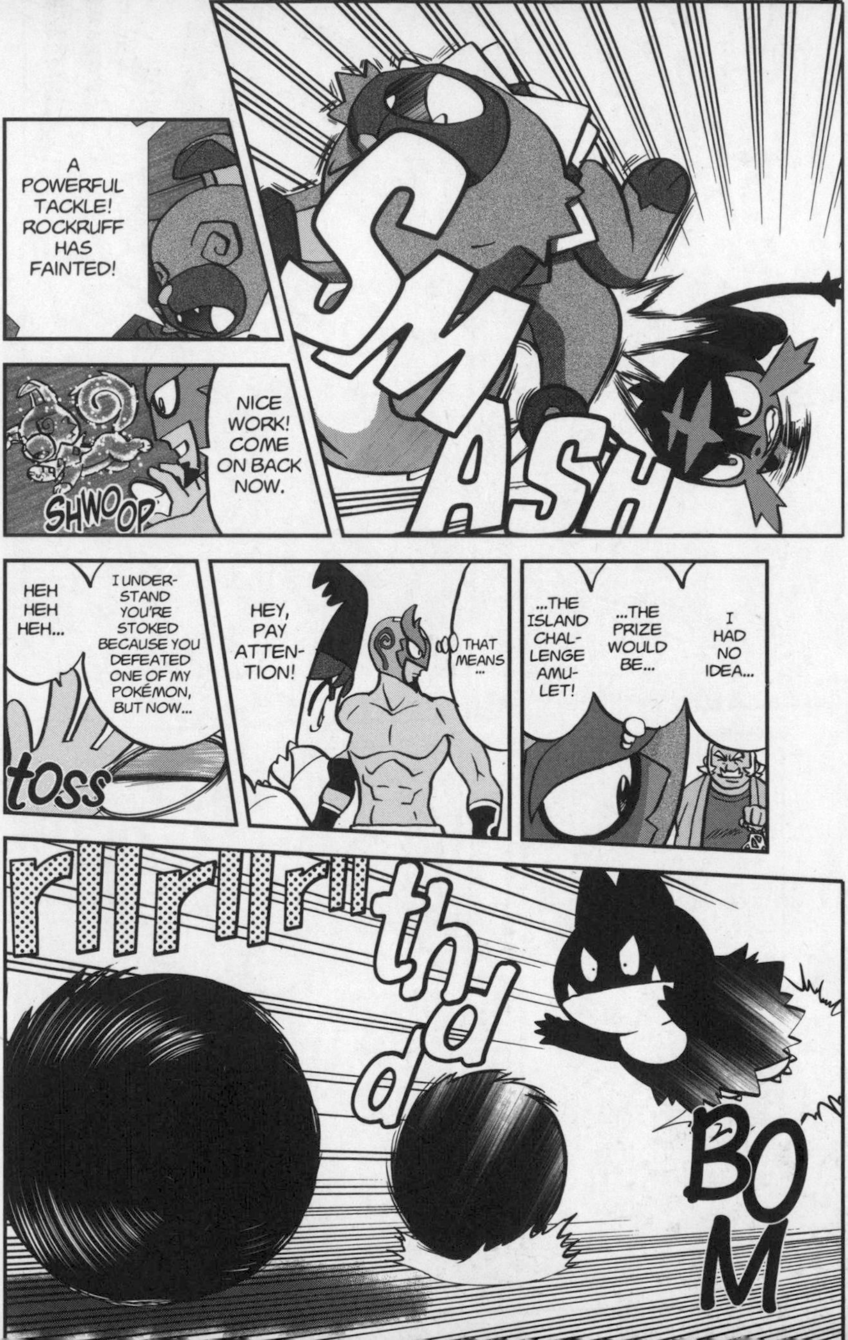
SMASH
A POWERFUL TACKLE! ROCKRUFF HAS FAINTED!
NICE WORK! COME ON BACK NOW.
SHWOOP
I HAD NO IDEA...
...THE PRIZE WOULD BE...
...THE ISLAND CHALLENGE AMULET!
THAT MEANS...
HEY, PAY ATTENTION!
I UNDERSTAND YOU'RE STOKED BECAUSE YOU DEFEATED ONE OF MY POKÉMON, BUT NOW...
HEH HEH HEH...
toss
BOOM
thdd
rllrllrll

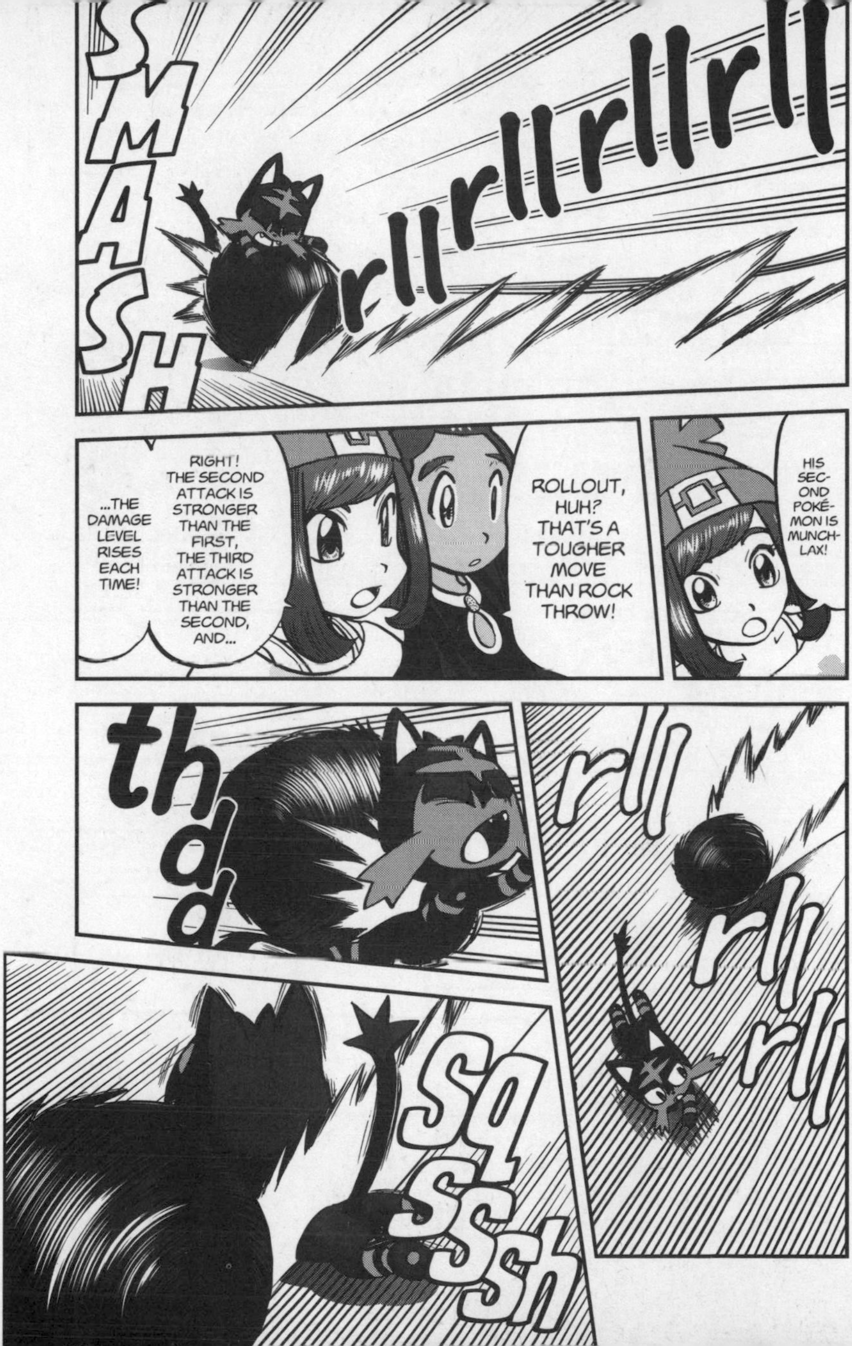
SMASH
rllrllrllrllrll
HIS SECOND POKÉMON IS MUNCHLAX!
ROLLOUT, HUH? THAT'S A TOUGHER MOVE THAN ROCK THROW!
RIGHT! THE SECOND ATTACK IS STRONGER THAN THE FIRST, THE THIRD ATTACK IS STRONGER THAN THE SECOND, AND...
...THE DAMAGE LEVEL RISES EACH TIME!
rll
rll
rll
thdd
sqsssh

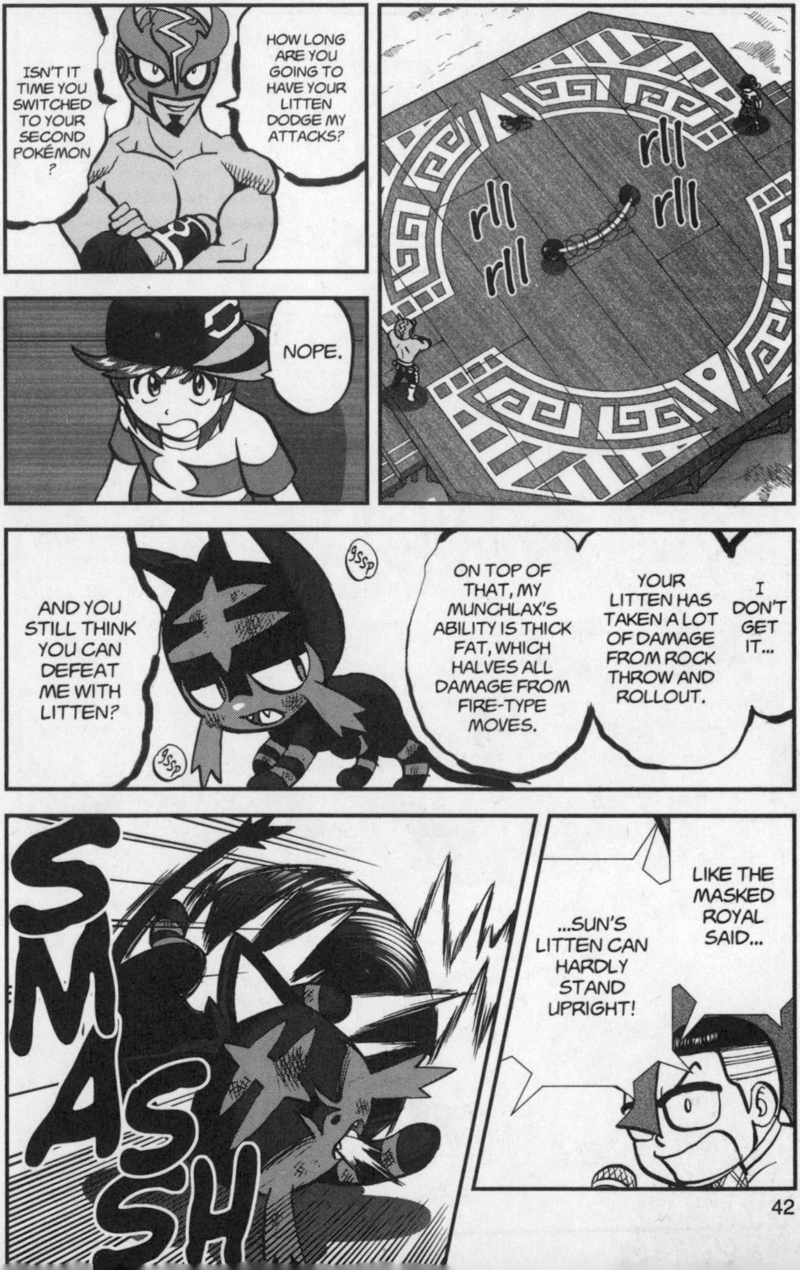
rll
rll
rll
rll
HOW LONG ARE YOU GOING TO HAVE YOUR LITTEN DODGE MY ATTACKS?
ISN'T IT TIME YOU SWITCHED TO YOUR SECOND POKÉMON?
NOPE.
I DON'T GET IT...
YOUR LITTEN HAS TAKEN A LOT OF DAMAGE FROM ROCK THROW AND ROLLOUT.
ON TOP OF THAT, MY MUNCHLAX'S ABILITY IS THICK FAT, WHICH HALVES ALL DAMAGE FROM FIRE-TYPE MOVES.
AND YOU STILL THINK YOU CAN DEFEAT ME WITH LITTEN?
gssp
gssp
LIKE THE MASKED ROYAL SAID...
...SUN'S LITTEN CAN HARDLY STAND UPRIGHT!
SMASH

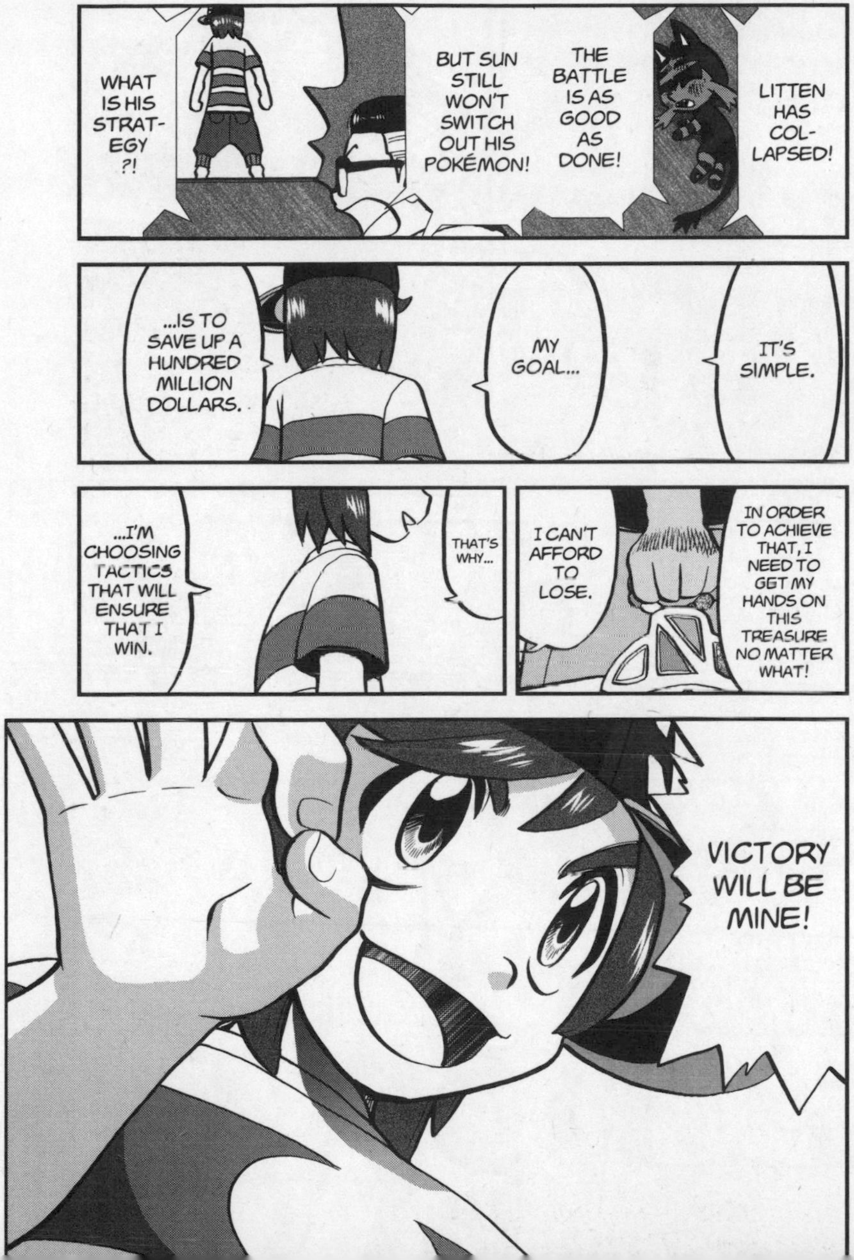
LITTEN HAS COLLAPSED!
THE BATTLE IS AS GOOD AS DONE!
BUT SUN STILL WON'T SWITCH OUT HIS POKÉMON!
WHAT IS HIS STRATEGY?!
IT'S SIMPLE.
MY GOAL...
...IS TO SAVE UP A HUNDRED MILLION DOLLARS.
IN ORDER TO ACHIEVE THAT, I NEED TO GET MY HANDS ON THIS TREASURE NO MATTER WHAT!
I CAN'T AFFORD TO LOSE.
THAT'S WHY...
...I'M CHOOSING TACTICS THAT WILL ENSURE THAT I WIN.
VICTORY WILL BE MINE!

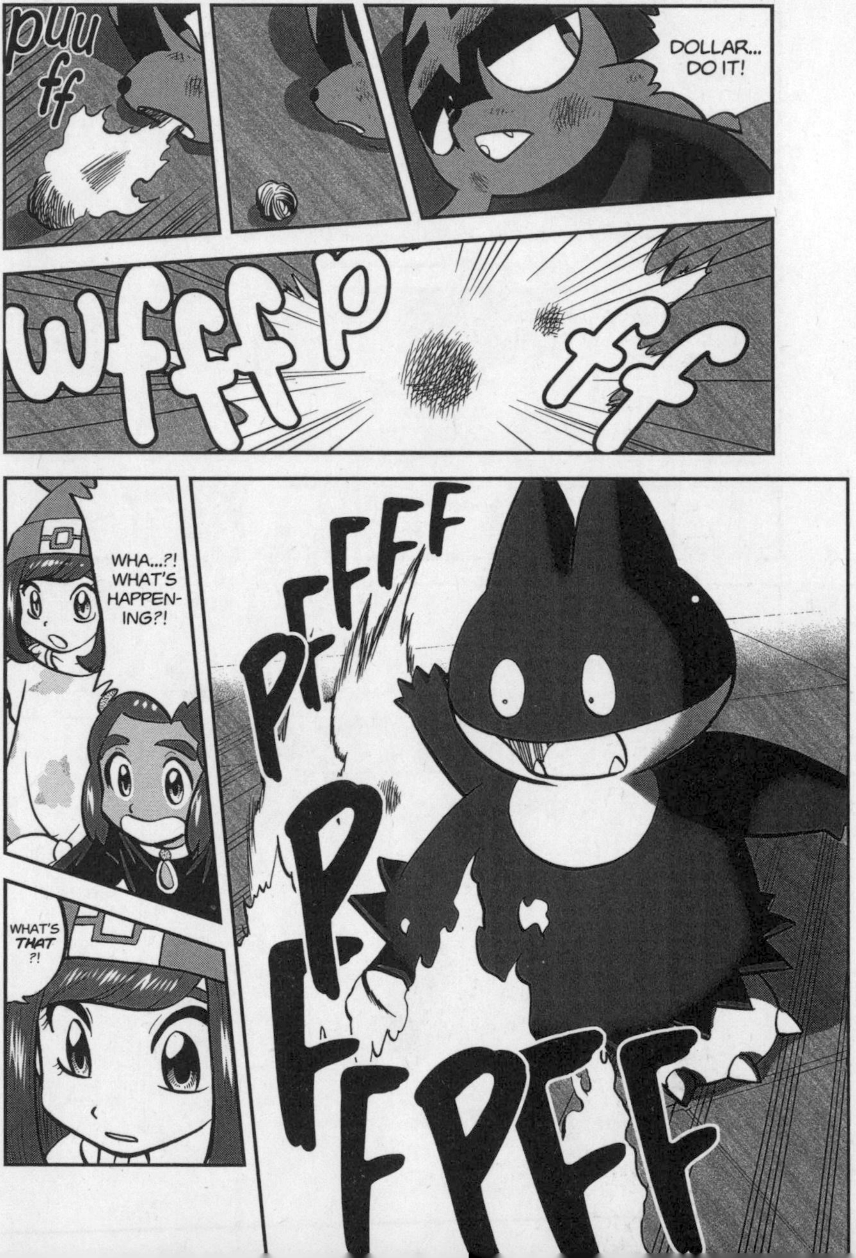
DOLLAR... DO IT!
puuff
wfffp ff
PFFFF
PPFPFF
WHA...?! WHAT'S HAPPEN-ING?!
WHAT'S *THAT* ?!

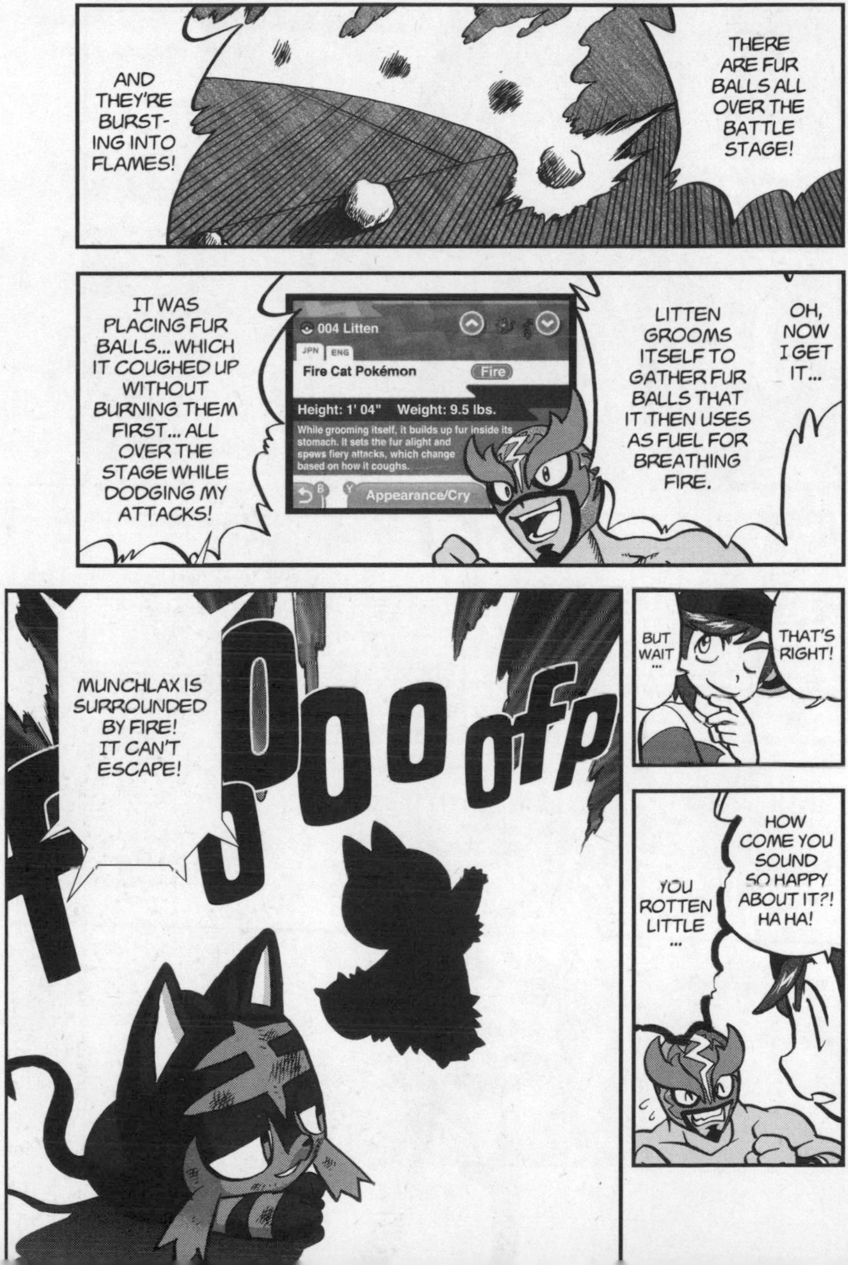
THERE ARE FUR BALLS ALL OVER THE BATTLE STAGE!
AND THEY'RE BURST-ING INTO FLAMES!
OH, NOW I GET IT...
LITTEN GROOMS ITSELF TO GATHER FUR BALLS THAT IT THEN USES AS FUEL FOR BREATHING FIRE.
004 Litten
JPN ENG
Fire Cat Pokémon
Fire
Height: 1' 04" Weight: 9.5 lbs.
While grooming itself, it builds up fur inside its stomach. It sets the fur alight and spews fiery attacks, which change based on how it coughs.
B Y Appearance/Cry
IT WAS PLACING FUR BALLS... WHICH IT COUGHED UP WITHOUT BURNING THEM FIRST... ALL OVER THE STAGE WHILE DODGING MY ATTACKS!
THAT'S RIGHT!
BUT WAIT...
HOW COME YOU SOUND SO HAPPY ABOUT IT?! HA HA!
YOU ROTTEN LITTLE...
MUNCHLAX IS SURROUNDED BY FIRE! IT CAN'T ESCAPE!

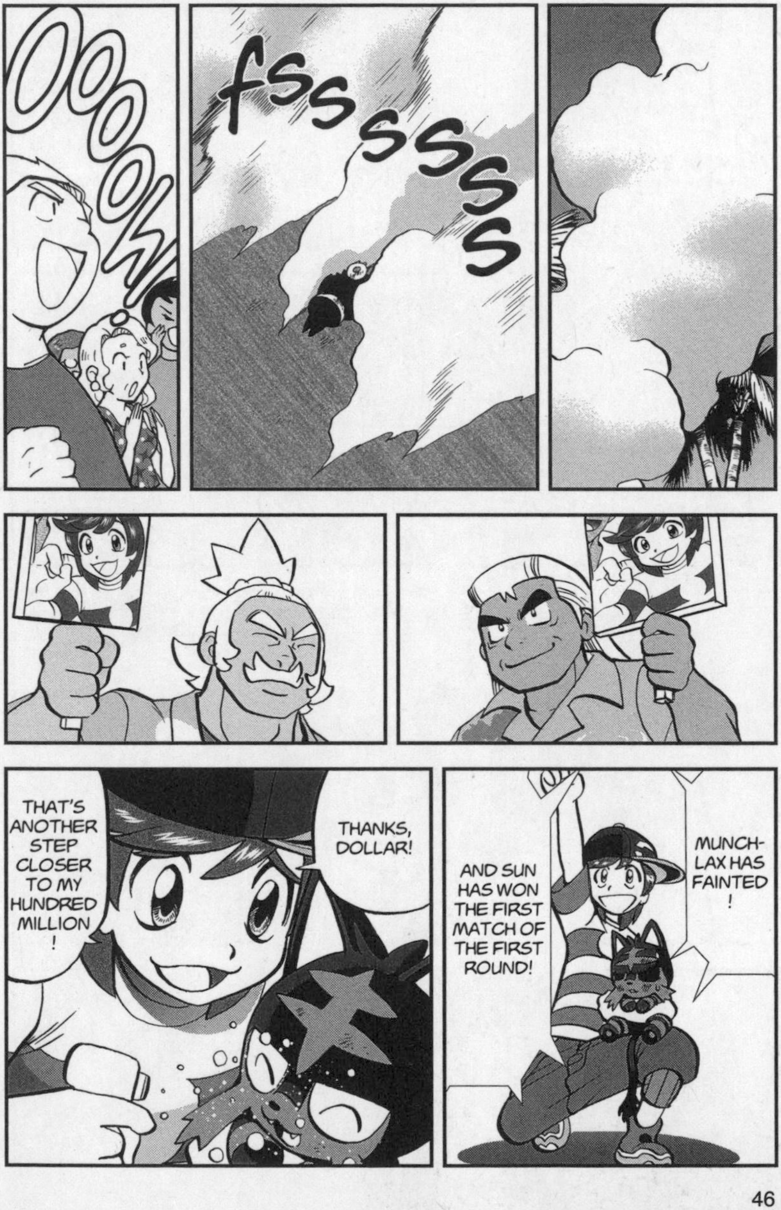
fsssssss
OOOOOW!
MUNCH-LAX HAS FAINTED!
AND SUN HAS WON THE FIRST MATCH OF THE FIRST ROUND!
THANKS, DOLLAR!
THAT'S ANOTHER STEP CLOSER TO MY HUNDRED MILLION!

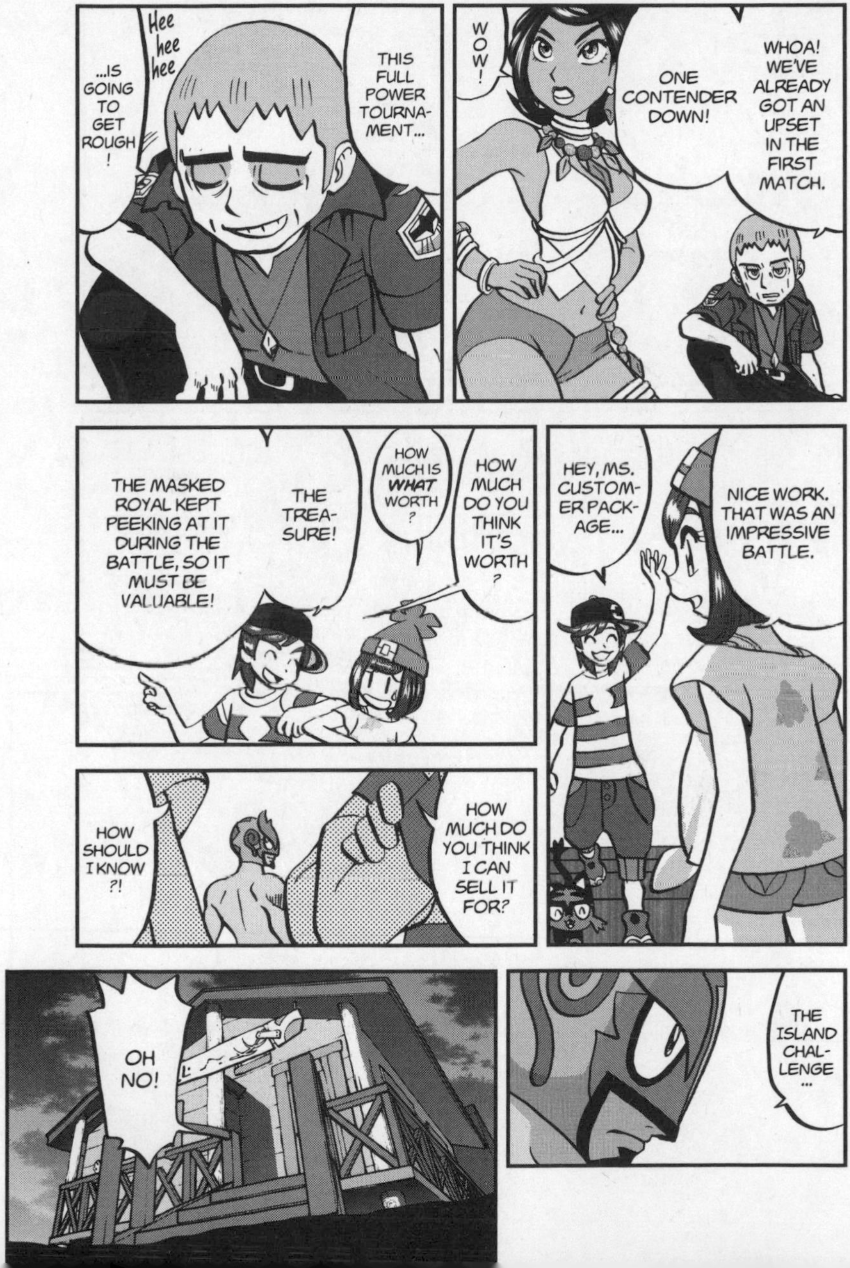
WHOA! WE'VE ALREADY GOT AN UPSET IN THE FIRST MATCH.
ONE CONTENDER DOWN!
WOW!
THIS FULL POWER TOURNAMENT...
...IS GOING TO GET ROUGH!
Hee hee hee
NICE WORK. THAT WAS AN IMPRESSIVE BATTLE.
HEY, MS. CUSTOMER PACKAGE...
HOW MUCH DO YOU THINK IT'S WORTH?
HOW MUCH IS WHAT WORTH?
THE TREASURE!
THE MASKED ROYAL KEPT PEEKING AT IT DURING THE BATTLE, SO IT MUST BE VALUABLE!
HOW MUCH DO YOU THINK I CAN SELL IT FOR?
HOW SHOULD I KNOW?!
THE ISLAND CHALLENGE...
OH NO!

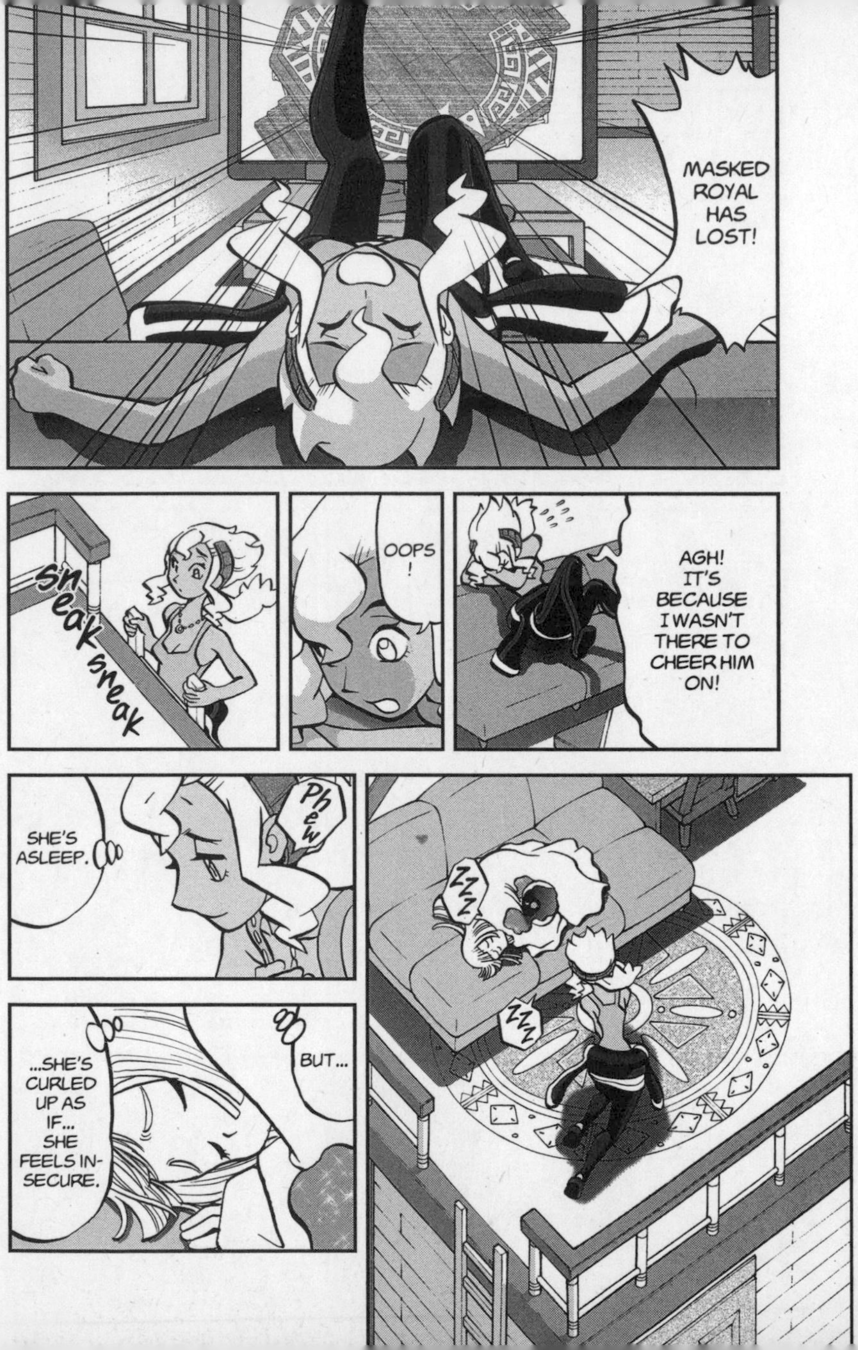
MASKED ROYAL HAS LOST!
AGH! IT'S BECAUSE I WASN'T THERE TO CHEER HIM ON!
OOPS!
sneak sneak
ZZZ
ZZZ
Phew
SHE'S ASLEEP.
BUT...
...SHE'S CURLED UP AS IF... SHE FEELS IN-SECURE.

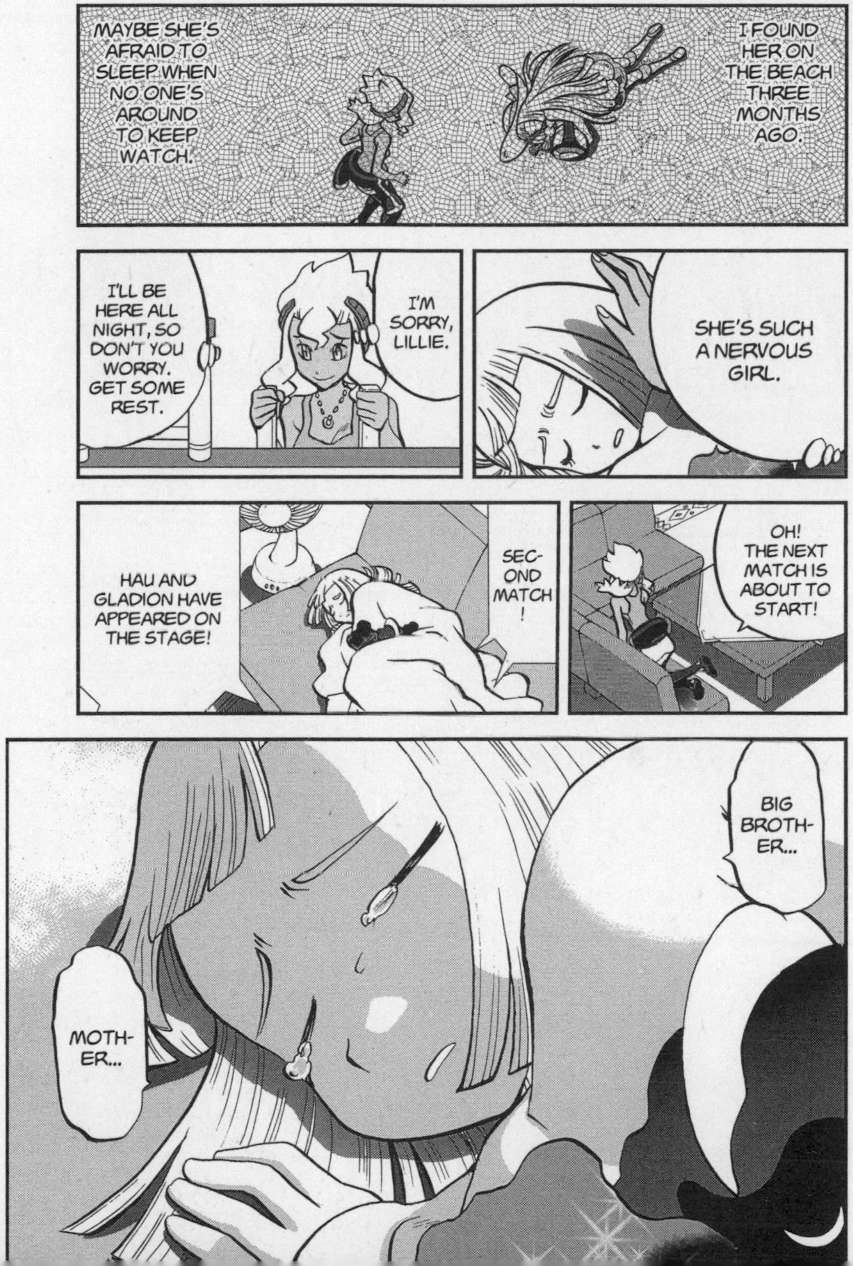
I FOUND HER ON THE BEACH THREE MONTHS AGO.
MAYBE SHE'S AFRAID TO SLEEP WHEN NO ONE'S AROUND TO KEEP WATCH.
SHE'S SUCH A NERVOUS GIRL.
I'M SORRY, LILLIE.
I'LL BE HERE ALL NIGHT, SO DON'T YOU WORRY. GET SOME REST.
OH! THE NEXT MATCH IS ABOUT TO START!
SEC-OND MATCH!
HAU AND GLADION HAVE APPEARED ON THE STAGE!
BIG BROTH-ER...
MOTH-ER...

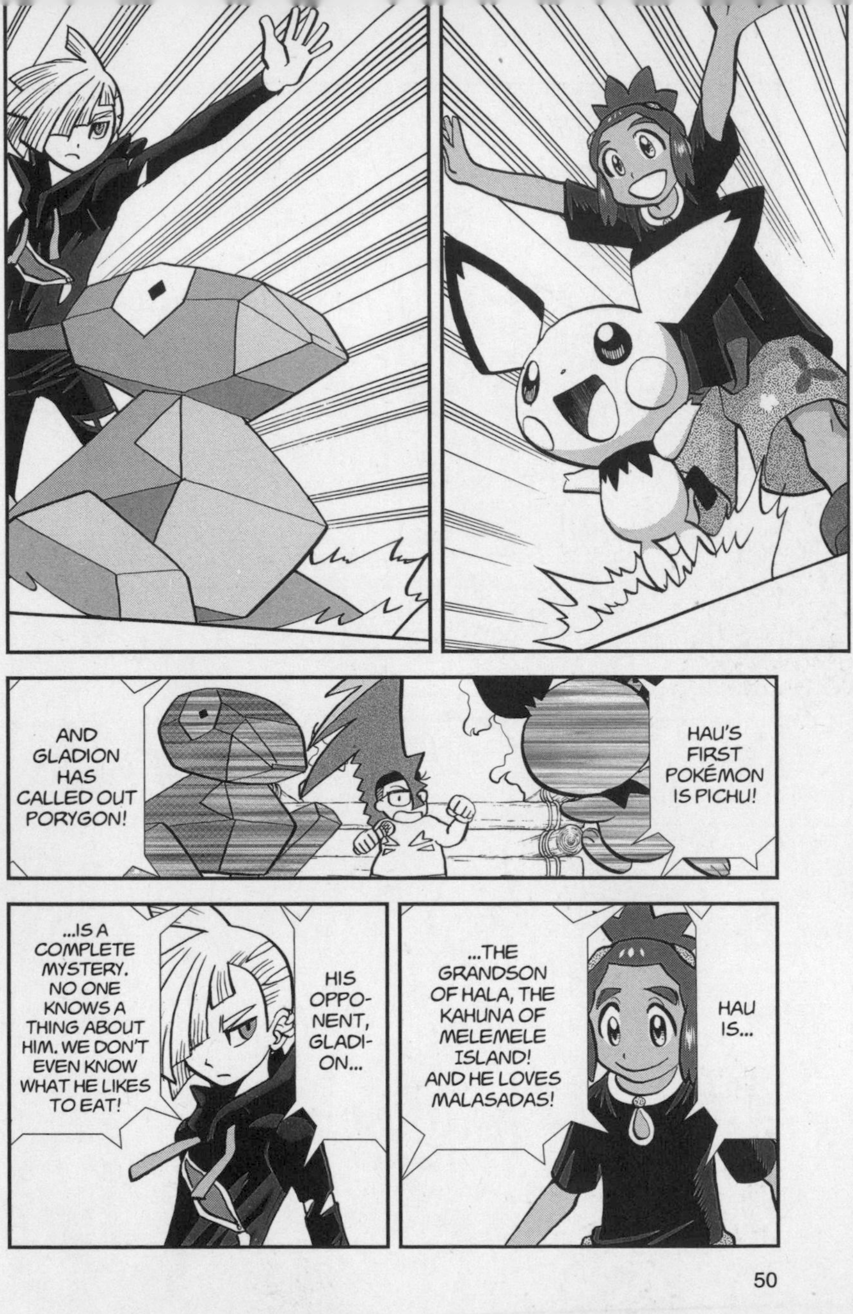
HAU'S FIRST POKÉMON IS PICHU!
AND GLADION HAS CALLED OUT PORYGON!
HAU IS...
...THE GRANDSON OF HALA, THE KAHUNA OF MELEMELE ISLAND! AND HE LOVES MALASADAS!
HIS OPPO-NENT, GLADI-ON...
...IS A COMPLETE MYSTERY. NO ONE KNOWS A THING ABOUT HIM. WE DON'T EVEN KNOW WHAT HE LIKES TO EAT!

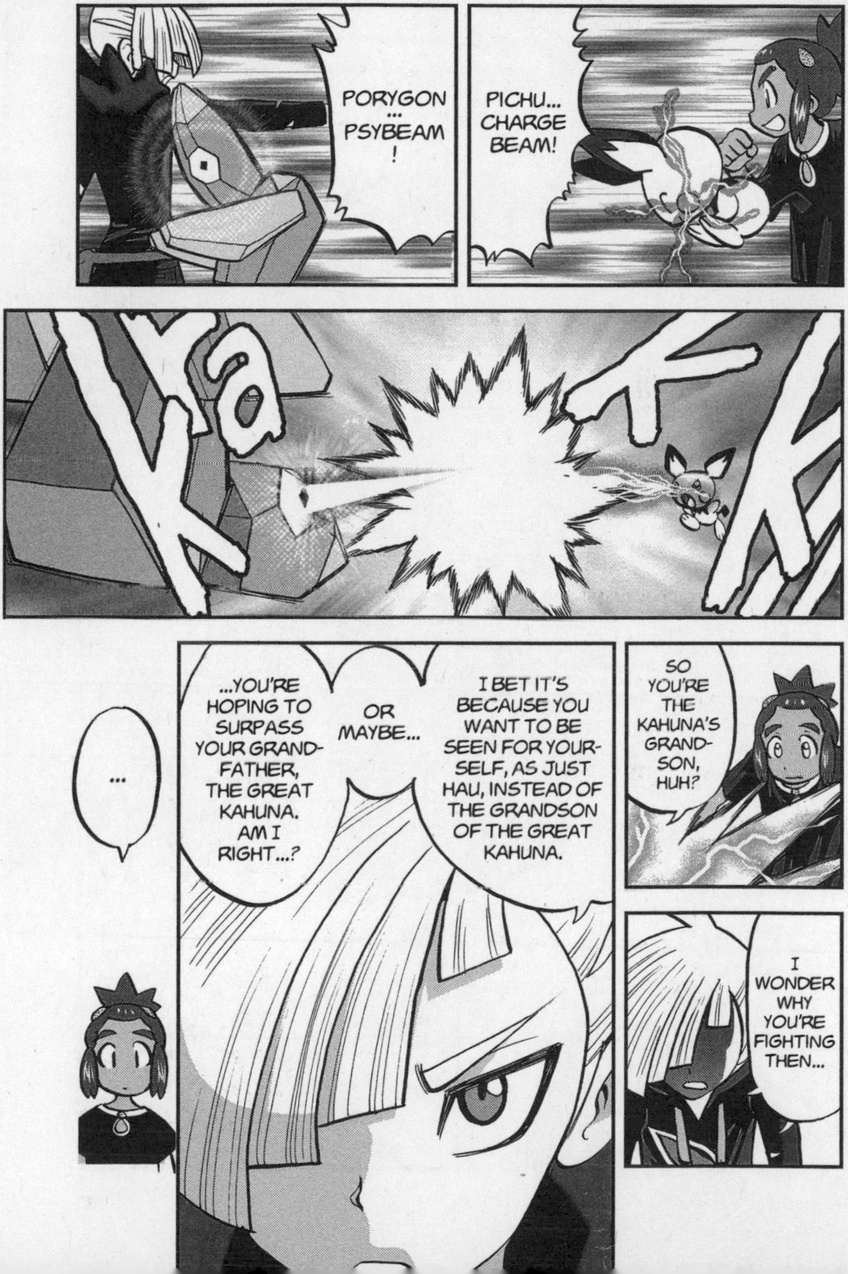
PICHU... CHARGE BEAM!
PORYGON ... PSYBEAM !
Ka
SO YOU'RE THE KAHUNA'S GRANDSON, HUH?
I WONDER WHY YOU'RE FIGHTING THEN...
I BET IT'S BECAUSE YOU WANT TO BE SEEN FOR YOURSELF, AS JUST HAU, INSTEAD OF THE GRANDSON OF THE GREAT KAHUNA.
OR MAYBE...
...YOU'RE HOPING TO SURPASS YOUR GRANDFATHER, THE GREAT KAHUNA. AM I RIGHT...?
...

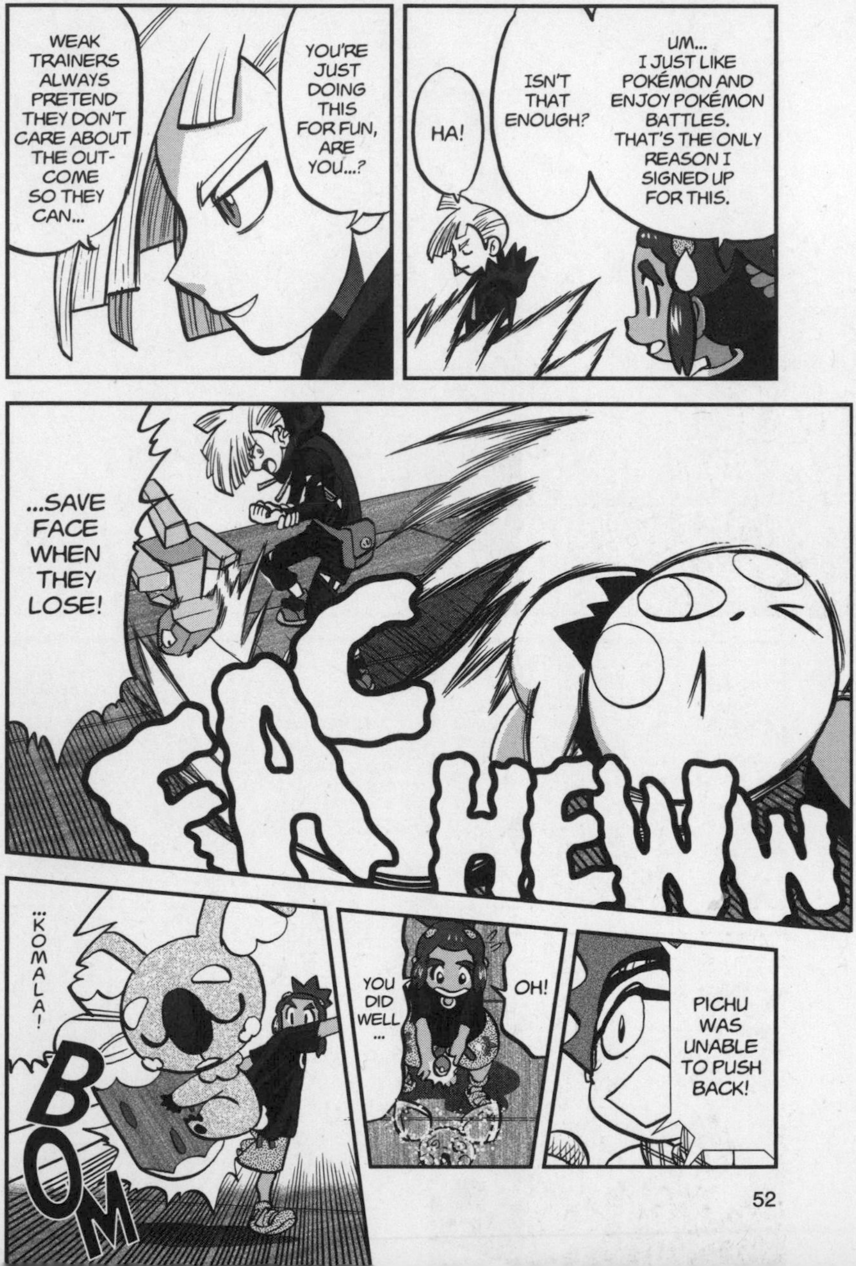
UM... I JUST LIKE POKÉMON AND ENJOY POKÉMON BATTLES. THAT'S THE ONLY REASON I SIGNED UP FOR THIS.
ISN'T THAT ENOUGH?
HA!
YOU'RE JUST DOING THIS FOR FUN, ARE YOU...?
WEAK TRAINERS ALWAYS PRETEND THEY DON'T CARE ABOUT THE OUT-COME SO THEY CAN...
...SAVE FACE WHEN THEY LOSE!
FA-HEWW
PICHU WAS UNABLE TO PUSH BACK!
OH!
YOU DID WELL...
...KOMALA!
BOOM

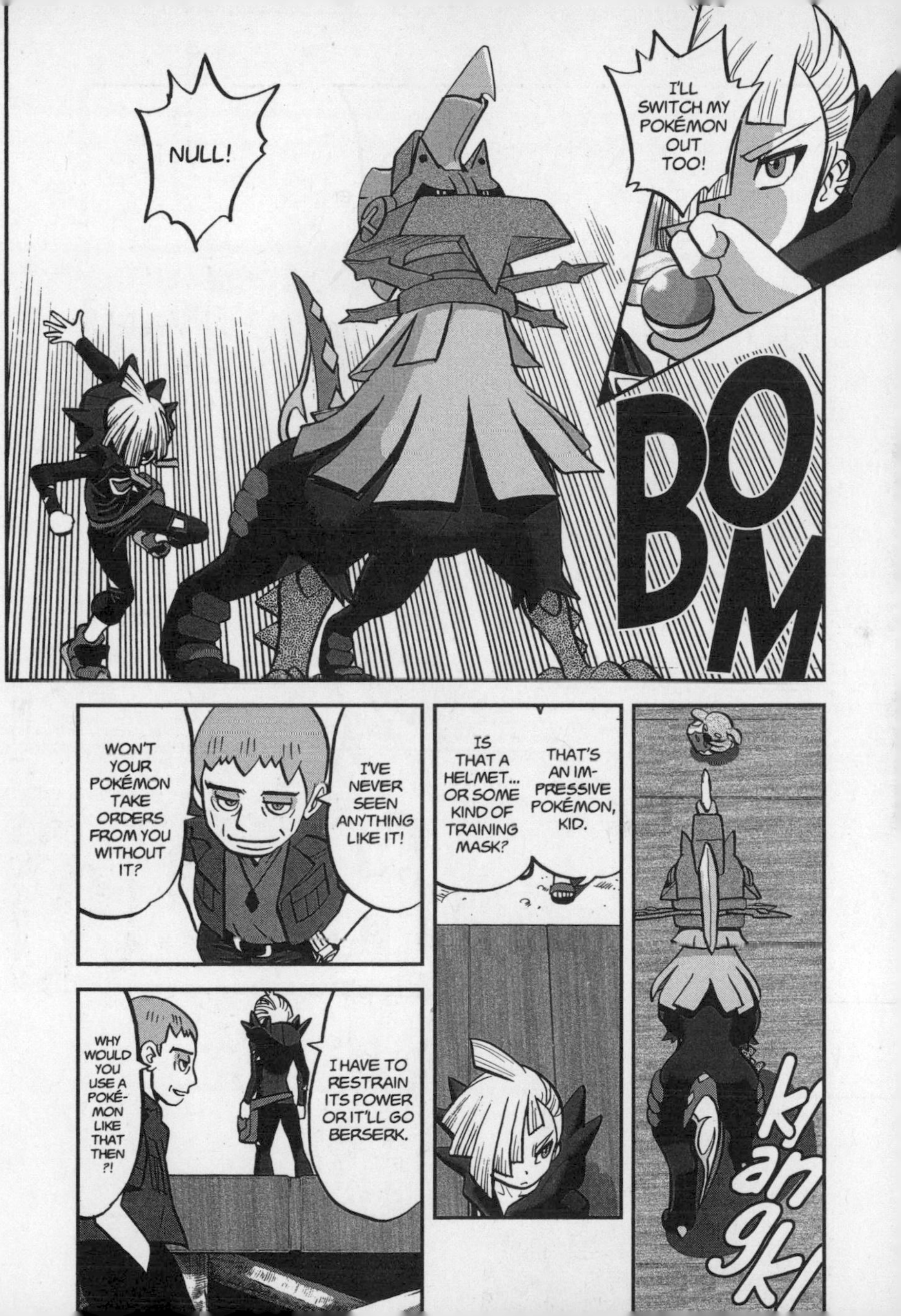
I'LL SWITCH MY POKÉMON OUT TOO!
BOOM
NULL!
klangkl
THAT'S AN IMPRESSIVE POKÉMON, KID.
IS THAT A HELMET... OR SOME KIND OF TRAINING MASK?
I'VE NEVER SEEN ANYTHING LIKE IT!
WON'T YOUR POKÉMON TAKE ORDERS FROM YOU WITHOUT IT?
I HAVE TO RESTRAIN ITS POWER OR IT'LL GO BERSERK.
WHY WOULD YOU USE A POKÉMON LIKE THAT THEN?!

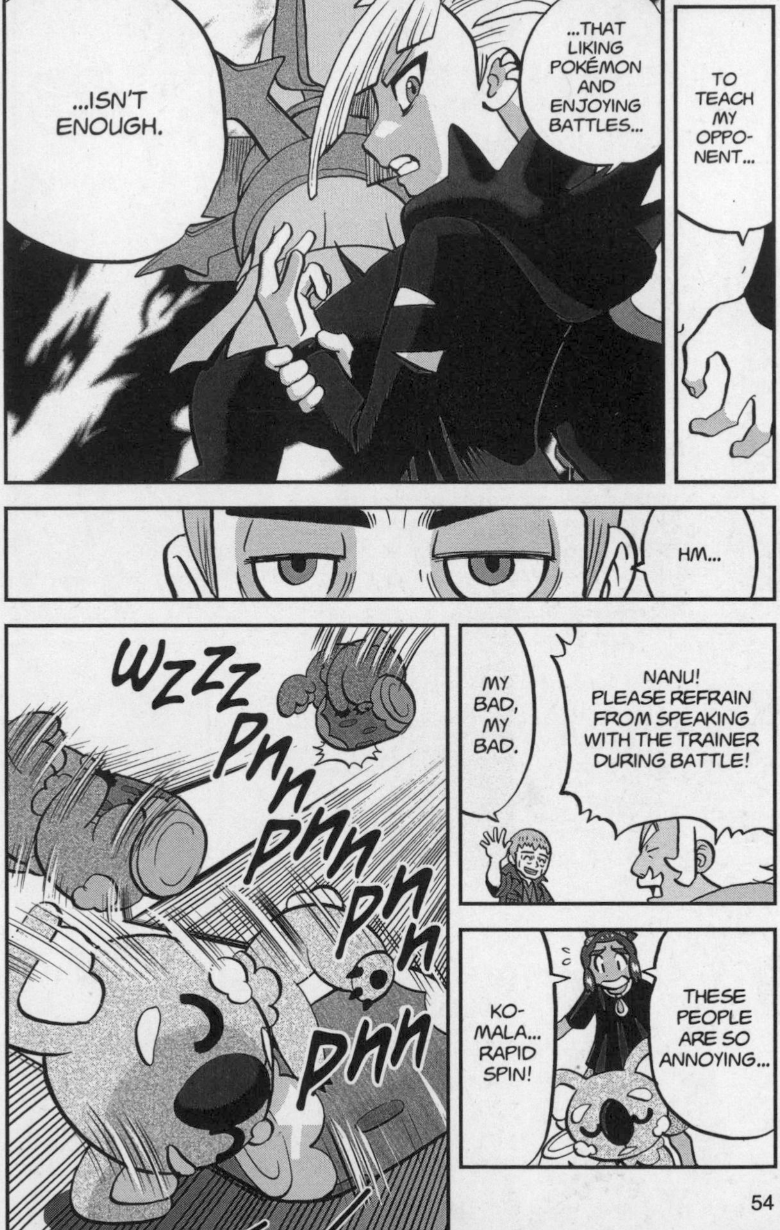
TO TEACH MY OPPONENT...
...THAT LIKING POKÉMON AND ENJOYING BATTLES...
...ISN'T ENOUGH.
HM...
NANU! PLEASE REFRAIN FROM SPEAKING WITH THE TRAINER DURING BATTLE!
MY BAD, MY BAD.
THESE PEOPLE ARE SO ANNOYING...
KO-MALA... RAPID SPIN!
WZZZ
PNN
PNNN
PNN
PNN
PNN

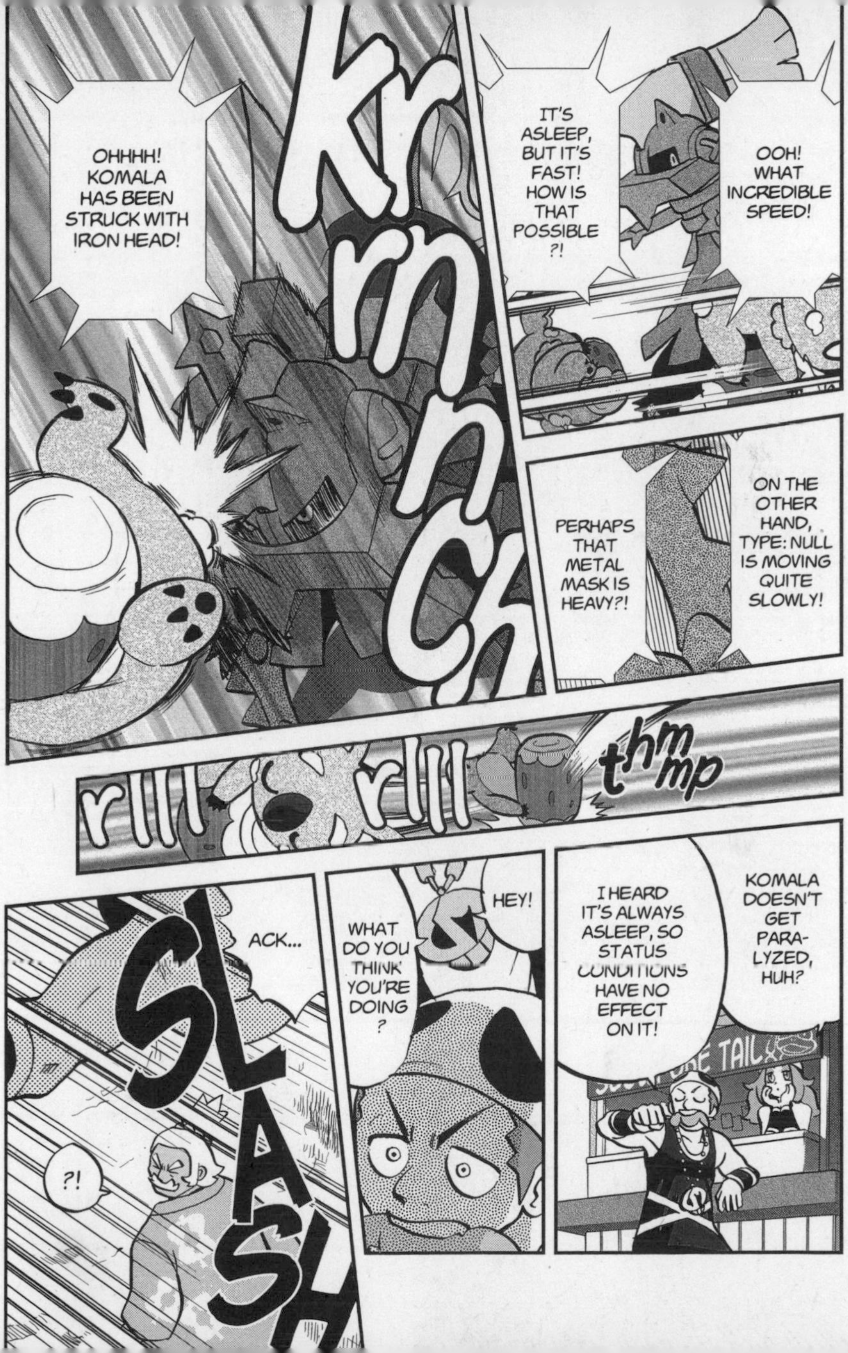
OOH! WHAT INCREDIBLE SPEED!
IT'S ASLEEP, BUT IT'S FAST! HOW IS THAT POSSIBLE?!
ON THE OTHER HAND, TYPE: NULL IS MOVING QUITE SLOWLY!
PERHAPS THAT METAL MASK IS HEAVY?!
OHHHH! KOMALA HAS BEEN STRUCK WITH IRON HEAD!
thmmp
rlll
rlll
KOMALA DOESN'T GET PARA-LYZED, HUH?
I HEARD IT'S ALWAYS ASLEEP, SO STATUS CONDITIONS HAVE NO EFFECT ON IT!
HEY!
WHAT DO YOU THINK YOU'RE DOING?
ACK...
SLASH
?!

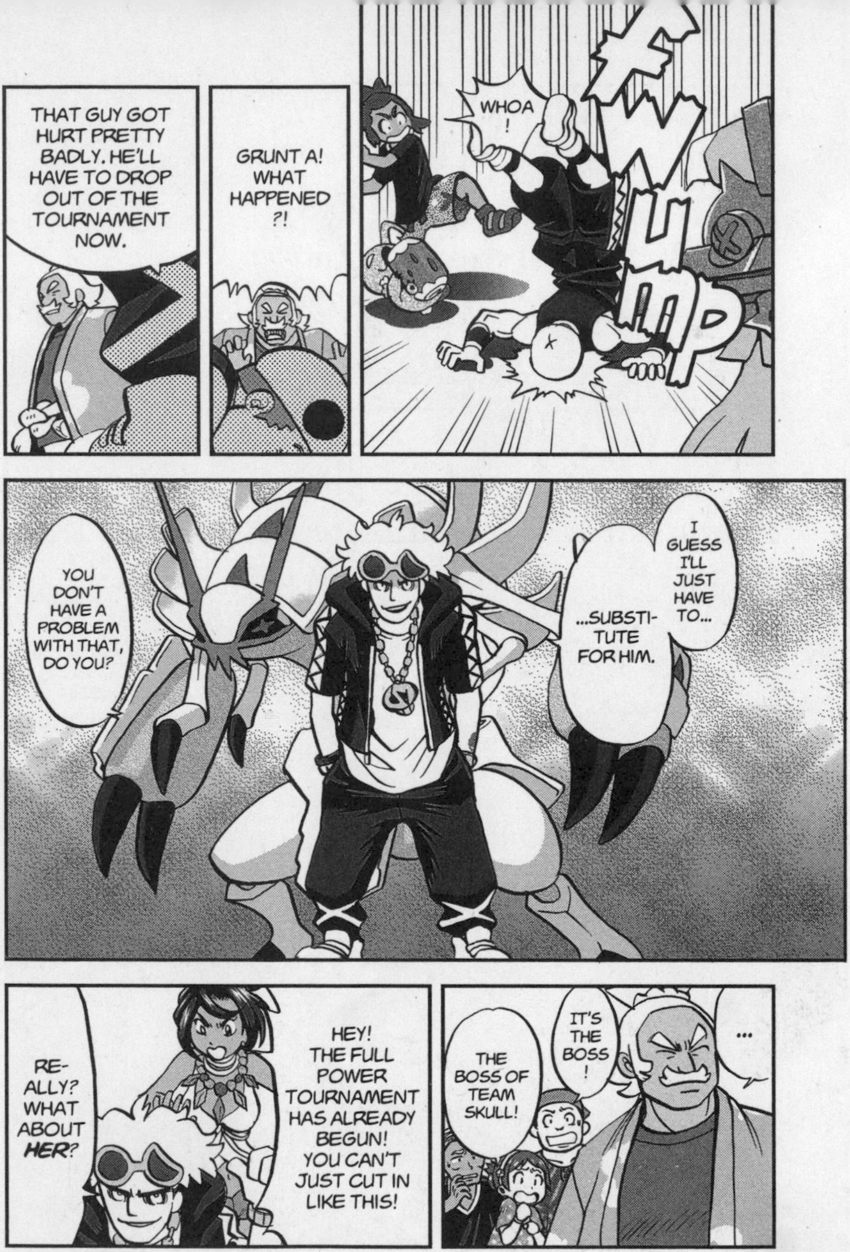
WHOA!
THUMP
GRUNT A! WHAT HAPPENED?!
THAT GUY GOT HURT PRETTY BADLY. HE'LL HAVE TO DROP OUT OF THE TOURNAMENT NOW.
I GUESS I'LL JUST HAVE TO...
...SUBSTITUTE FOR HIM.
YOU DON'T HAVE A PROBLEM WITH THAT, DO YOU?
...
IT'S THE BOSS!
THE BOSS OF TEAM SKULL!
HEY! THE FULL POWER TOURNAMENT HAS ALREADY BEGUN! YOU CAN'T JUST CUT IN LIKE THIS!
RE-ALLY? WHAT ABOUT HER?

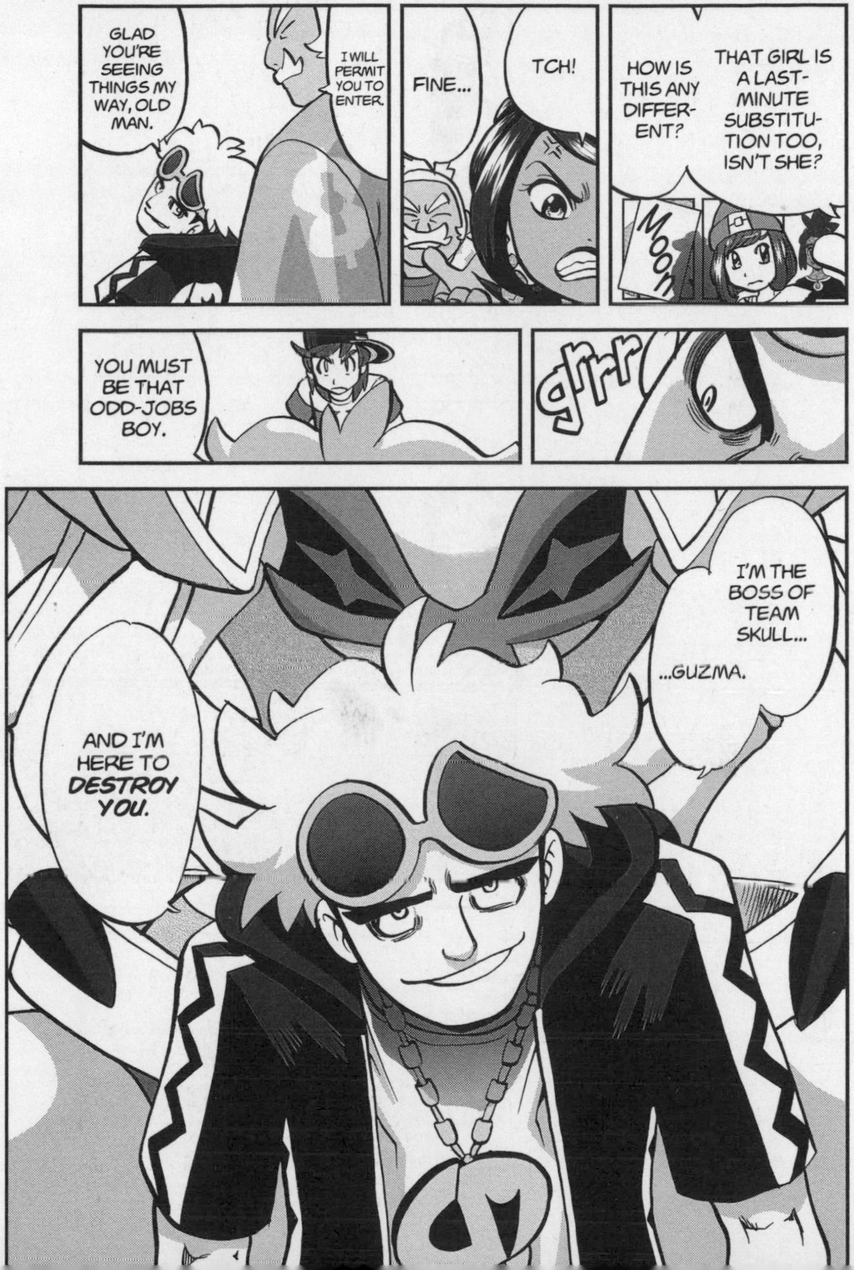
THAT GIRL IS A LAST-MINUTE SUBSTITUTION TOO, ISN'T SHE?
HOW IS THIS ANY DIFFERENT?
MOON
TCH!
FINE...
I WILL PERMIT YOU TO ENTER.
GLAD YOU'RE SEEING THINGS MY WAY, OLD MAN.
grrr
YOU MUST BE THAT ODD-JOBS BOY.
I'M THE BOSS OF TEAM SKULL...
...GUZMA.
AND I'M HERE TO **DESTROY YOU.**

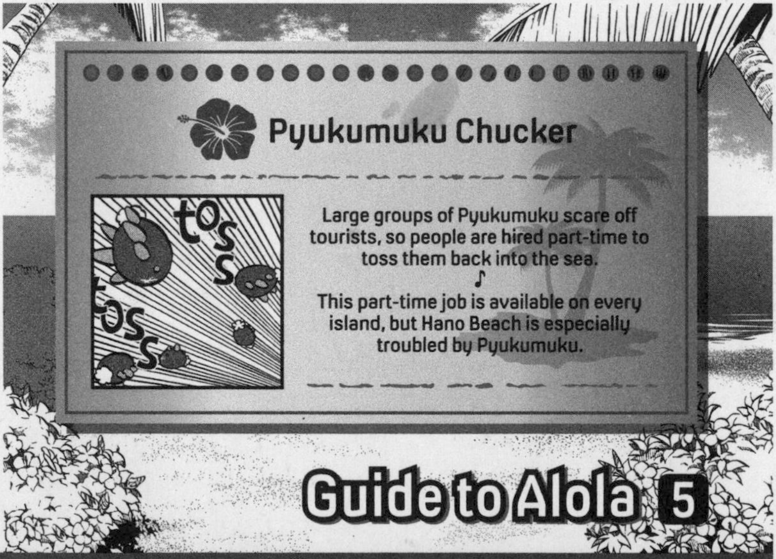
Pyukumuku Chucker
toss
toss
Large groups of Pyukumuku scare off tourists, so people are hired part-time to toss them back into the sea.
♪
This part-time job is available on every island, but Hano Beach is especially troubled by Pyukumuku.
Guide to Alola 5

Adventure 6
The Party Crasher and Guzma the Destroyer

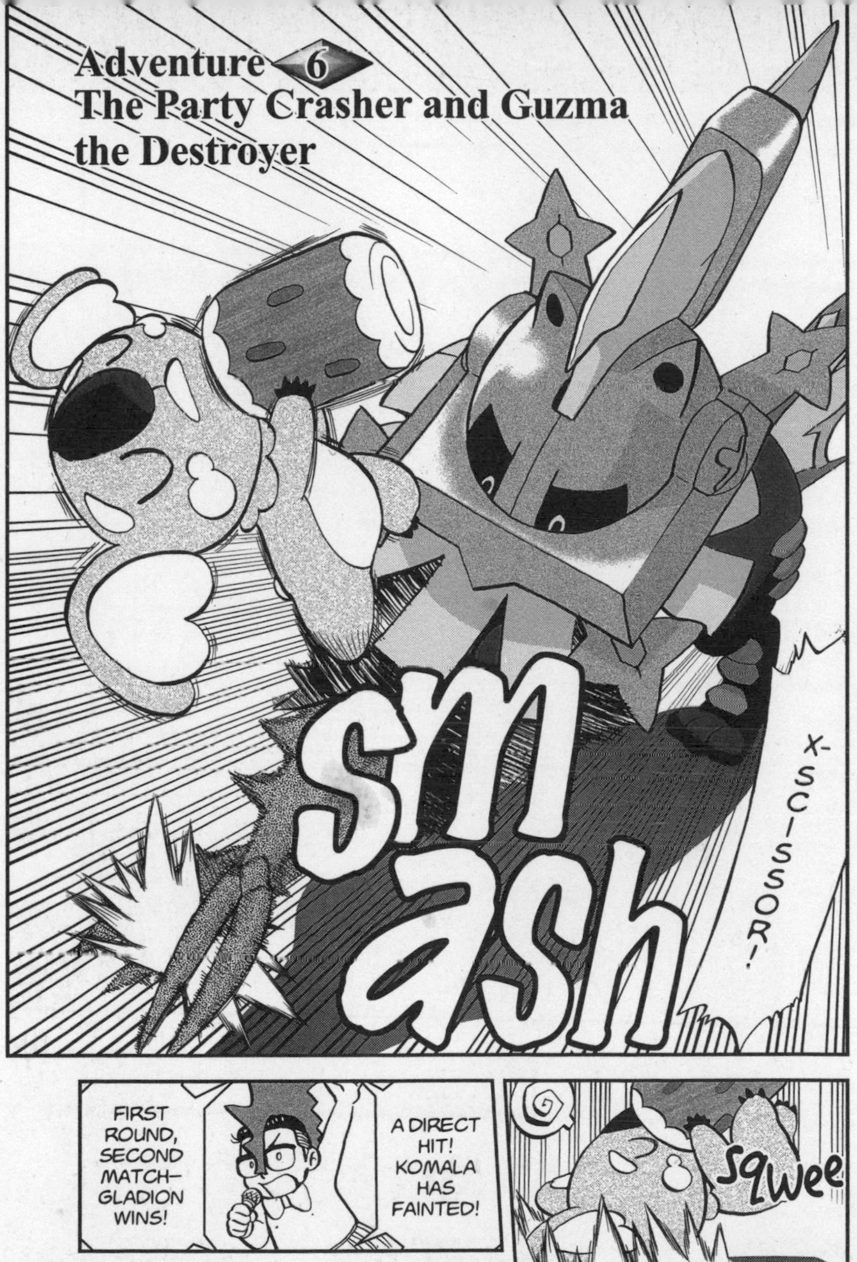
SMASH
X-SCISSOR!
SQWEE
A DIRECT HIT! KOMALA HAS FAINTED!
FIRST ROUND, SECOND MATCH— GLADION WINS!

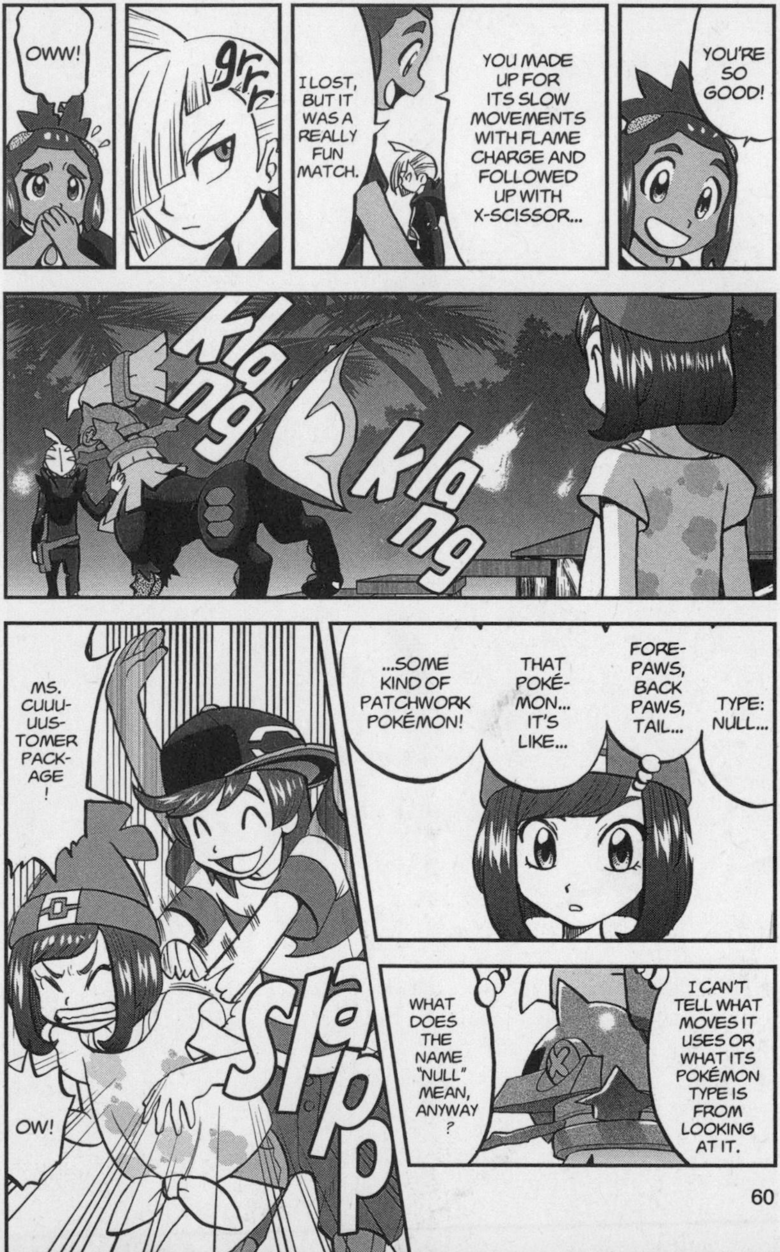
YOU'RE SO GOOD!
YOU MADE UP FOR ITS SLOW MOVEMENTS WITH FLAME CHARGE AND FOLLOWED UP WITH X-SCISSOR...
I LOST, BUT IT WAS A REALLY FUN MATCH.
grrr
OWW!
klang
klang
TYPE: NULL...
FORE-PAWS, BACK PAWS, TAIL...
THAT POKÉMON... IT'S LIKE...
...SOME KIND OF PATCHWORK POKÉMON!
I CAN'T TELL WHAT MOVES IT USES OR WHAT ITS POKÉMON TYPE IS FROM LOOKING AT IT.
WHAT DOES THE NAME "NULL" MEAN, ANYWAY?
MS. CUUUUUSTOMER PACKAGE!
slap
OW!

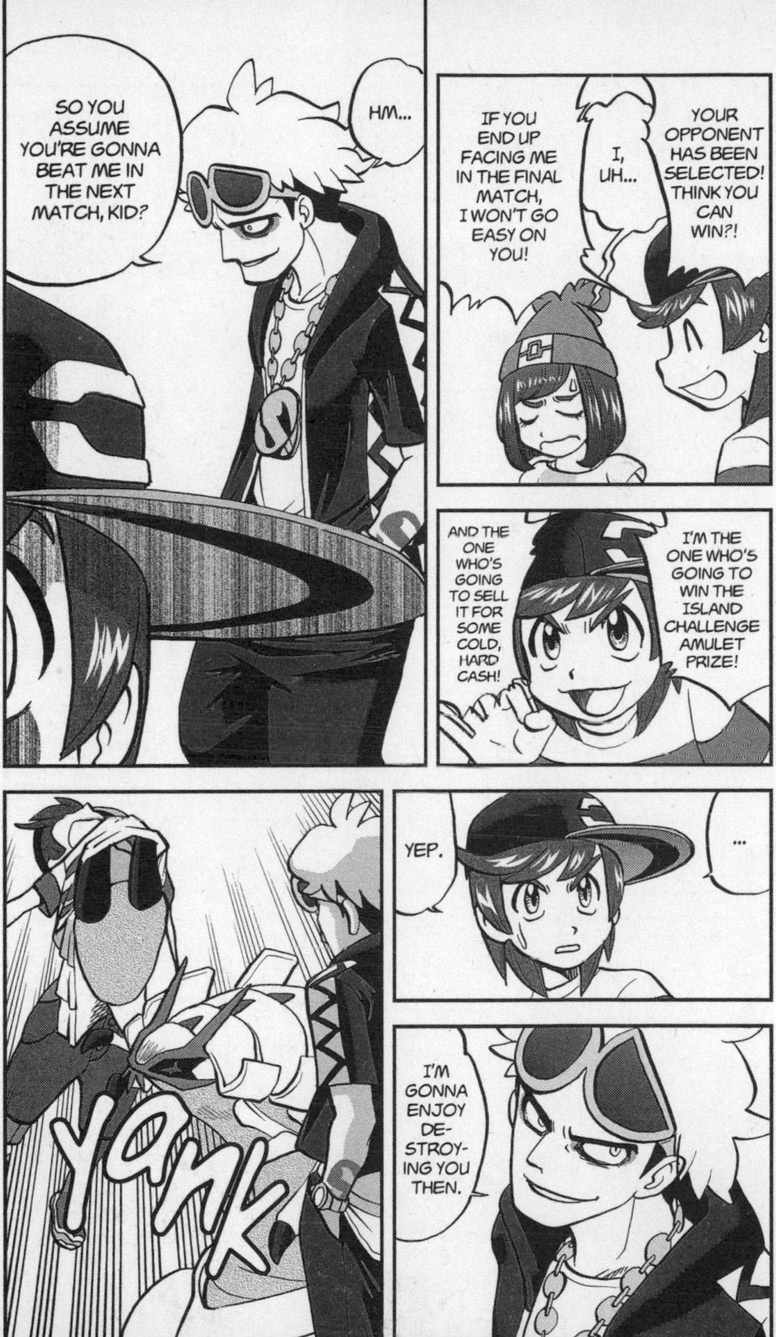
YOUR OPPONENT HAS BEEN SELECTED! THINK YOU CAN WIN?!
I, UH...
IF YOU END UP FACING ME IN THE FINAL MATCH, I WON'T GO EASY ON YOU!
I'M THE ONE WHO'S GOING TO WIN THE ISLAND CHALLENGE AMULET PRIZE!
AND THE ONE WHO'S GOING TO SELL IT FOR SOME COLD, HARD CASH!
HM...
SO YOU ASSUME YOU'RE GONNA BEAT ME IN THE NEXT MATCH, KID?
...
YEP.
I'M GONNA ENJOY DE-STROYING YOU THEN.
YANK

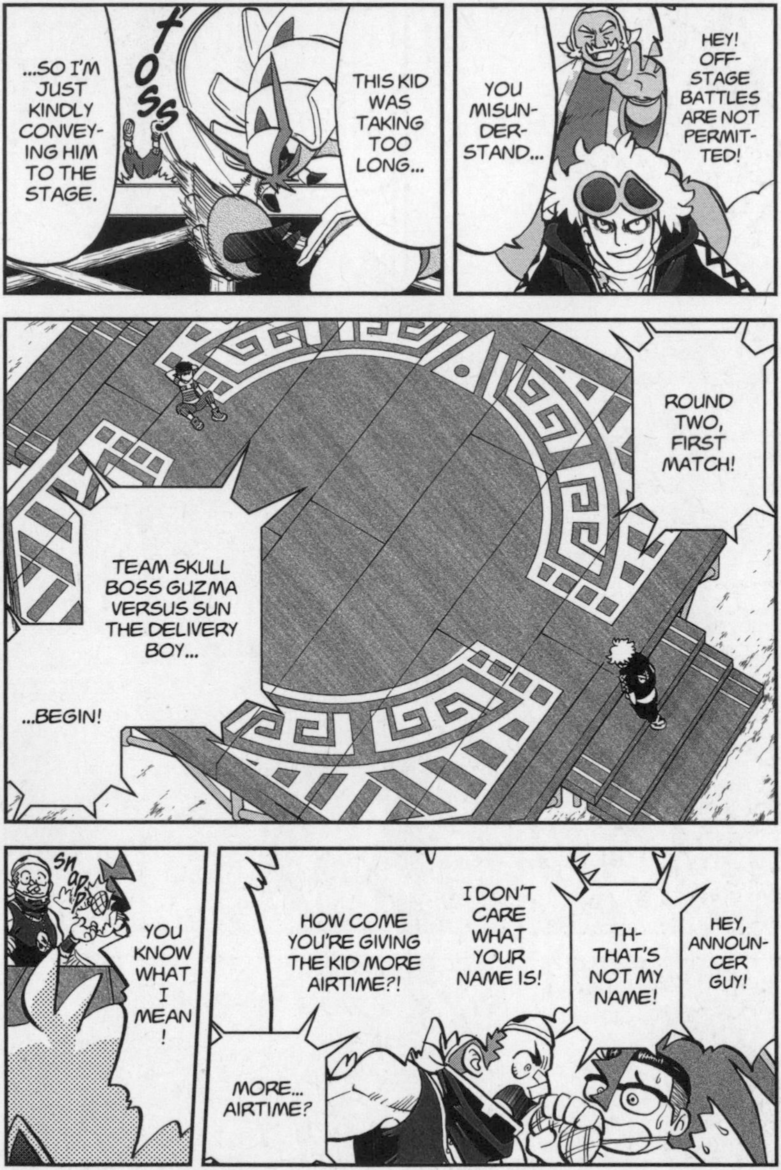
HEY! OFF-STAGE BATTLES ARE NOT PERMITTED!
YOU MISUNDERSTAND...
THIS KID WAS TAKING TOO LONG...
TOSS
...SO I'M JUST KINDLY CONVEYING HIM TO THE STAGE.
ROUND TWO, FIRST MATCH!
TEAM SKULL BOSS GUZMA VERSUS SUN THE DELIVERY BOY...
...BEGIN!
HEY, ANNOUNCER GUY!
TH-THAT'S NOT MY NAME!
I DON'T CARE WHAT YOUR NAME IS!
HOW COME YOU'RE GIVING THE KID MORE AIRTIME?!
MORE... AIRTIME?
SNAP
YOU KNOW WHAT I MEAN!

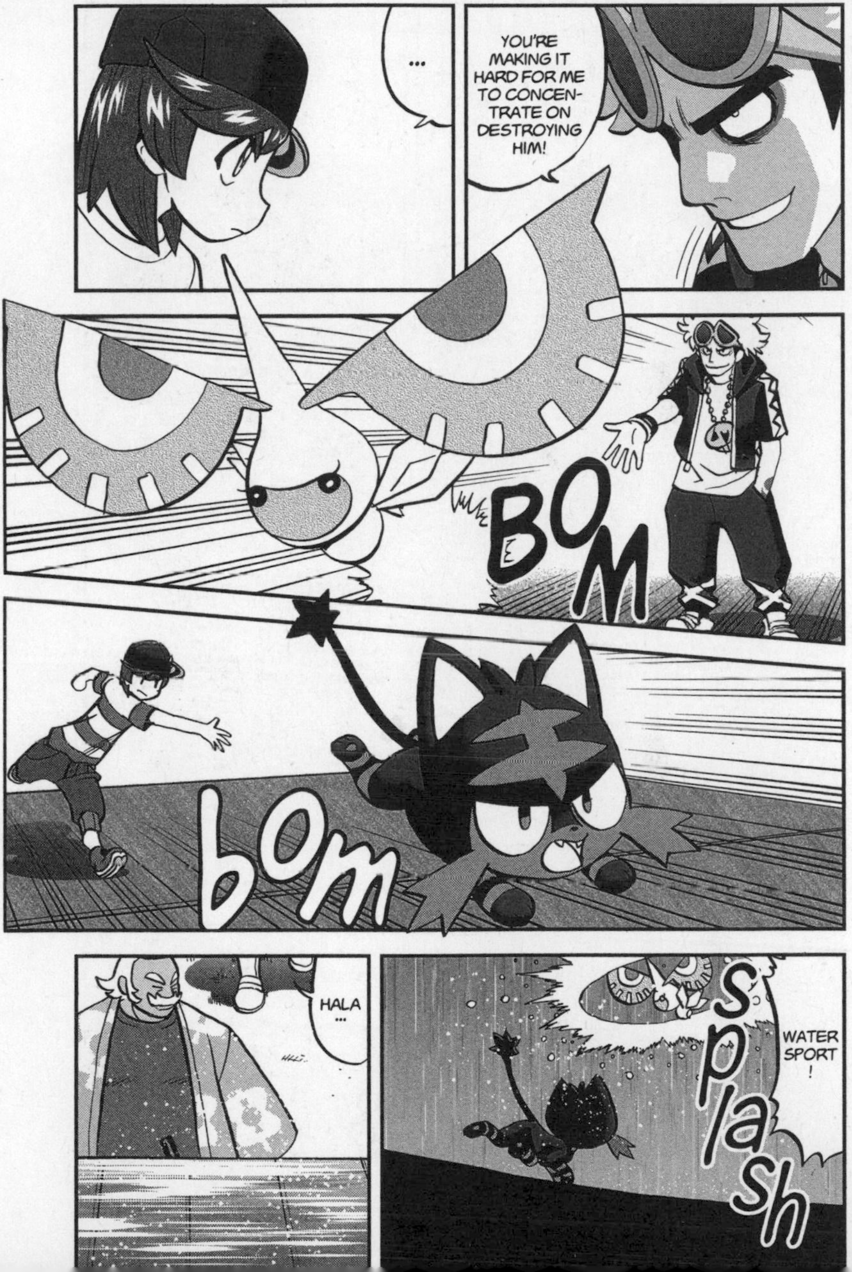
YOU'RE MAKING IT HARD FOR ME TO CONCEN-TRATE ON DESTROYING HIM!
...
BOM
bom
splash
WATER SPORT!
HALA ...

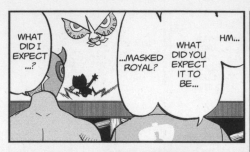

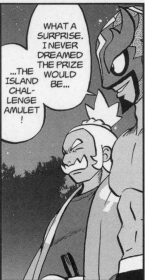

WHAT A SURPRISE. I NEVER DREAMED THE PRIZE WOULD BE...
...THE ISLAND CHAL-LENGE AMULET!
HM...
WHAT DID YOU EXPECT IT TO BE...
...MASKED ROYAL?
WHAT DID I EXPECT...?
I THOUGHT THE WINNER WOULD JUST QUALIFY TO FIGHT YOU.
THAT THE PRIZE WOULD BE THE RIGHT TO FIGHT THE KAHUNA. THAT'S THE REASON I'VE BEEN TRAINING SO HARD FOR THIS.
I LOST...
...BUT I HAD REALLY HOPED TO FACE YOU.
HA HA HA! I'M HON-ORED!
HOW-EVER...
...I BELIEVE THE ISLAND CHALLENGE AMULET IS WORTH MORE THAN THAT.
YES... I KNOW THAT MORE THAN ANY-BODY.
AFTER ALL, THE ISLAND CHALLENGE HAS BEEN A TRADITION SINCE ANCIENT TIMES.
YET IT HASN'T TAKEN PLACE DURING THE PAST FEW YEARS BECAUSE YOU WERE UNABLE TO FIND A TRAINER WORTHY OF IT.

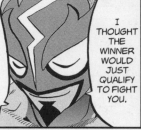

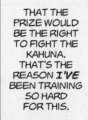

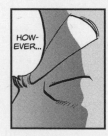

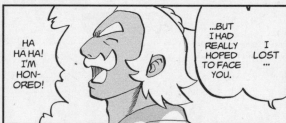

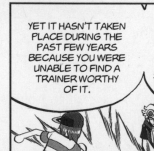

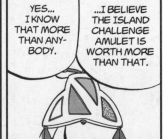

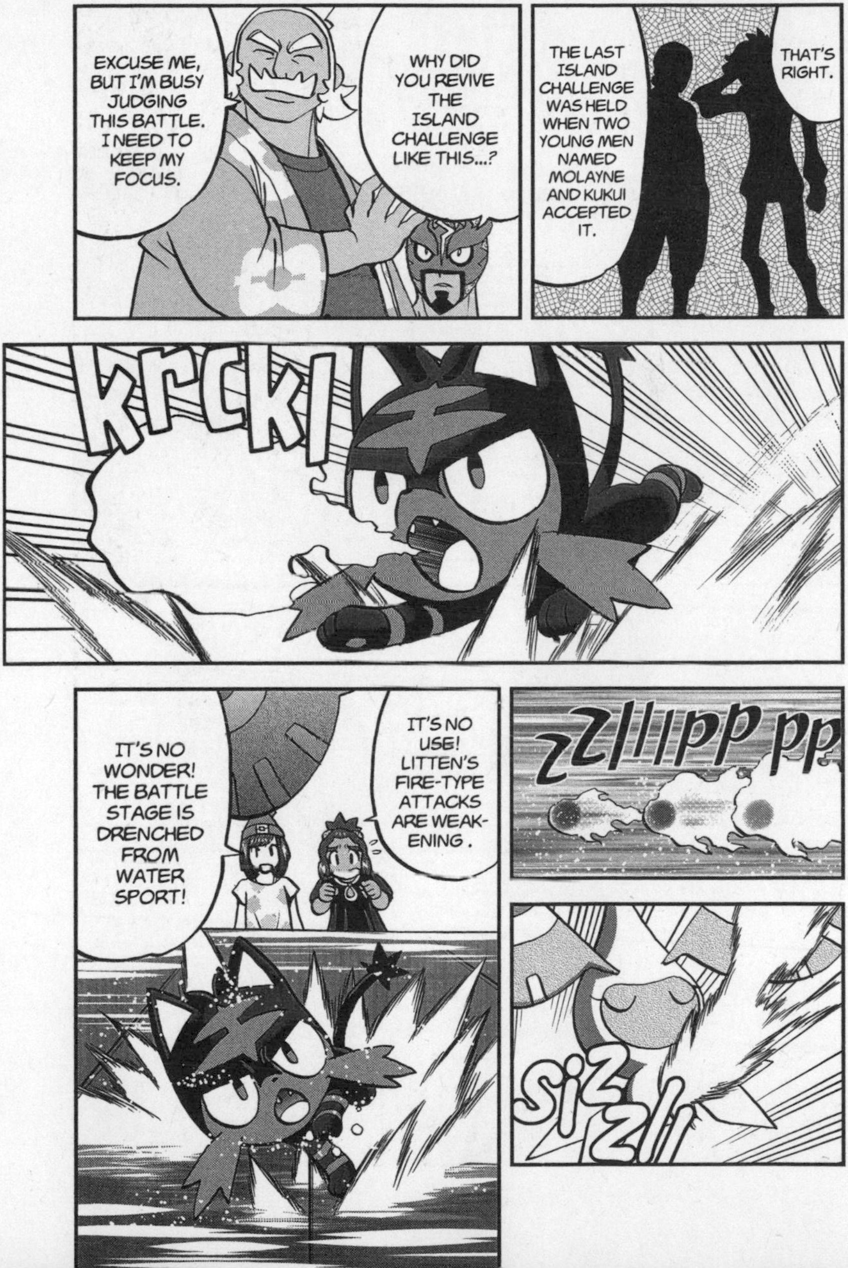
THAT'S RIGHT.
THE LAST ISLAND CHALLENGE WAS HELD WHEN TWO YOUNG MEN NAMED MOLAYNE AND KUKUI ACCEPTED IT.
WHY DID YOU REVIVE THE ISLAND CHALLENGE LIKE THIS...?
EXCUSE ME, BUT I'M BUSY JUDGING THIS BATTLE. I NEED TO KEEP MY FOCUS.
krckl
zzllpp pp
sizzl
IT'S NO USE! LITTEN'S FIRE-TYPE ATTACKS ARE WEAK-ENING.
IT'S NO WONDER! THE BATTLE STAGE IS DRENCHED FROM WATER SPORT!

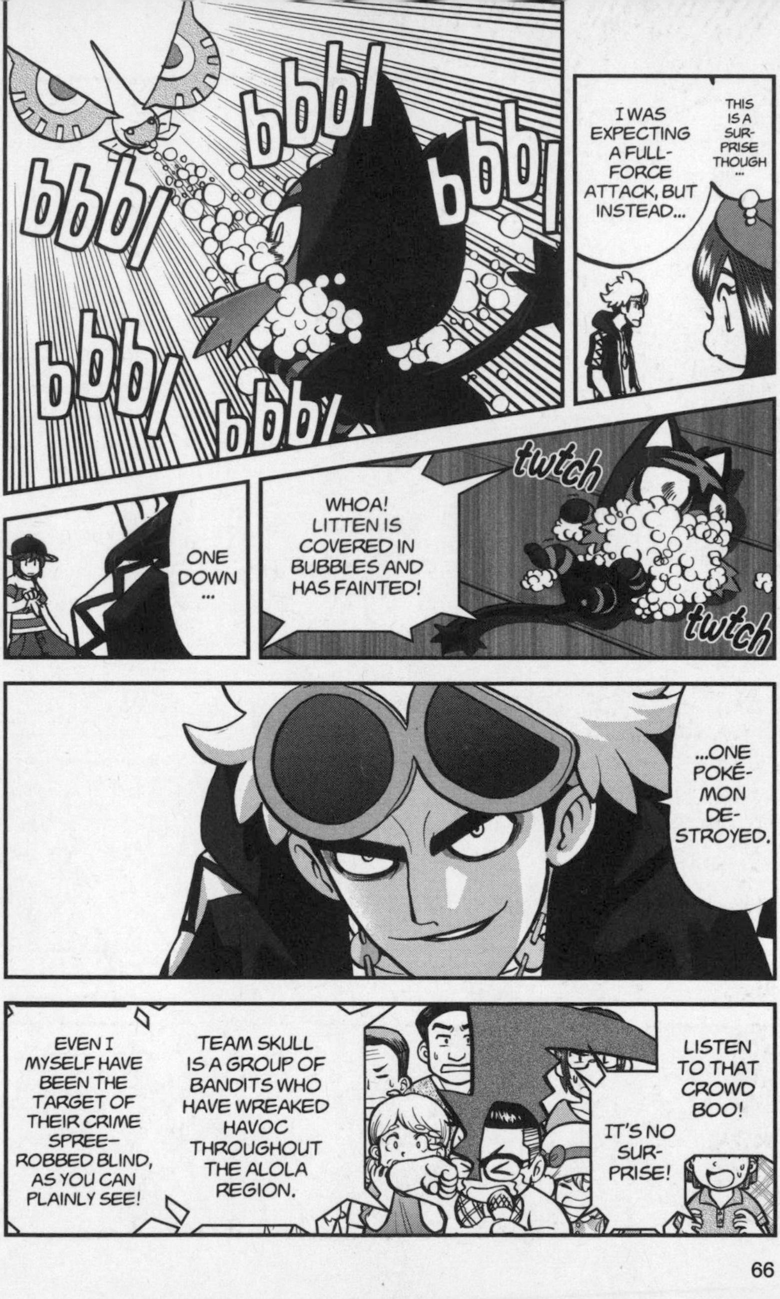
I WAS EXPECTING A FULL-FORCE ATTACK, BUT INSTEAD...
THIS IS A SUR-PRISE THOUGH...
bbbl
bbbl
bbbl
bbbl
bbbl
twtch
WHOA! LITTEN IS COVERED IN BUBBLES AND HAS FAINTED!
twtch
ONE DOWN...
...ONE POKÉ-MON DE-STROYED.
LISTEN TO THAT CROWD BOO!
IT'S NO SUR-PRISE!
TEAM SKULL IS A GROUP OF BANDITS WHO HAVE WREAKED HAVOC THROUGHOUT THE ALOLA REGION.
EVEN I MYSELF HAVE BEEN THE TARGET OF THEIR CRIME SPREE—ROBBED BLIND, AS YOU CAN PLAINLY SEE!

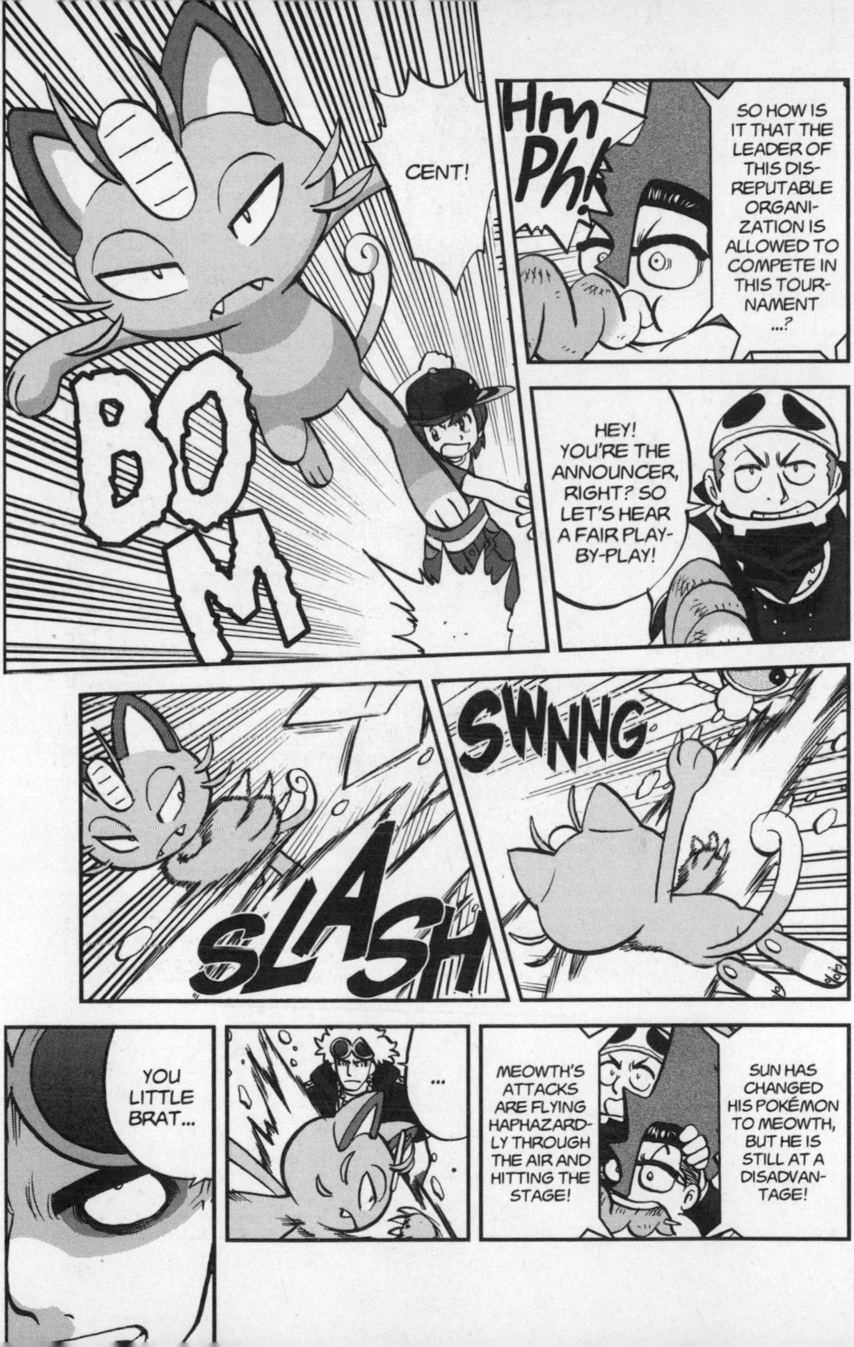
CENT!
BOOM
HmPh!
SO HOW IS IT THAT THE LEADER OF THIS DISREPUTABLE ORGANIZATION IS ALLOWED TO COMPETE IN THIS TOURNAMENT ...?
HEY! YOU'RE THE ANNOUNCER, RIGHT? SO LET'S HEAR A FAIR PLAY-BY-PLAY!
SLASH
SWNNG
YOU LITTLE BRAT...
...
MEOWTH'S ATTACKS ARE FLYING HAPHAZARDLY THROUGH THE AIR AND HITTING THE STAGE!
SUN HAS CHANGED HIS POKÉMON TO MEOWTH, BUT HE IS STILL AT A DISADVANTAGE!

NIGHT SLASH!

IT'S ABOUT TO CRASH!

MASQUERAIN IS SLOWLY FALLING!

W-WHAT?! WHAT DO YOU MEAN?!

OH, GUZMA IS IN TROUBLE!

SLA

SSSH

MASQUERAIN IS DOWN! BOTH TRAINERS HAVE ONLY ONE POKÉMON LEFT!

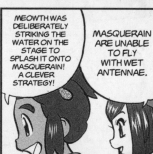

MEOWTH WAS DELIBERATELY STRIKING THE WATER ON THE STAGE TO SPLASH IT ONTO MASQUERAIN! A CLEVER STRATEGY!

MASQUERAIN ARE UNABLE TO FLY WITH WET ANTENNAE.

fwump

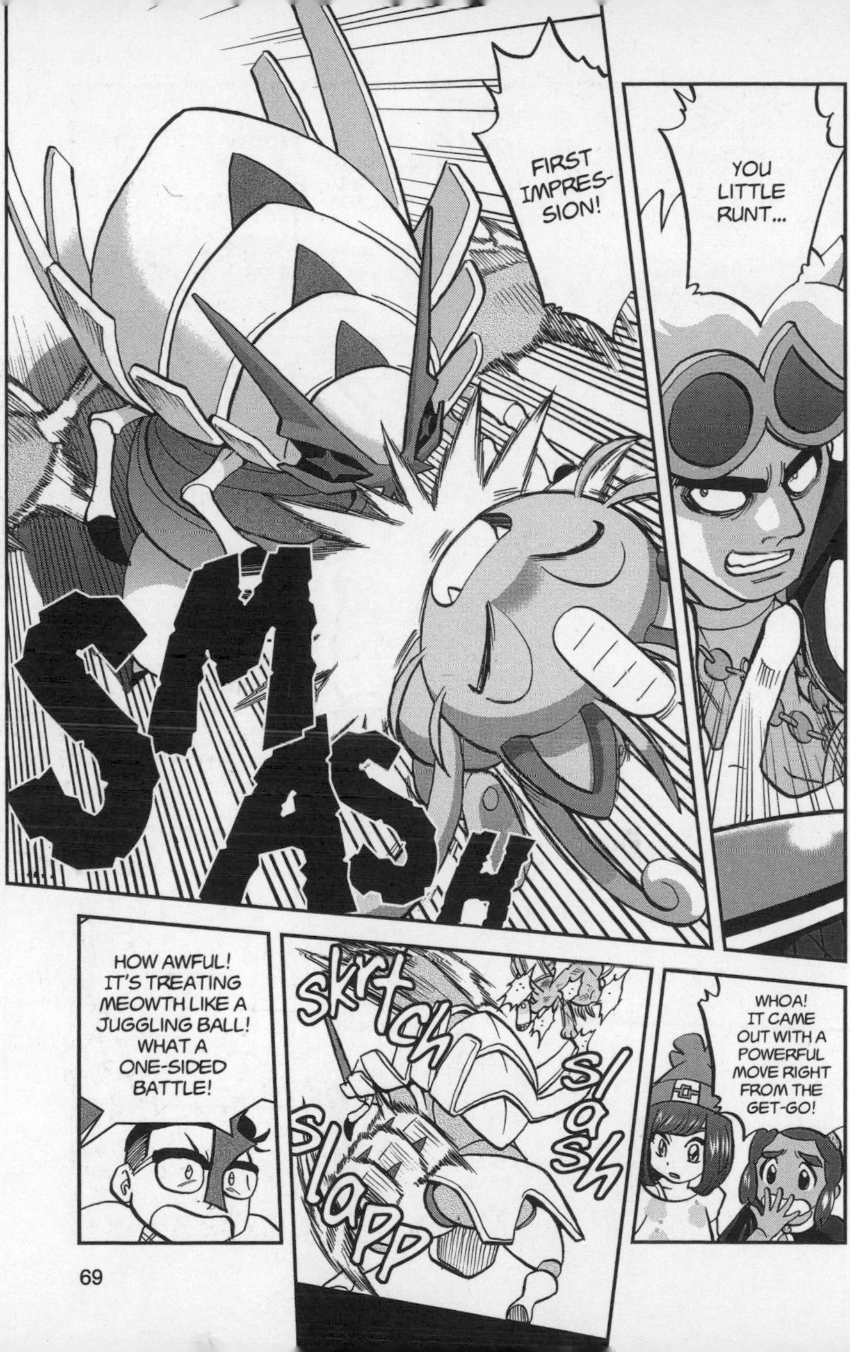
YOU LITTLE RUNT...
FIRST IMPRES-SION!
SMASH
WHOA! IT CAME OUT WITH A POWERFUL MOVE RIGHT FROM THE GET-GO!
skrtch
slash
slapp
HOW AWFUL! IT'S TREATING MEOWTH LIKE A JUGGLING BALL! WHAT A ONE-SIDED BATTLE!

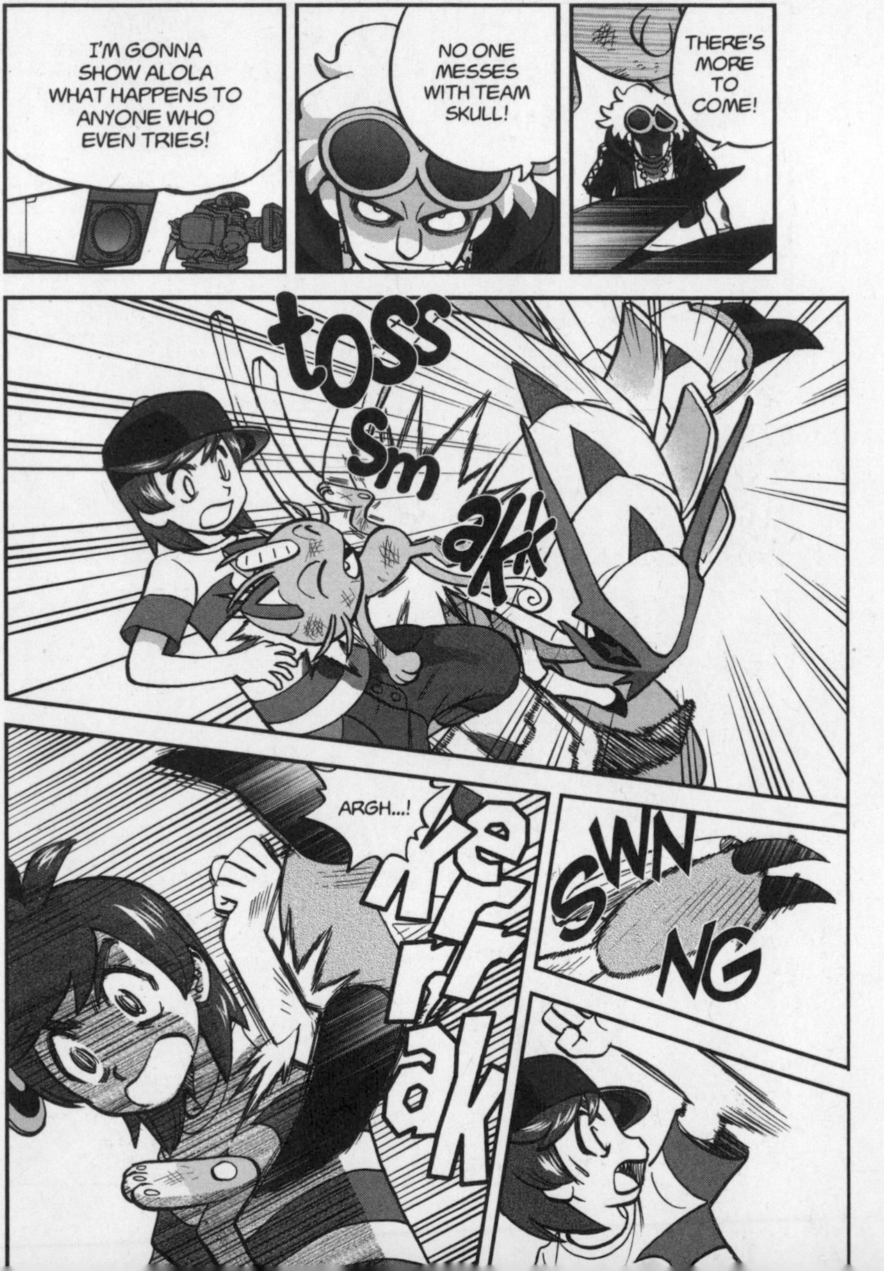
I'M GONNA SHOW ALOLA WHAT HAPPENS TO ANYONE WHO EVEN TRIES!
NO ONE MESSES WITH TEAM SKULL!
THERE'S MORE TO COME!
toss
smakk
ARGH...!
SWNNG

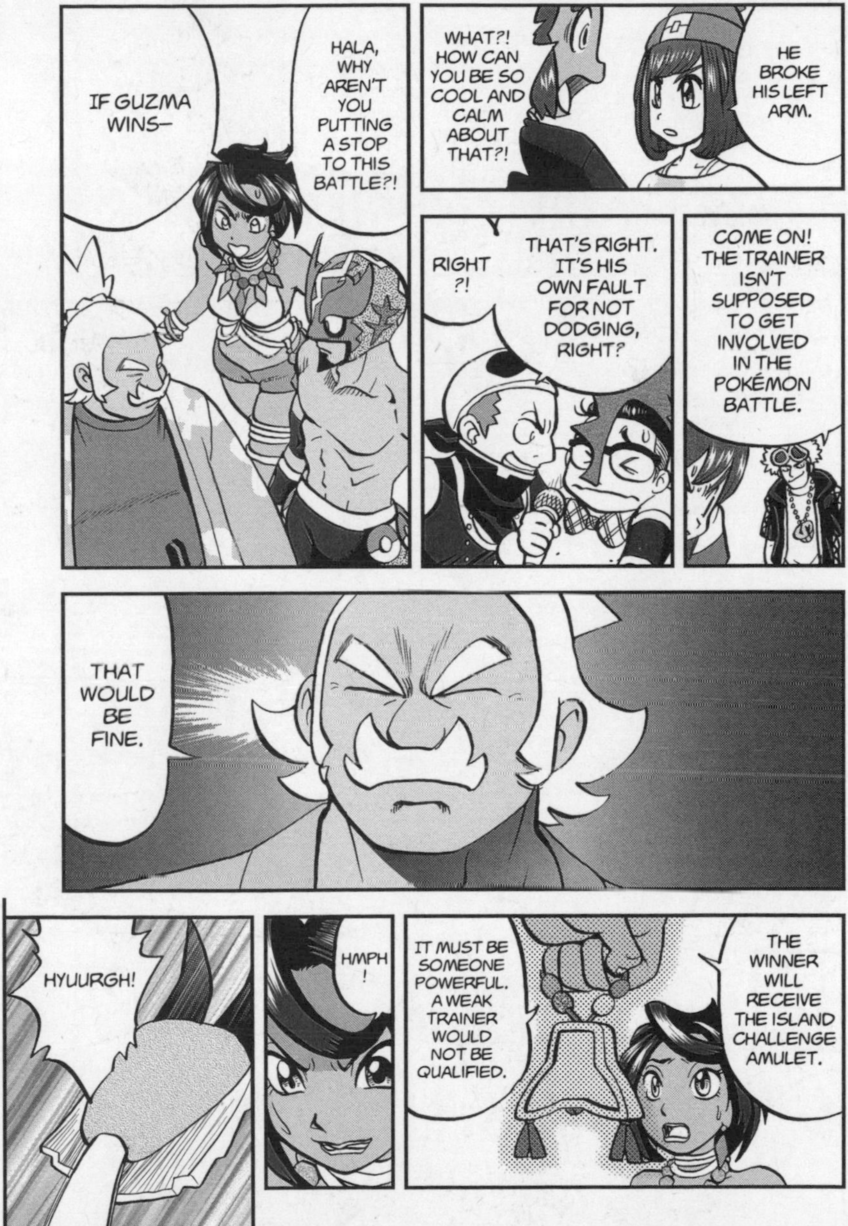
HE BROKE HIS LEFT ARM.
WHAT?! HOW CAN YOU BE SO COOL AND CALM ABOUT THAT?!
COME ON! THE TRAINER ISN'T SUPPOSED TO GET INVOLVED IN THE POKÉMON BATTLE.
THAT'S RIGHT. IT'S HIS OWN FAULT FOR NOT DODGING, RIGHT?
RIGHT?!
HALA, WHY AREN'T YOU PUTTING A STOP TO THIS BATTLE?!
IF GUZMA WINS—
THAT WOULD BE FINE.
THE WINNER WILL RECEIVE THE ISLAND CHALLENGE AMULET.
IT MUST BE SOMEONE POWERFUL. A WEAK TRAINER WOULD NOT BE QUALIFIED.
HMPH!
HYUURGH!

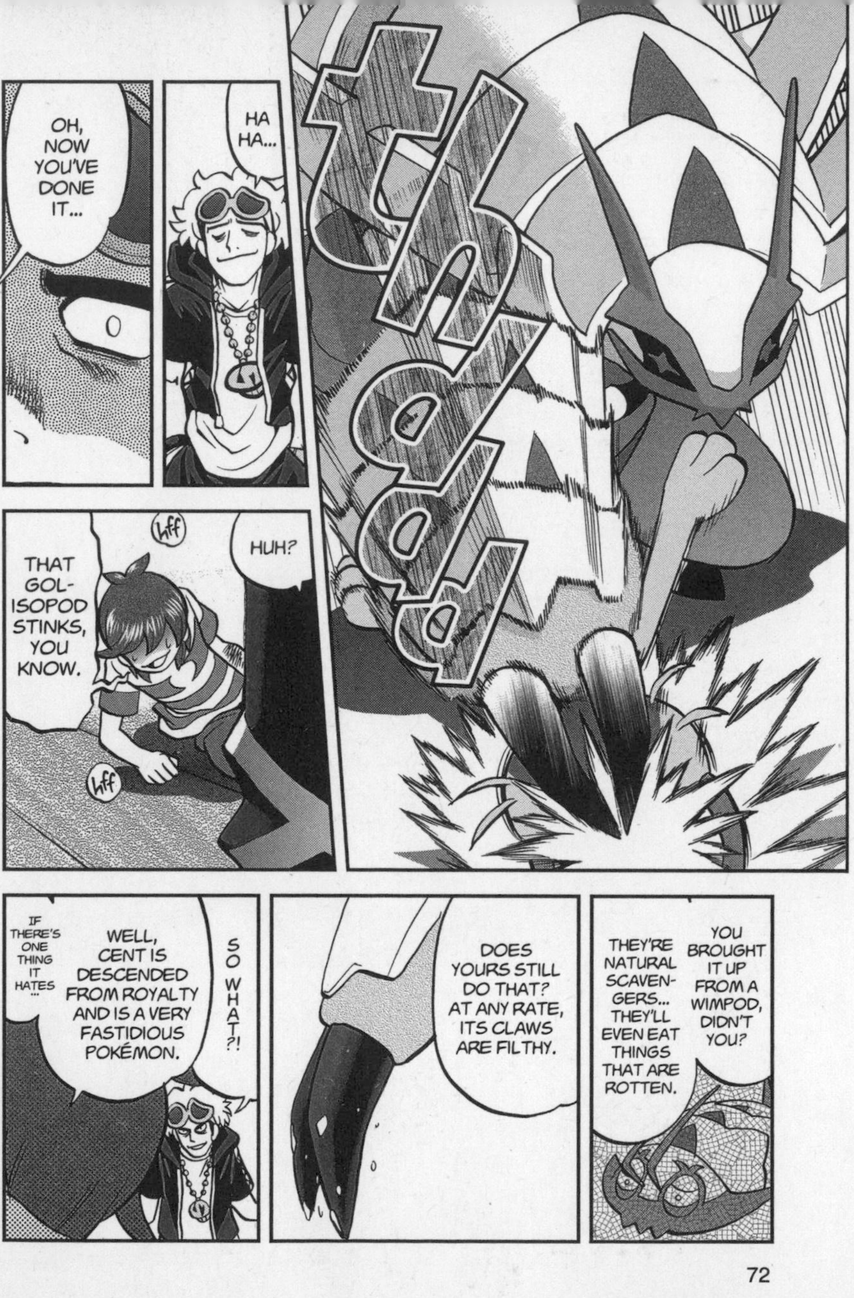

HA HA...
OH, NOW YOU'VE DONE IT...
HUH?
hff
THAT GOL-ISOPOD STINKS, YOU KNOW.
hff
YOU BROUGHT IT UP FROM A WIMPOD, DIDN'T YOU?
THEY'RE NATURAL SCAVEN-GERS... THEY'LL EVEN EAT THINGS THAT ARE ROTTEN.
DOES YOURS STILL DO THAT? AT ANY RATE, ITS CLAWS ARE FILTHY.
SO WHAT?!
WELL, CENT IS DESCENDED FROM ROYALTY AND IS A VERY FASTIDIOUS POKÉMON.
IF THERE'S ONE THING IT HATES...

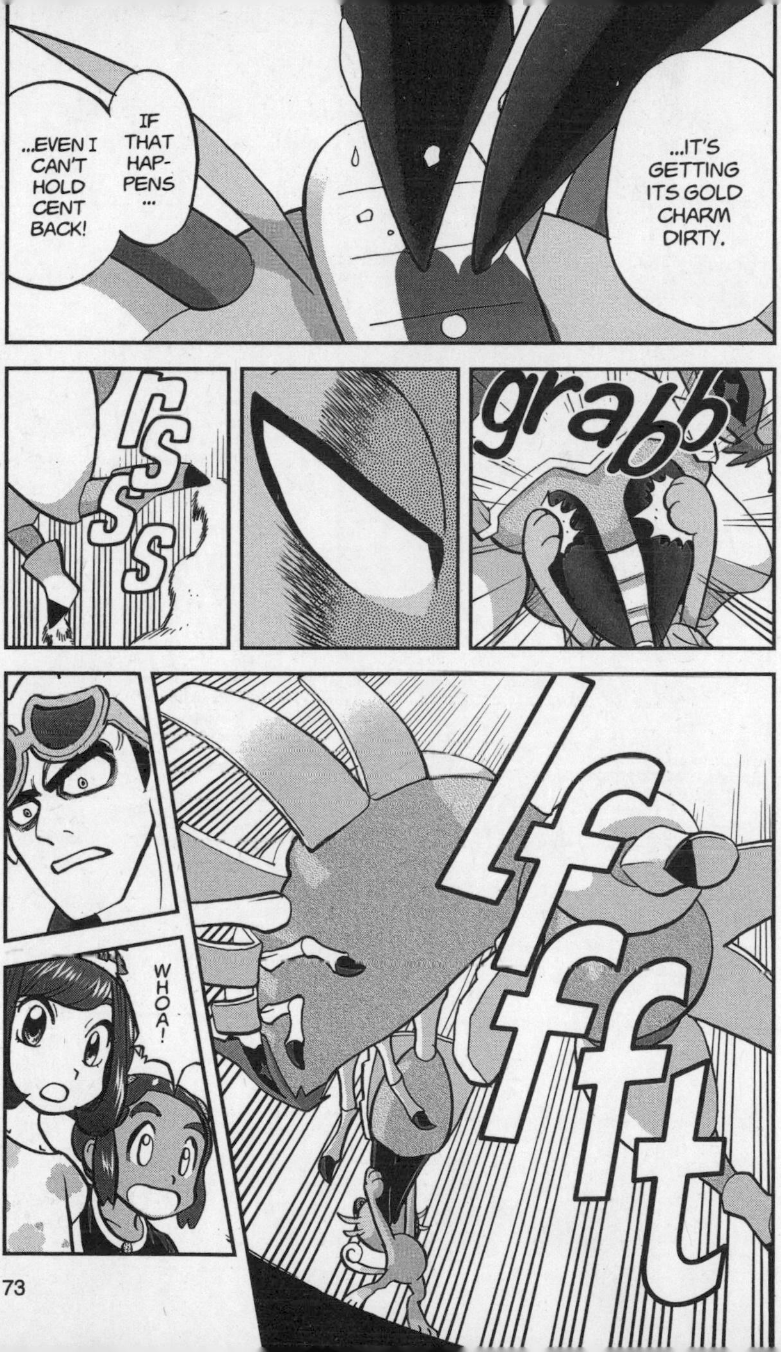
...IT'S GETTING ITS GOLD CHARM DIRTY.
IF THAT HAP-PENS ...
...EVEN I CAN'T HOLD CENT BACK!
grabb
rsss
ffft
WHOA!

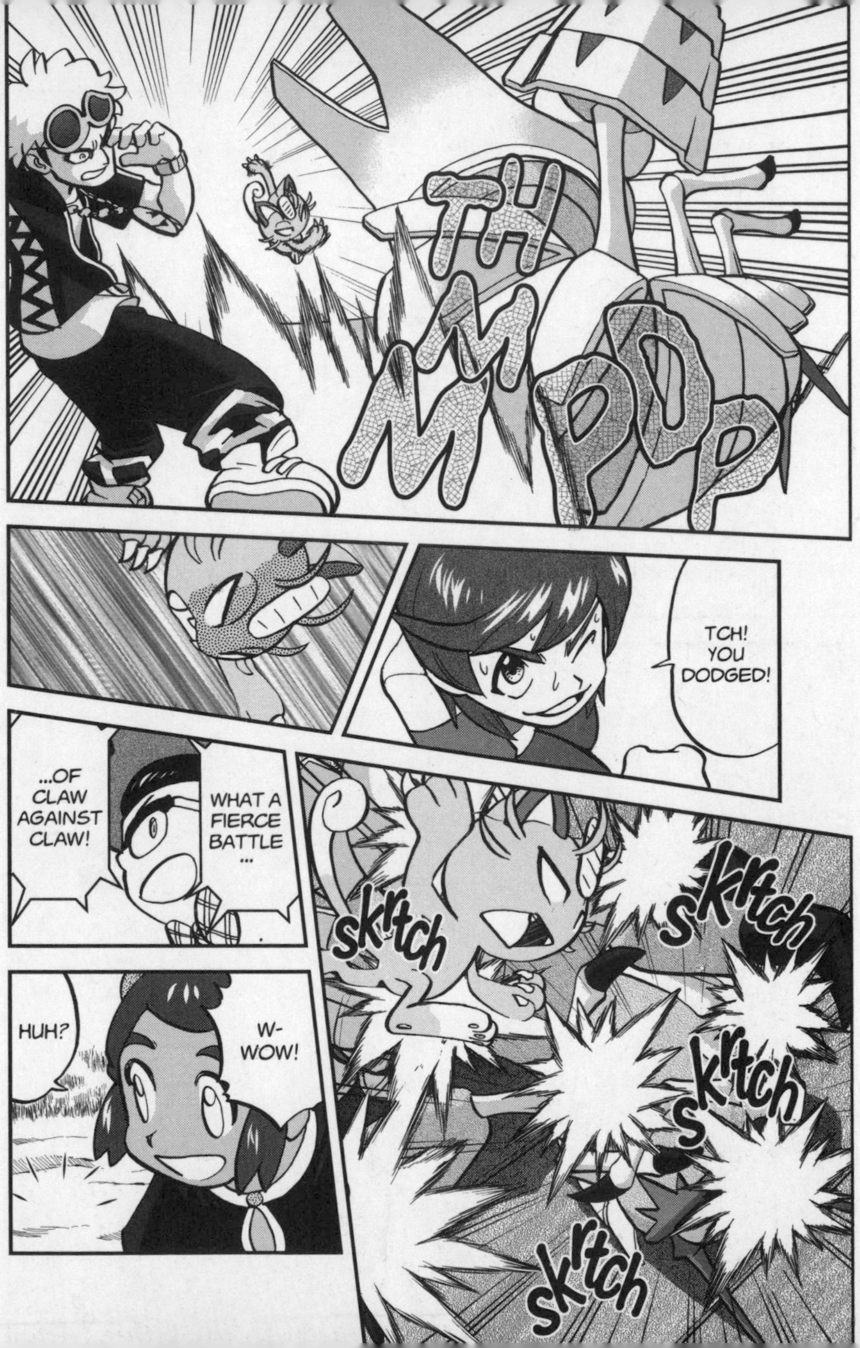
THMMPOP
TCH! YOU DODGED!
skrtch
skrtch
skrtch
skrtch
WHAT A FIERCE BATTLE ...
...OF CLAW AGAINST CLAW!
W-WOW!
HUH?

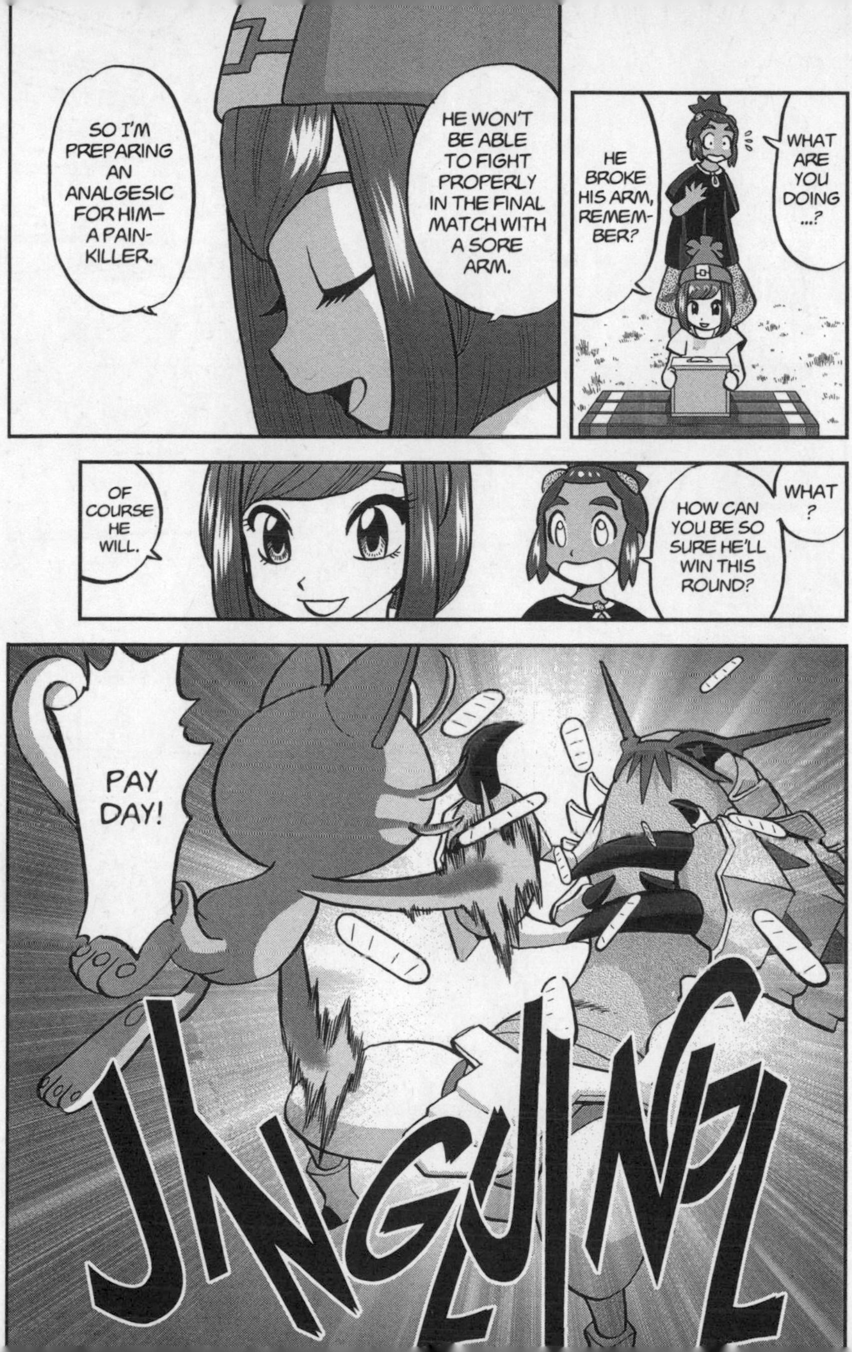
WHAT ARE YOU DOING ...?
HE BROKE HIS ARM, REMEMBER?
HE WON'T BE ABLE TO FIGHT PROPERLY IN THE FINAL MATCH WITH A SORE ARM.
SO I'M PREPARING AN ANALGESIC FOR HIM—A PAIN-KILLER.
WHAT?
HOW CAN YOU BE SO SURE HE'LL WIN THIS ROUND?
OF COURSE HE WILL.
PAY DAY!
JINGLING

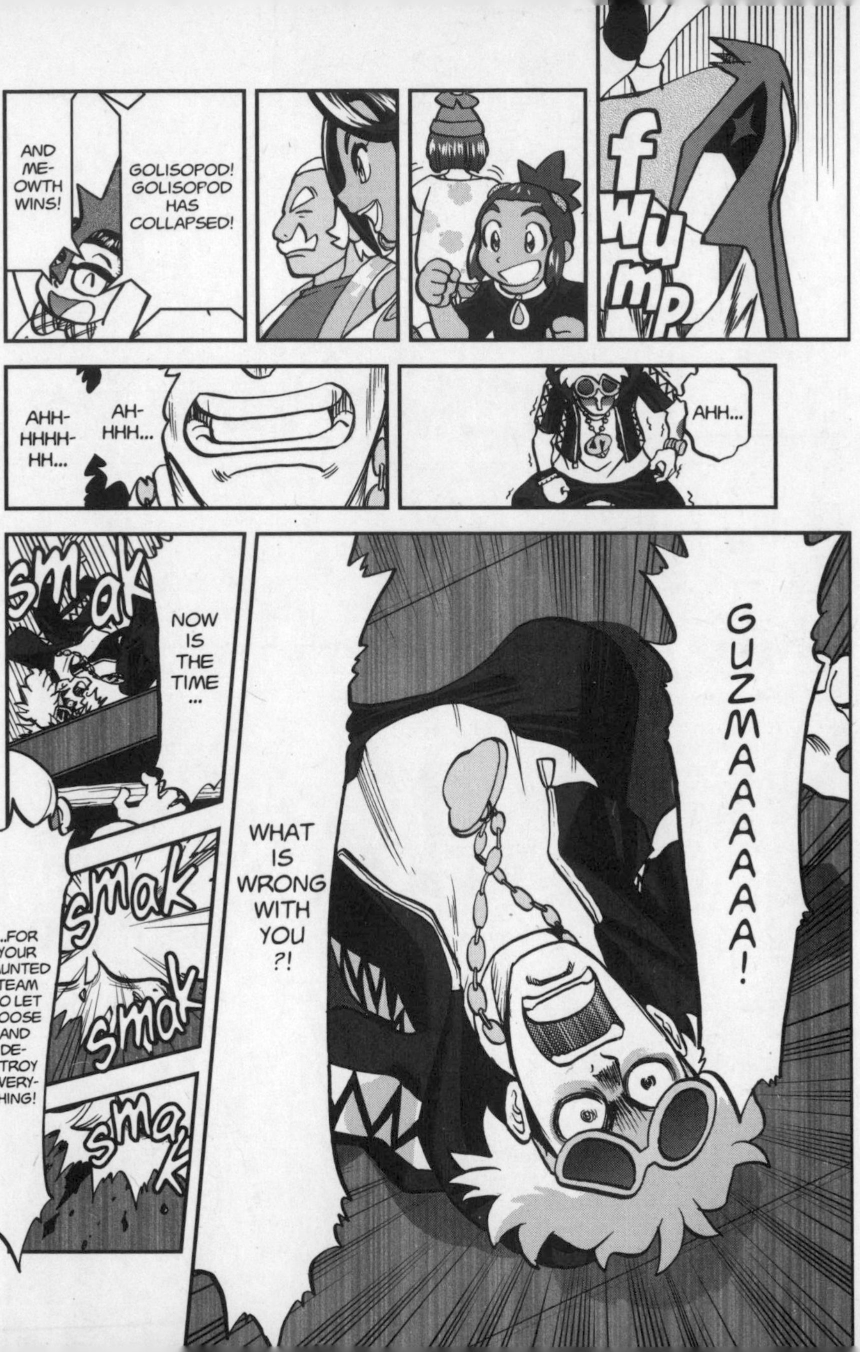
fwump
GOLISOPOD! GOLISOPOD HAS COLLAPSED!
AND ME-OWTH WINS!
AHH...
AH-HHH...
AHH-HHHH-HH...
GUZMAAAAAAAA!
WHAT IS WRONG WITH YOU ?!
smak
NOW IS THE TIME...
smak
smak
smak
...FOR YOUR VAUNTED TEAM TO LET LOOSE AND DE-STROY EVERY-THING!

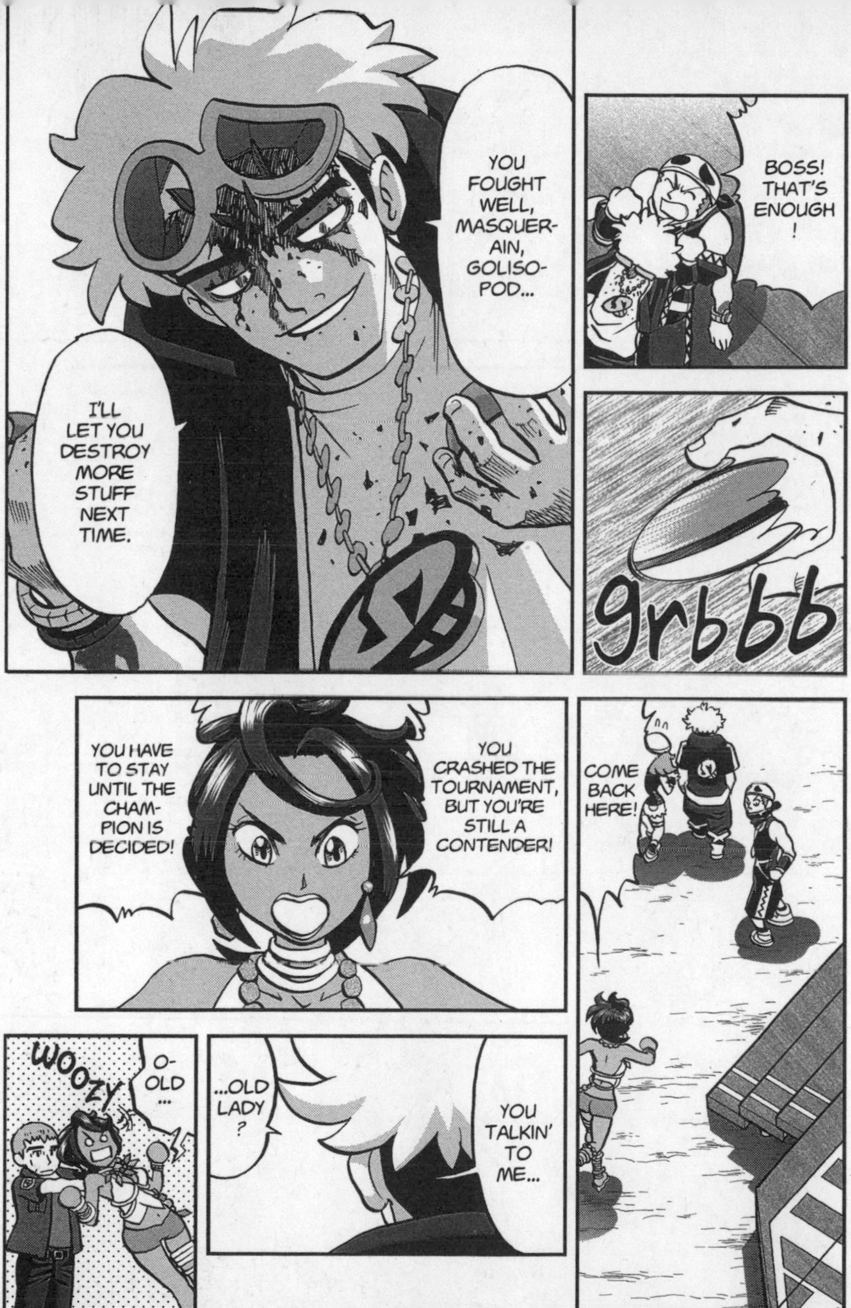
BOSS! THAT'S ENOUGH!
grbbb
YOU FOUGHT WELL, MASQUER-AIN, GOLISO-POD...
I'LL LET YOU DESTROY MORE STUFF NEXT TIME.
COME BACK HERE!
YOU CRASHED THE TOURNAMENT, BUT YOU'RE STILL A CONTENDER!
YOU HAVE TO STAY UNTIL THE CHAM-PION IS DECIDED!
YOU TALKIN' TO ME...
...OLD LADY?
O-OLD...
WOOZY

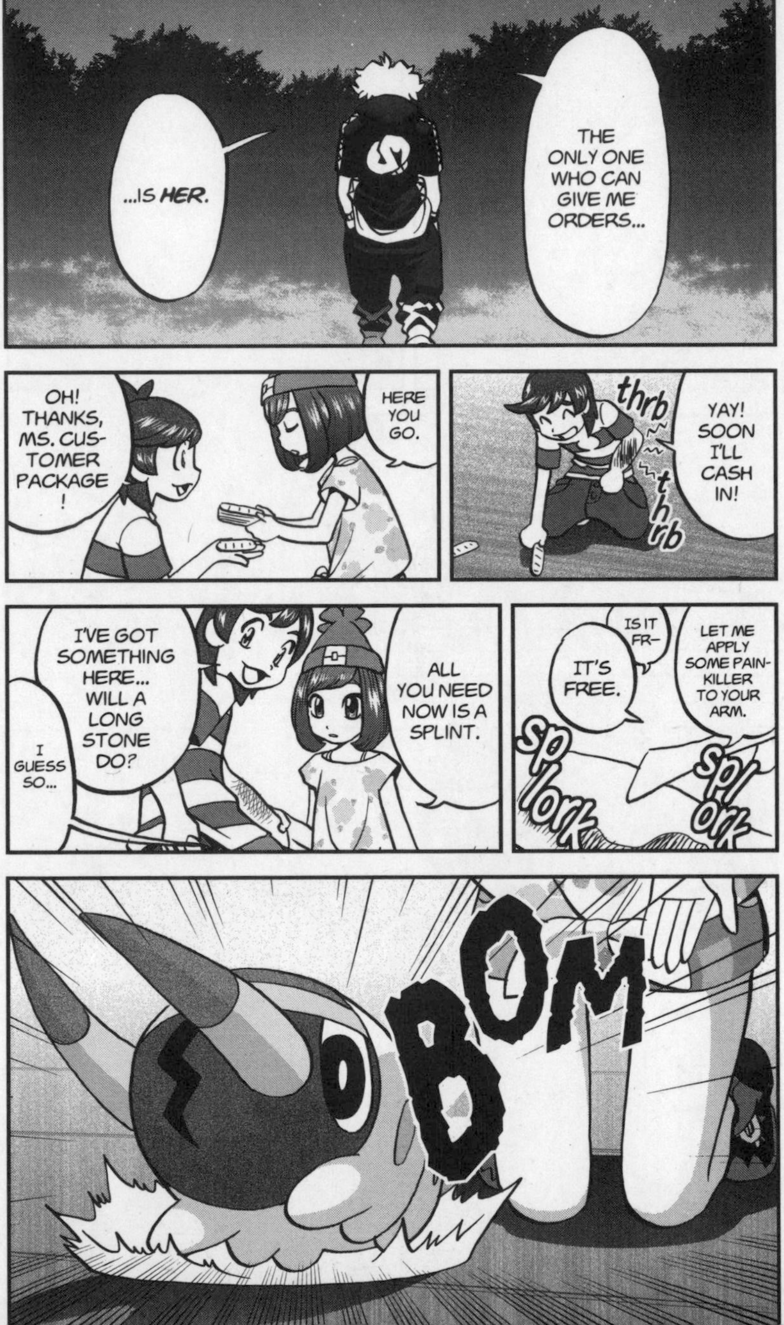
THE ONLY ONE WHO CAN GIVE ME ORDERS...
...IS HER.
YAY! SOON I'LL CASH IN!
thrb thrb
HERE YOU GO.
OH! THANKS, MS. CUSTOMER PACKAGE!
LET ME APPLY SOME PAINKILLER TO YOUR ARM.
IS IT FR–
IT'S FREE.
splork splork
ALL YOU NEED NOW IS A SPLINT.
I'VE GOT SOMETHING HERE... WILL A LONG STONE DO?
I GUESS SO...
BOM

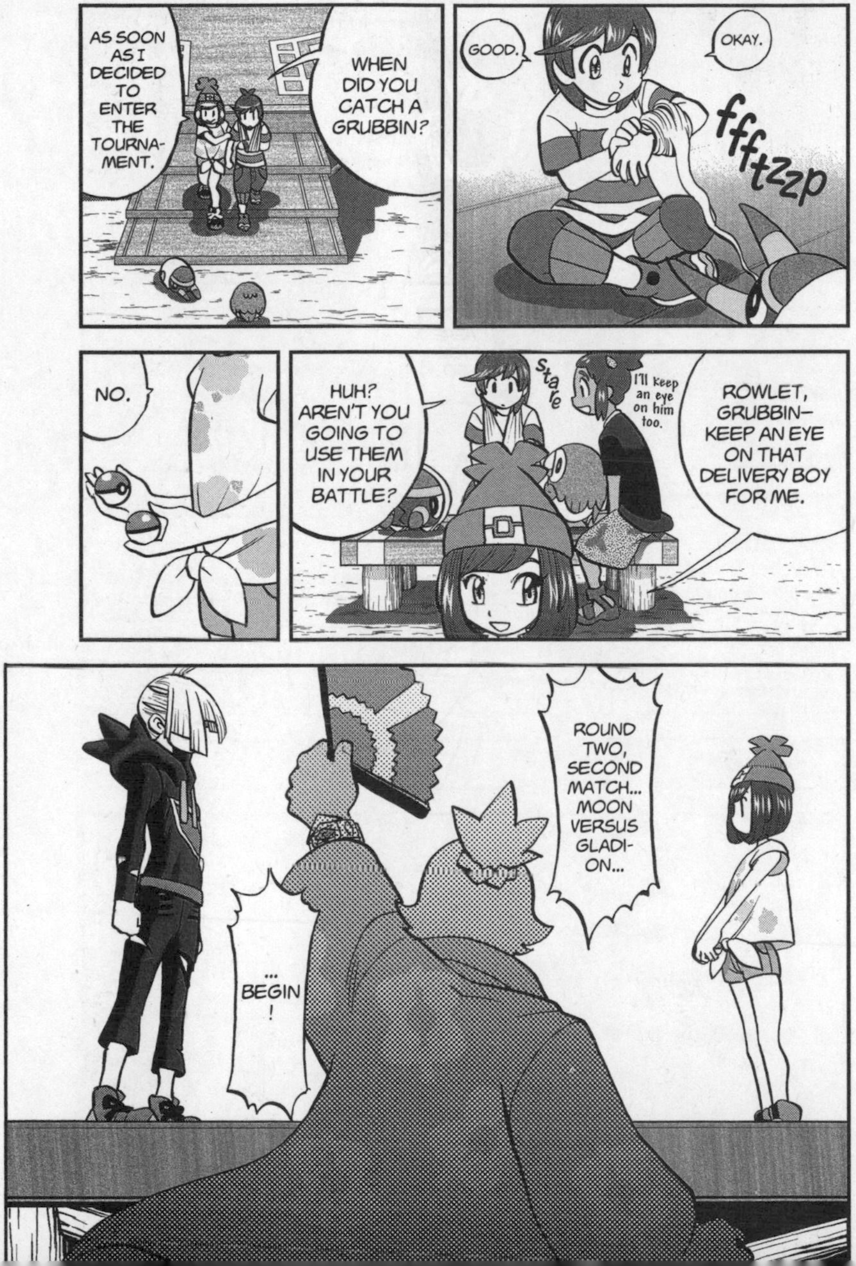
OKAY.
GOOD.
ffftzzp
WHEN DID YOU CATCH A GRUBBIN?
AS SOON AS I DECIDED TO ENTER THE TOURNAMENT.
ROWLET, GRUBBIN— KEEP AN EYE ON THAT DELIVERY BOY FOR ME.
I'll keep an eye on him too.
stare
HUH? AREN'T YOU GOING TO USE THEM IN YOUR BATTLE?
NO.
ROUND TWO, SECOND MATCH... MOON VERSUS GLADION...
...BEGIN!

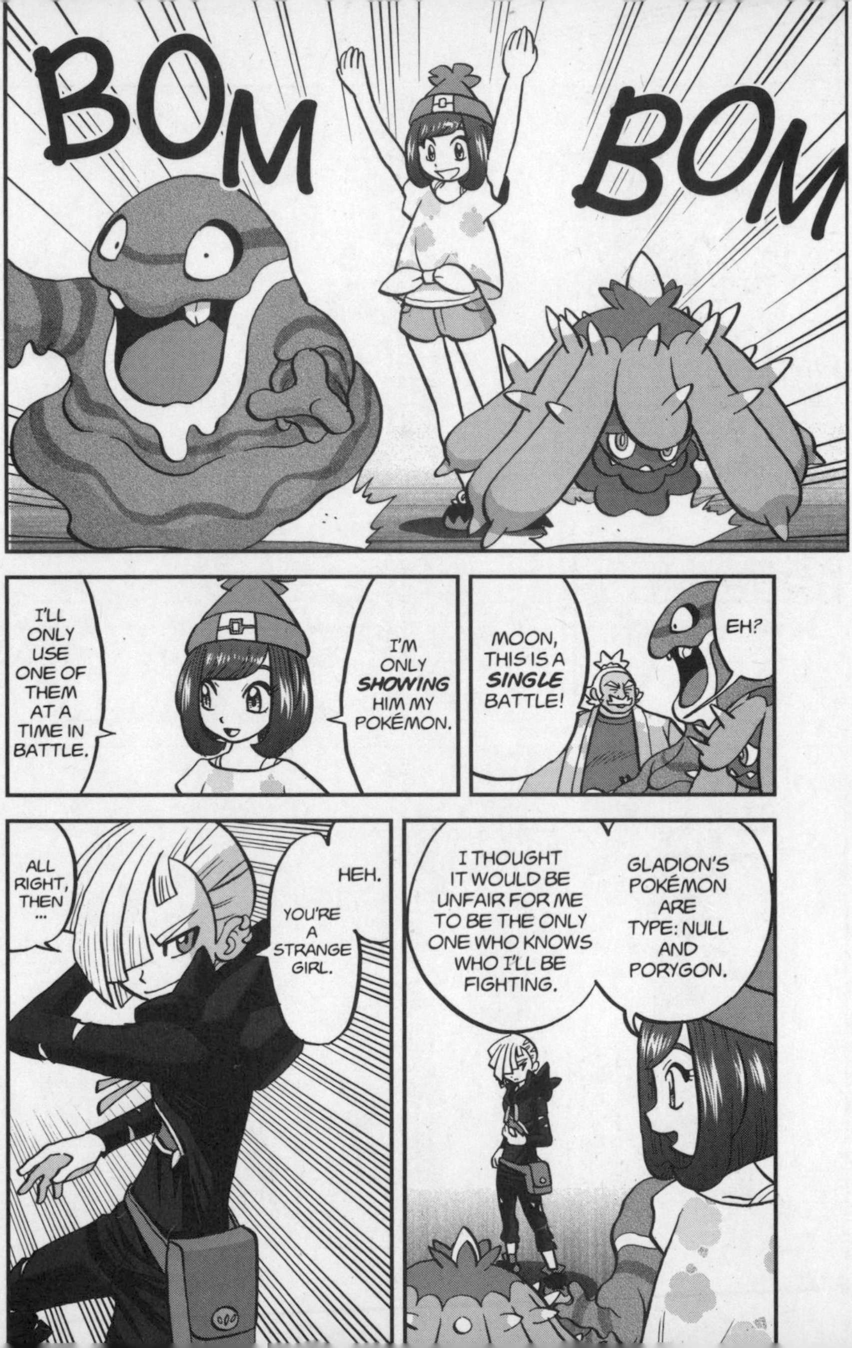
BOM
BOM
EH?
MOON, THIS IS A SINGLE BATTLE!
I'M ONLY SHOWING HIM MY POKÉMON.
I'LL ONLY USE ONE OF THEM AT A TIME IN BATTLE.
GLADION'S POKÉMON ARE TYPE: NULL AND PORYGON.
I THOUGHT IT WOULD BE UNFAIR FOR ME TO BE THE ONLY ONE WHO KNOWS WHO I'LL BE FIGHTING.
HEH.
YOU'RE A STRANGE GIRL.
ALL RIGHT, THEN ...

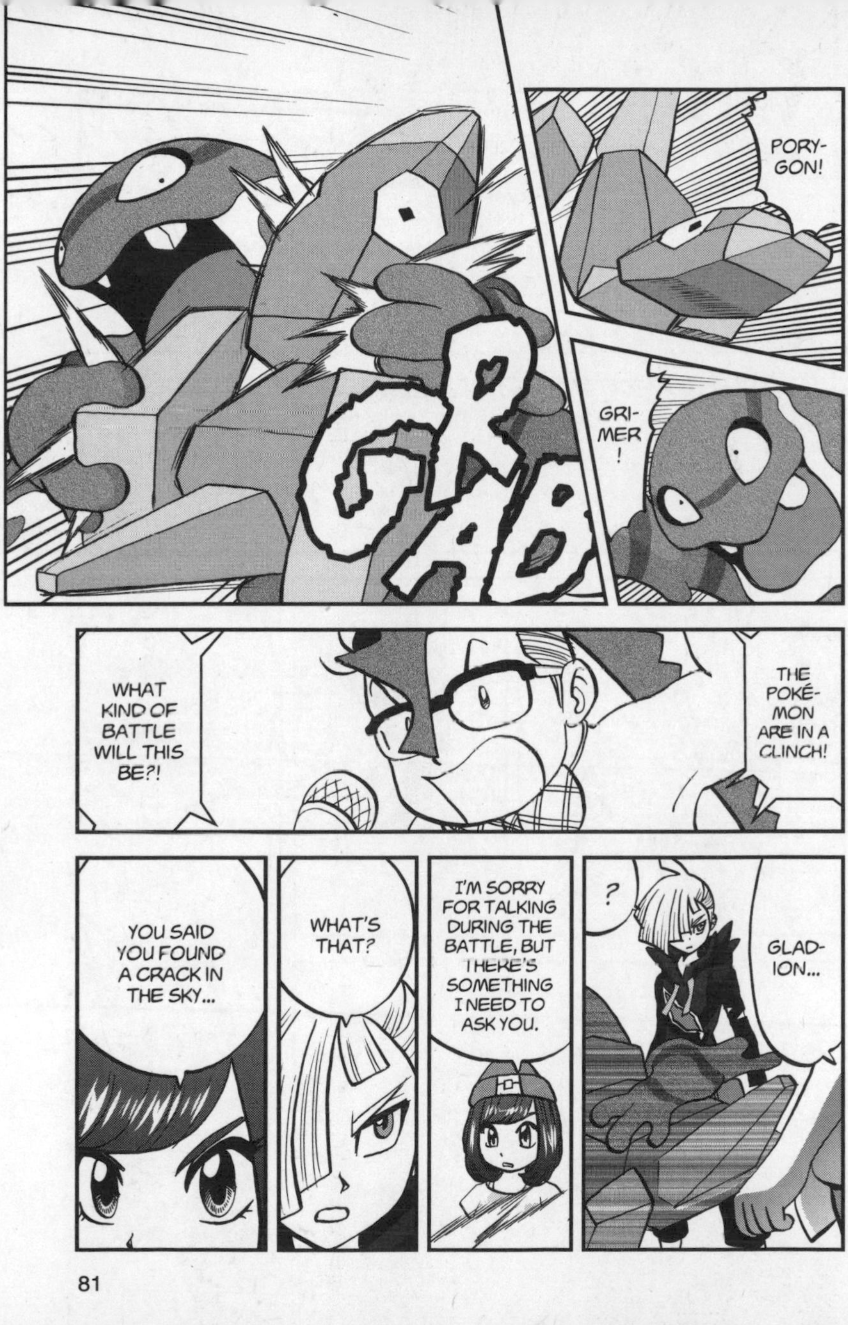
PORY-GON!
GRI-MER!
GRAB
THE POKÉ-MON ARE IN A CLINCH!
WHAT KIND OF BATTLE WILL THIS BE?!
GLAD-ION...
?
I'M SORRY FOR TALKING DURING THE BATTLE, BUT THERE'S SOMETHING I NEED TO ASK YOU.
WHAT'S THAT?
YOU SAID YOU FOUND A CRACK IN THE SKY...

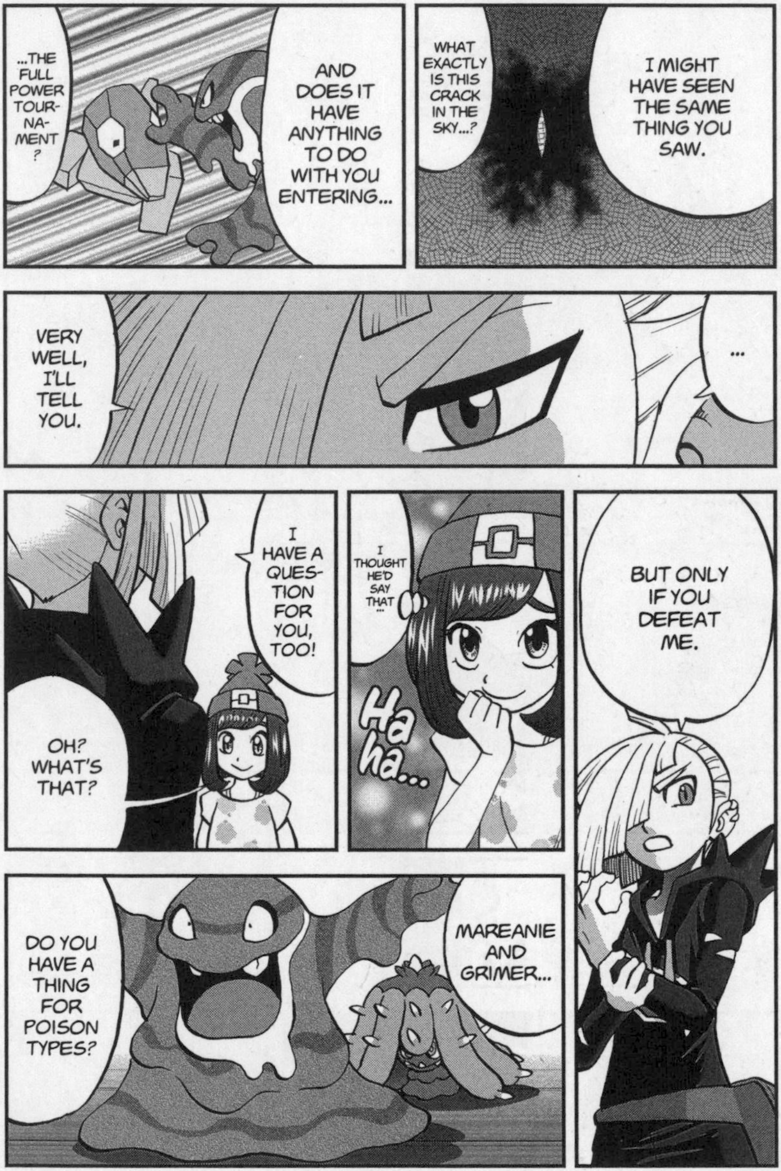
I MIGHT HAVE SEEN THE SAME THING YOU SAW.
WHAT EXACTLY IS THIS CRACK IN THE SKY...?
AND DOES IT HAVE ANYTHING TO DO WITH YOU ENTERING...
...THE FULL POWER TOURNAMENT?
...
VERY WELL, I'LL TELL YOU.
BUT ONLY IF YOU DEFEAT ME.
I THOUGHT HE'D SAY THAT...
Ha ha...
I HAVE A QUESTION FOR YOU, TOO!
OH? WHAT'S THAT?
MAREANIE AND GRIMER...
DO YOU HAVE A THING FOR POISON TYPES?

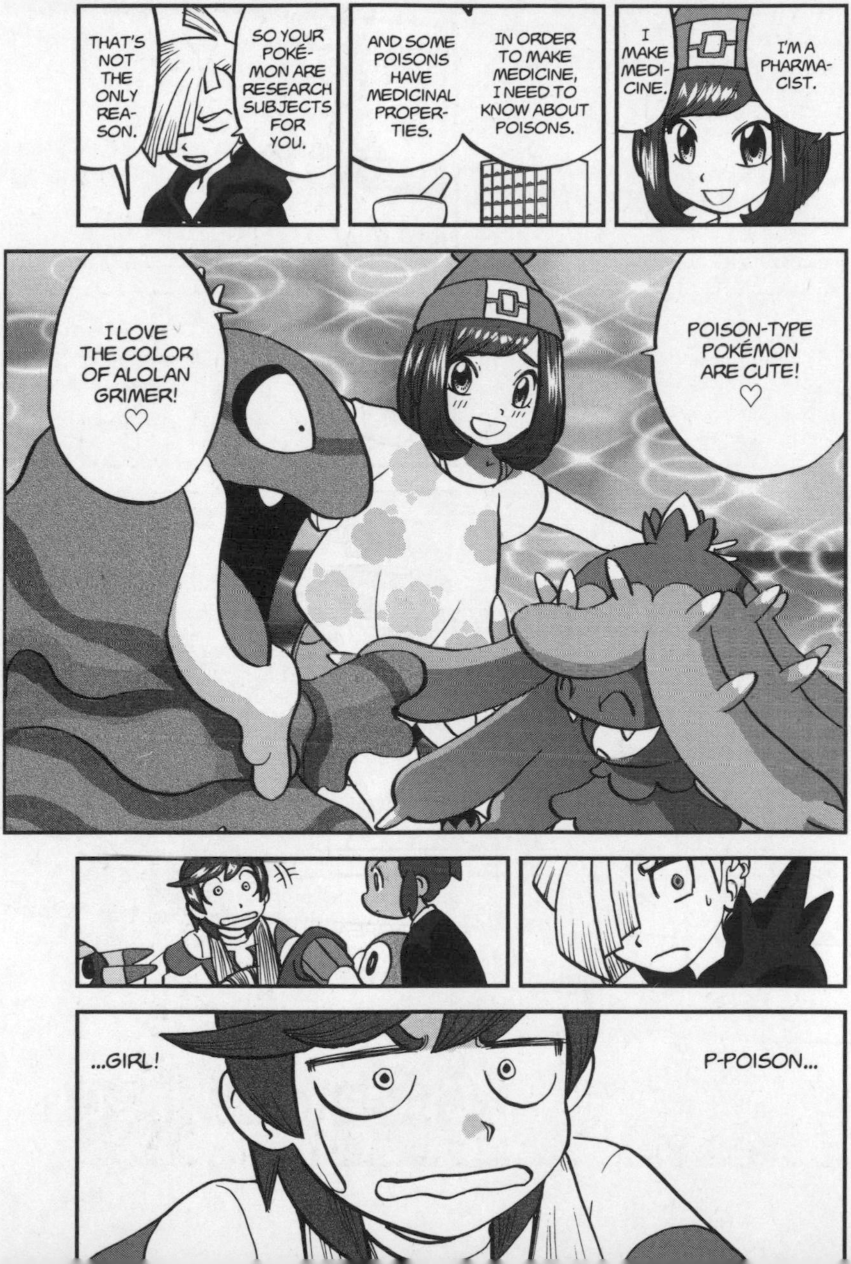
I'M A PHARMACIST.
I MAKE MEDICINE.
IN ORDER TO MAKE MEDICINE, I NEED TO KNOW ABOUT POISONS.
AND SOME POISONS HAVE MEDICINAL PROPERTIES.
SO YOUR POKÉMON ARE RESEARCH SUBJECTS FOR YOU.
THAT'S NOT THE ONLY REASON.
POISON-TYPE POKÉMON ARE CUTE! ♡
I LOVE THE COLOR OF ALOLAN GRIMER! ♡
P-POISON...
...GIRL!

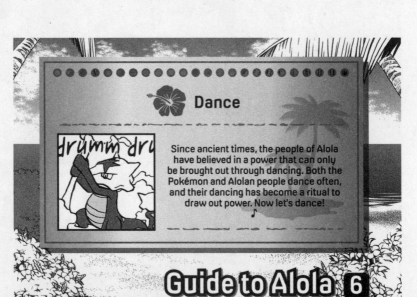

Dance

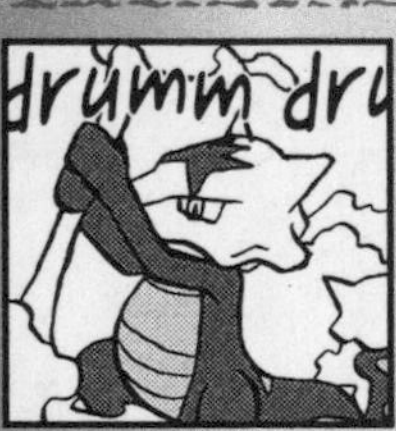
drumm dru

Since ancient times, the people of Alola have believed in a power that can only be brought out through dancing. Both the Pokémon and Alolan people dance often, and their dancing has become a ritual to draw out power. Now let's dance! ♪

Guide to Alola 6

Adventure 7
The Final Match and a Surprising Finale!

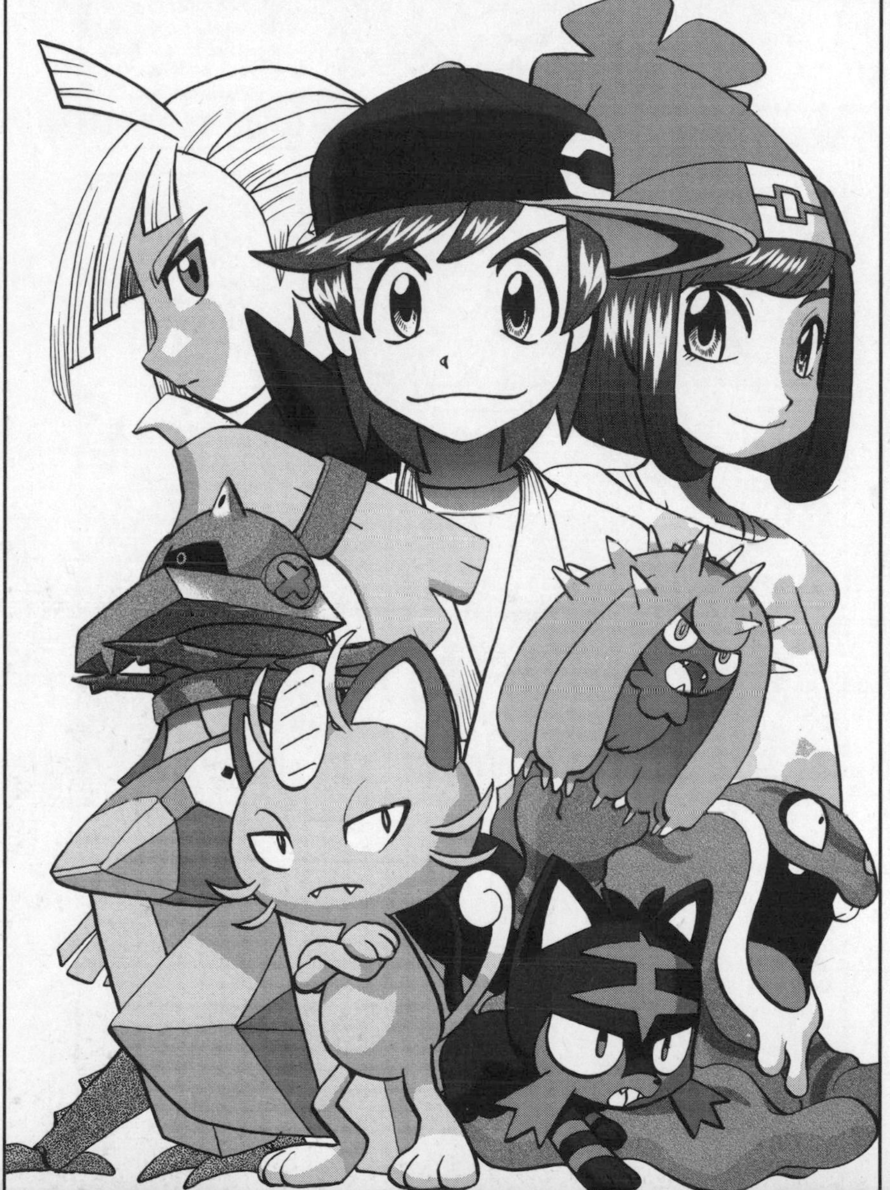

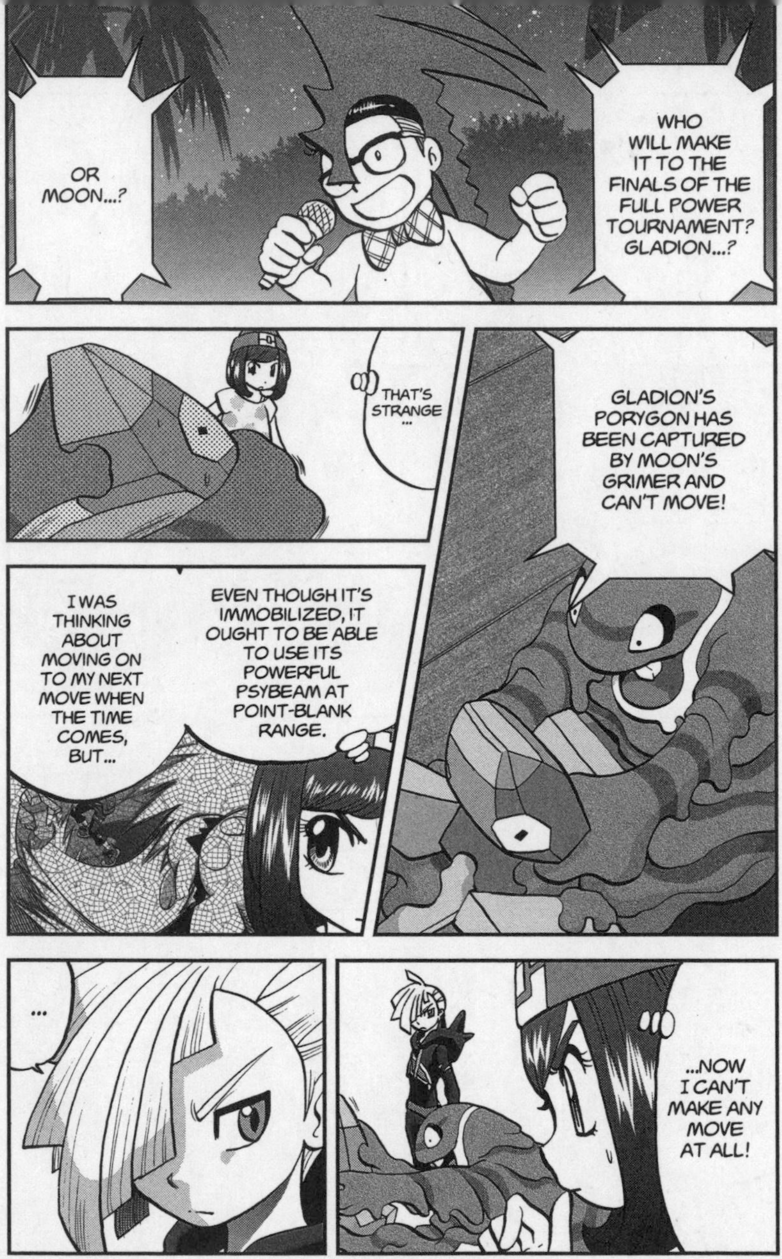
WHO WILL MAKE IT TO THE FINALS OF THE FULL POWER TOURNAMENT? GLADION...?
OR MOON...?
GLADION'S PORYGON HAS BEEN CAPTURED BY MOON'S GRIMER AND CAN'T MOVE!
THAT'S STRANGE...
EVEN THOUGH IT'S IMMOBILIZED, IT OUGHT TO BE ABLE TO USE ITS POWERFUL PSYBEAM AT POINT-BLANK RANGE.
I WAS THINKING ABOUT MOVING ON TO MY NEXT MOVE WHEN THE TIME COMES, BUT...
...NOW I CAN'T MAKE ANY MOVE AT ALL!
...

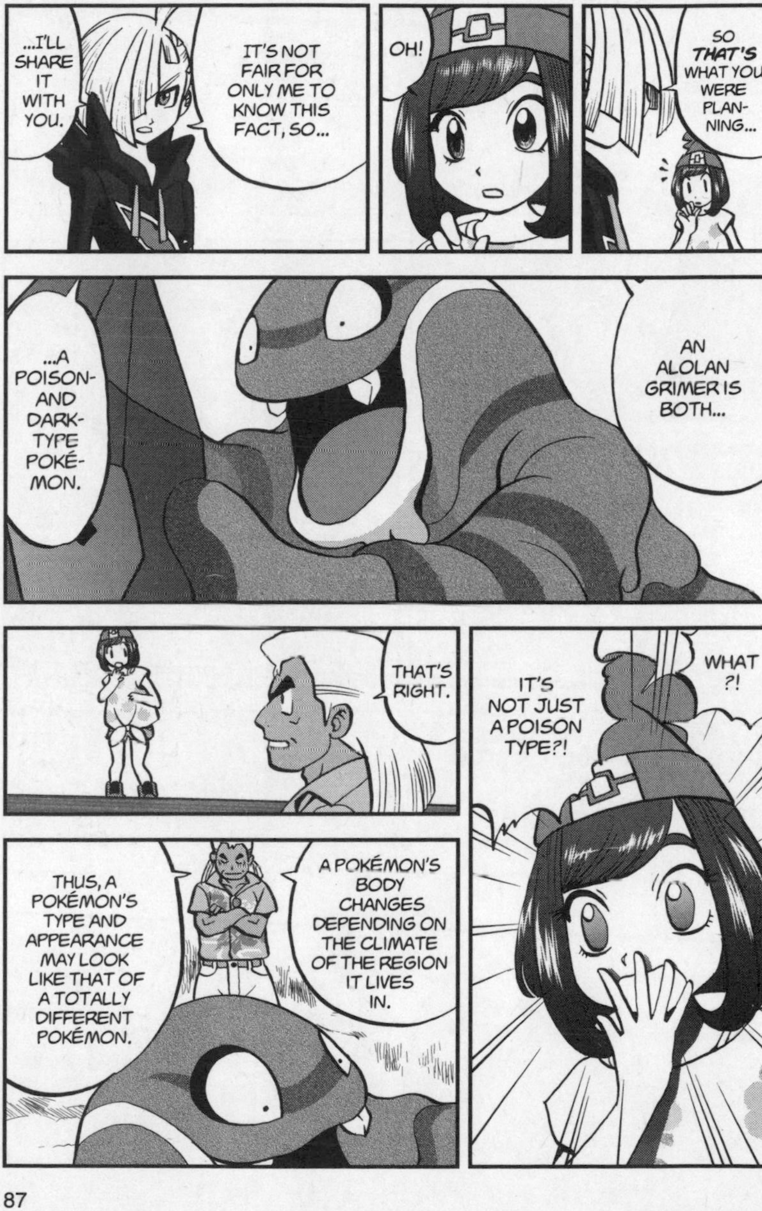
SO **THAT'S** WHAT YOU WERE PLAN-NING...
OH!
IT'S NOT FAIR FOR ONLY ME TO KNOW THIS FACT, SO...
...I'LL SHARE IT WITH YOU.
AN ALOLAN GRIMER IS BOTH...
...A POISON- AND DARK-TYPE POKÉ-MON.
WHAT?!
IT'S NOT JUST A POISON TYPE?!
THAT'S RIGHT.
A POKÉMON'S BODY CHANGES DEPENDING ON THE CLIMATE OF THE REGION IT LIVES IN.
THUS, A POKÉMON'S TYPE AND APPEARANCE MAY LOOK LIKE THAT OF A TOTALLY DIFFERENT POKÉMON.

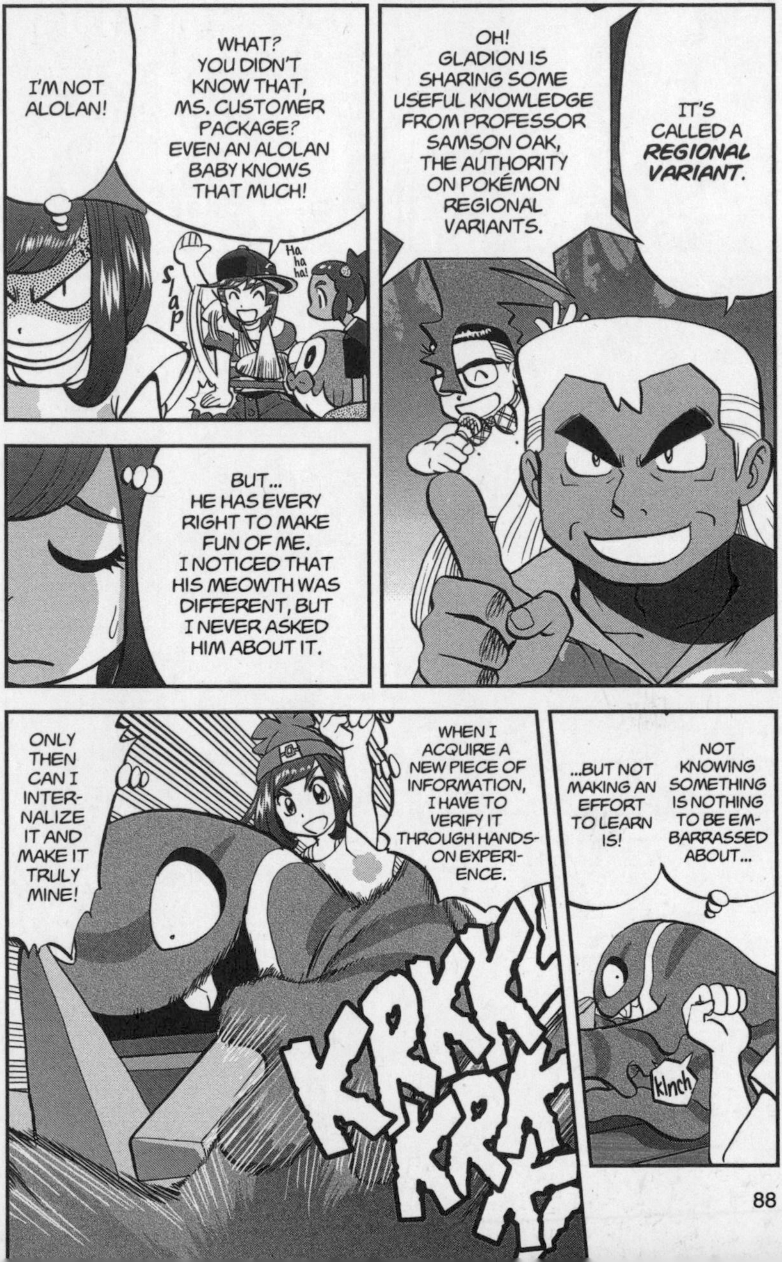
IT'S CALLED A ***REGIONAL VARIANT***.
OH! GLADION IS SHARING SOME USEFUL KNOWLEDGE FROM PROFESSOR SAMSON OAK, THE AUTHORITY ON POKÉMON REGIONAL VARIANTS.
WHAT? YOU DIDN'T KNOW THAT, MS. CUSTOMER PACKAGE? EVEN AN ALOLAN BABY KNOWS THAT MUCH!
Ha ha ha!
I'M NOT ALOLAN!
slap
BUT... HE HAS EVERY RIGHT TO MAKE FUN OF ME. I NOTICED THAT HIS MEOWTH WAS DIFFERENT, BUT I NEVER ASKED HIM ABOUT IT.
NOT KNOWING SOMETHING IS NOTHING TO BE EM-BARRASSED ABOUT...
...BUT NOT MAKING AN EFFORT TO LEARN IS!
klnch
WHEN I ACQUIRE A NEW PIECE OF INFORMATION, I HAVE TO VERIFY IT THROUGH HANDS-ON EXPERI-ENCE.
ONLY THEN CAN I INTER-NALIZE IT AND MAKE IT TRULY MINE!
KRKK KRK

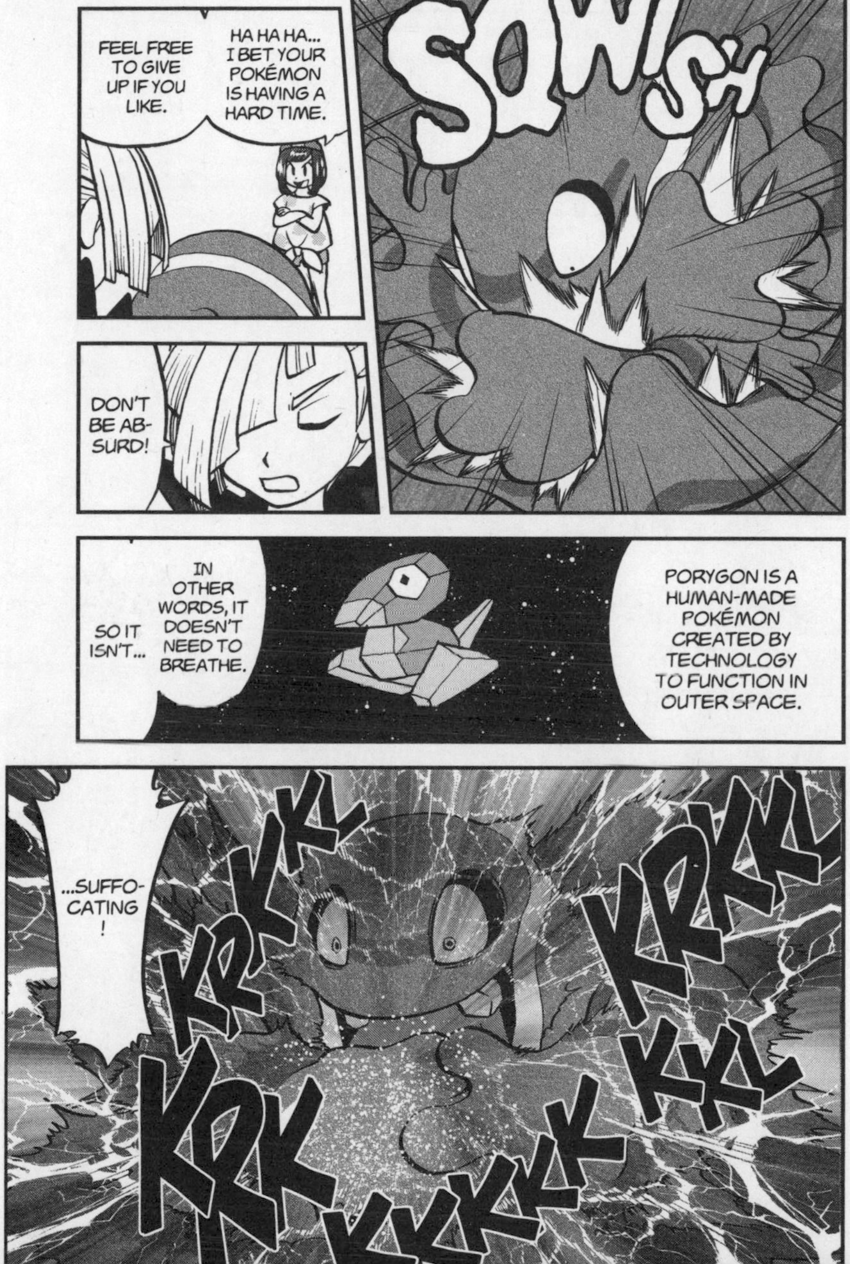
SQWISH
HA HA HA... I BET YOUR POKÉMON IS HAVING A HARD TIME.
FEEL FREE TO GIVE UP IF YOU LIKE.
DON'T BE ABSURD!
PORYGON IS A HUMAN-MADE POKÉMON CREATED BY TECHNOLOGY TO FUNCTION IN OUTER SPACE.
IN OTHER WORDS, IT DOESN'T NEED TO BREATHE.
SO IT ISN'T...
KRKKL
KKL
KRKKL
KRK
KKKKK
...SUFFOCATING!

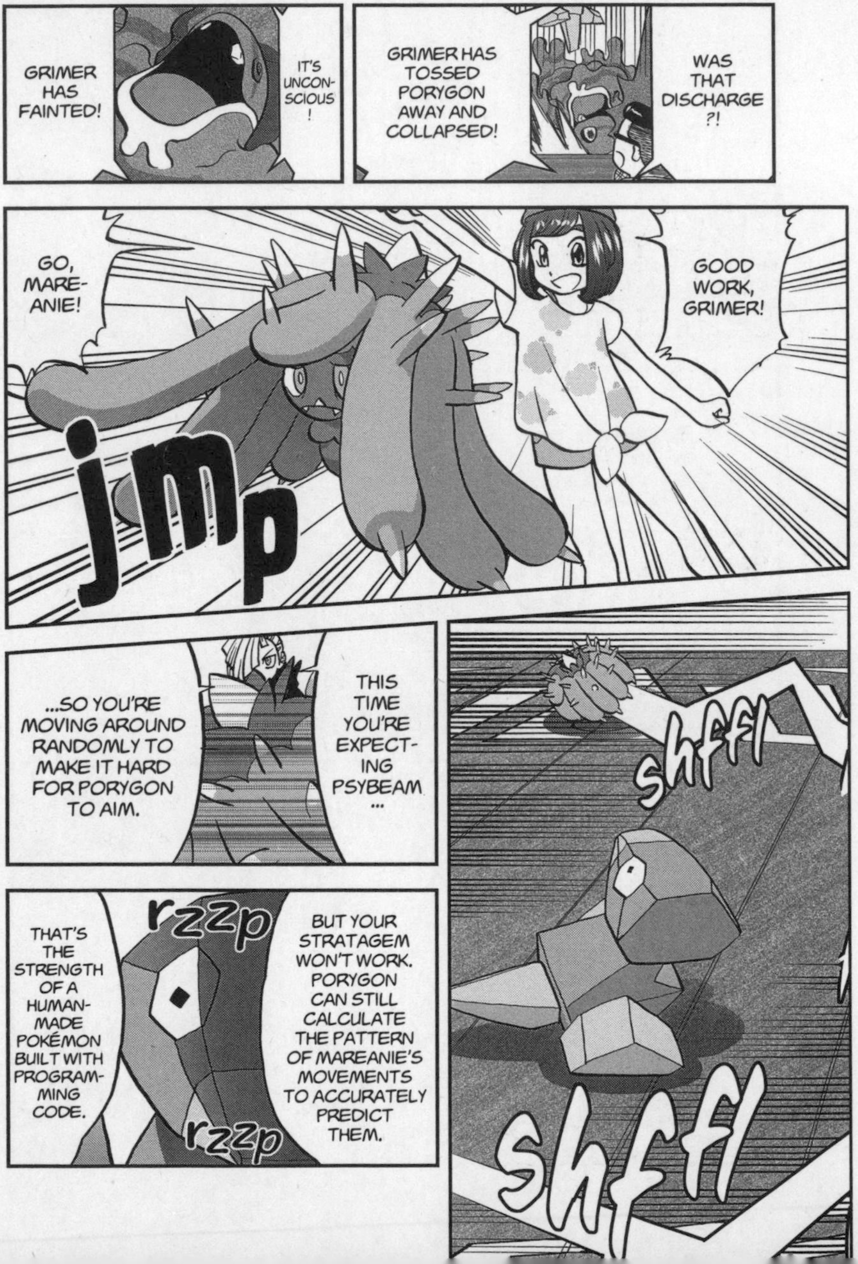
WAS THAT DISCHARGE?!
GRIMER HAS TOSSED PORYGON AWAY AND COLLAPSED!
IT'S UNCONSCIOUS!
GRIMER HAS FAINTED!
GOOD WORK, GRIMER!
GO, MAREANIE!
jmp
shffl
shffl
THIS TIME YOU'RE EXPECTING PSYBEAM...
...SO YOU'RE MOVING AROUND RANDOMLY TO MAKE IT HARD FOR PORYGON TO AIM.
BUT YOUR STRATAGEM WON'T WORK. PORYGON CAN STILL CALCULATE THE PATTERN OF MAREANIE'S MOVEMENTS TO ACCURATELY PREDICT THEM.
rzzp
THAT'S THE STRENGTH OF A HUMAN-MADE POKÉMON BUILT WITH PROGRAMMING CODE.
rzzp

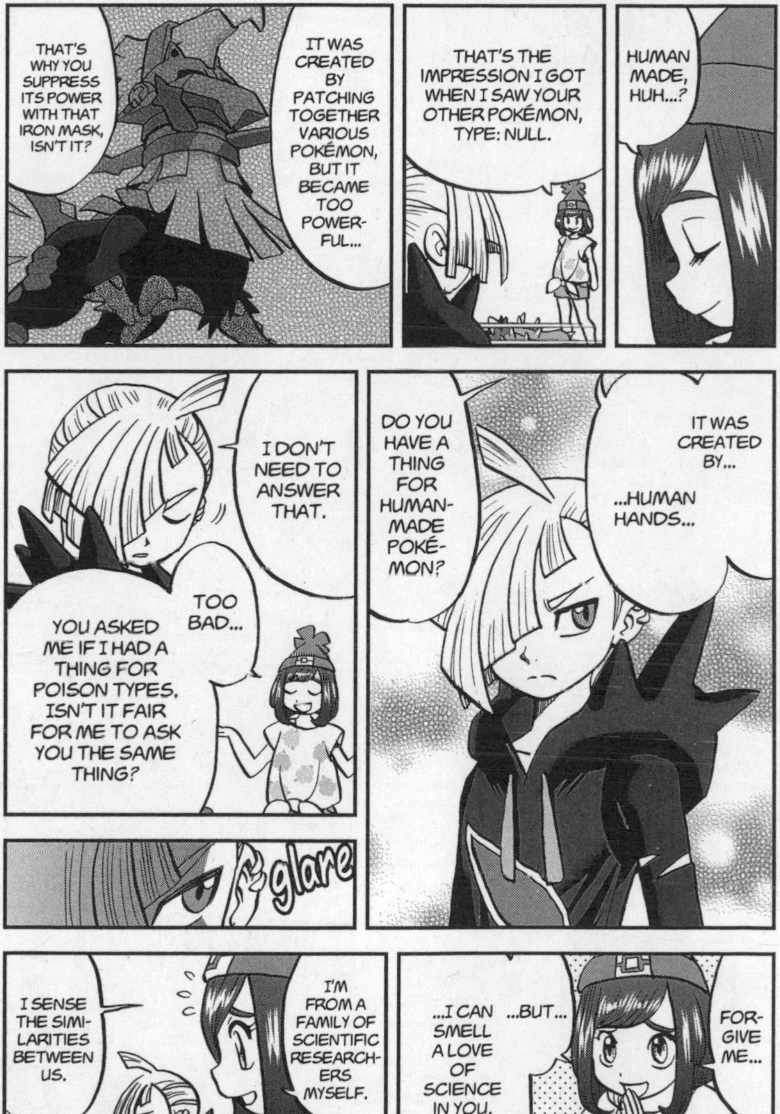

HUMAN MADE, HUH...?
THAT'S THE IMPRESSION I GOT WHEN I SAW YOUR OTHER POKÉMON, TYPE: NULL.
IT WAS CREATED BY PATCHING TOGETHER VARIOUS POKÉMON, BUT IT BECAME TOO POWER-FUL...
THAT'S WHY YOU SUPPRESS ITS POWER WITH THAT IRON MASK, ISN'T IT?
IT WAS CREATED BY...
...HUMAN HANDS...
DO YOU HAVE A THING FOR HUMAN-MADE POKÉ-MON?
I DON'T NEED TO ANSWER THAT.
TOO BAD...
YOU ASKED ME IF I HAD A THING FOR POISON TYPES. ISN'T IT FAIR FOR ME TO ASK YOU THE SAME THING?
glare
FOR-GIVE ME...
...BUT...
...I CAN SMELL A LOVE OF SCIENCE IN YOU.
I'M FROM A FAMILY OF SCIENTIFIC RESEARCH-ERS MYSELF.
I SENSE THE SIMI-LARITIES BETWEEN US.

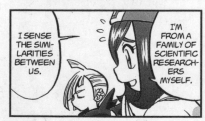

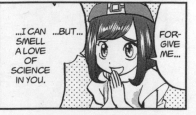

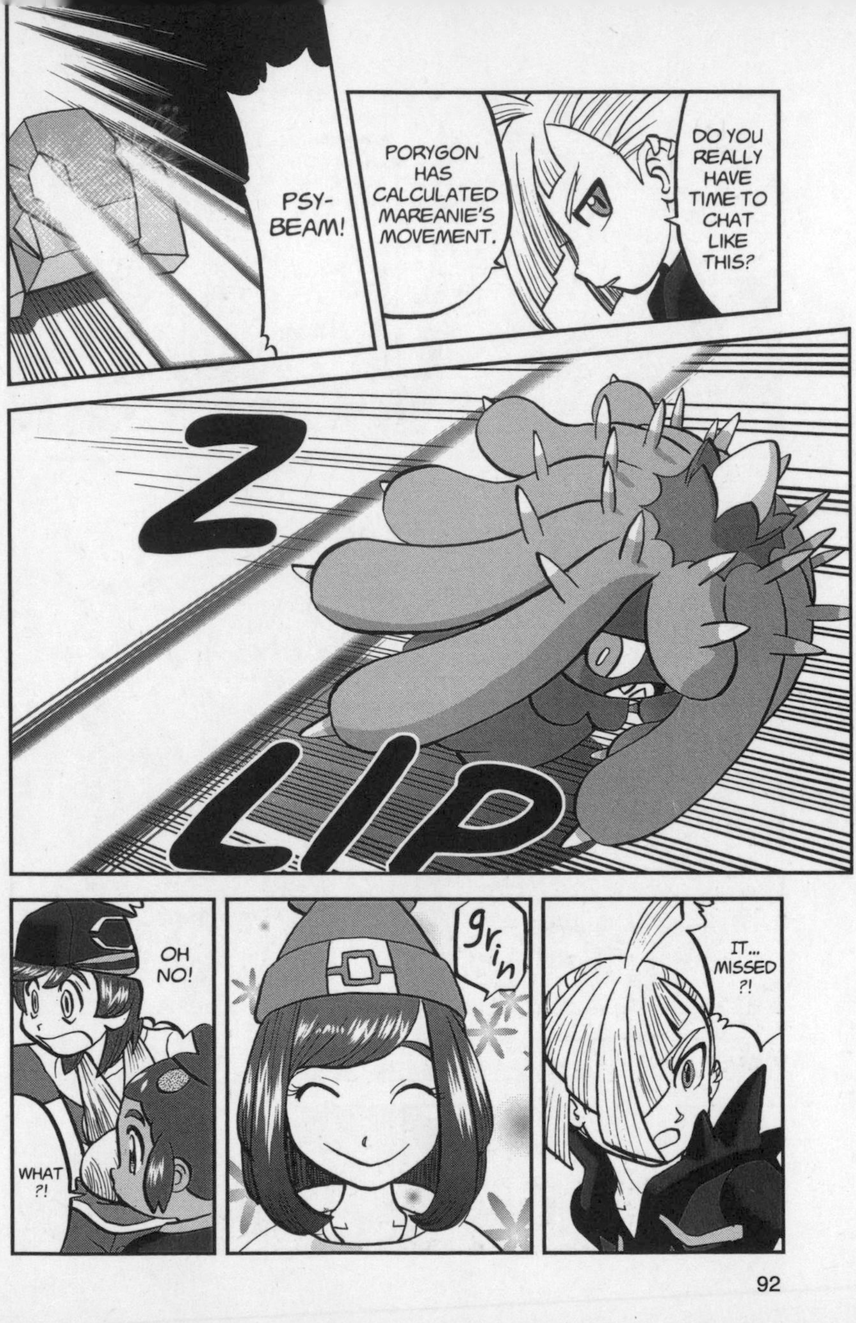
DO YOU REALLY HAVE TIME TO CHAT LIKE THIS?
PORYGON HAS CALCULATED MAREANIE'S MOVEMENT.
PSY-BEAM!
ZZLIP
IT... MISSED?!
grin
OH NO!
WHAT?!

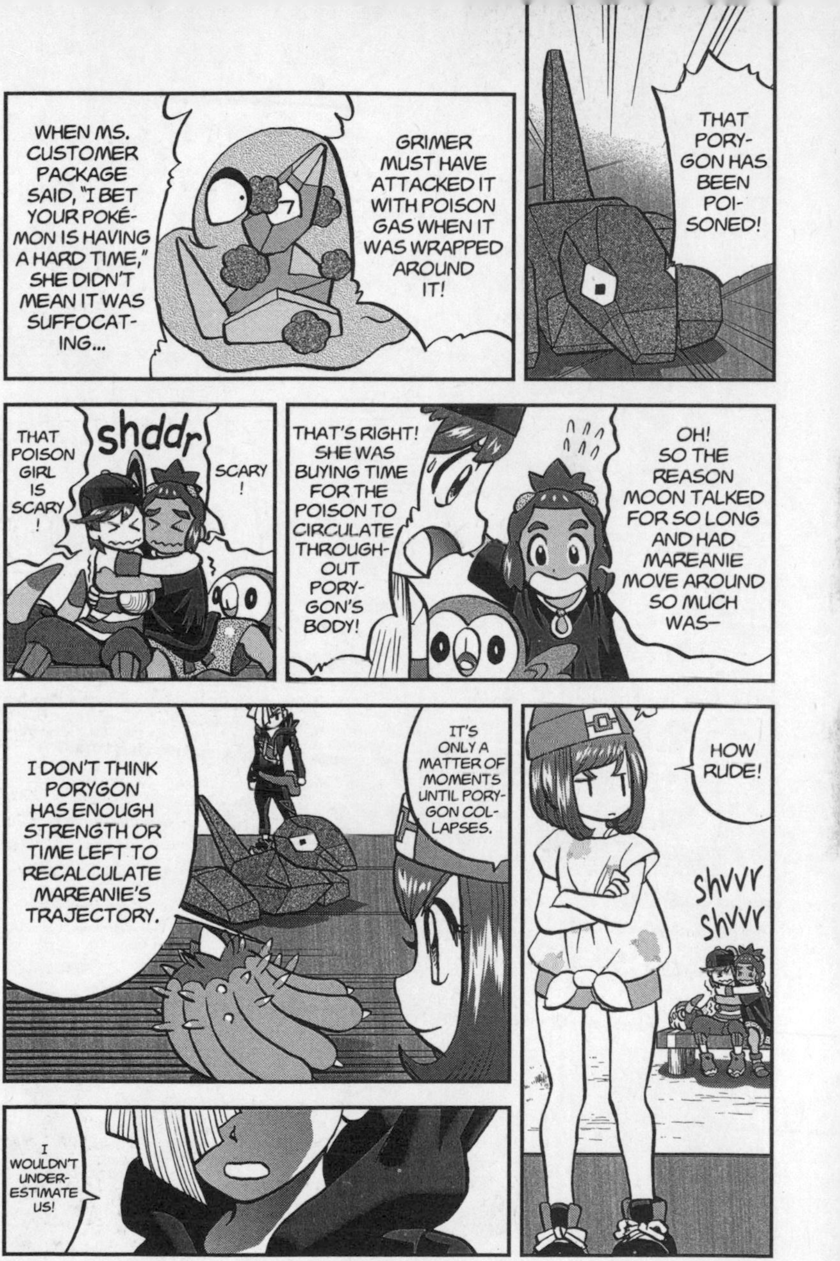
THAT PORYGON HAS BEEN POISONED!
GRIMER MUST HAVE ATTACKED IT WITH POISON GAS WHEN IT WAS WRAPPED AROUND IT!
WHEN MS. CUSTOMER PACKAGE SAID, "I BET YOUR POKÉMON IS HAVING A HARD TIME," SHE DIDN'T MEAN IT WAS SUFFOCATING...
OH! SO THE REASON MOON TALKED FOR SO LONG AND HAD MAREANIE MOVE AROUND SO MUCH WAS—
THAT'S RIGHT! SHE WAS BUYING TIME FOR THE POISON TO CIRCULATE THROUGHOUT PORYGON'S BODY!
SCARY!
shddr
THAT POISON GIRL IS SCARY!
HOW RUDE!
shvvr shvvr
IT'S ONLY A MATTER OF MOMENTS UNTIL PORYGON COLLAPSES.
I DON'T THINK PORYGON HAS ENOUGH STRENGTH OR TIME LEFT TO RECALCULATE MAREANIE'S TRAJECTORY.
I WOULDN'T UNDERESTIMATE US!

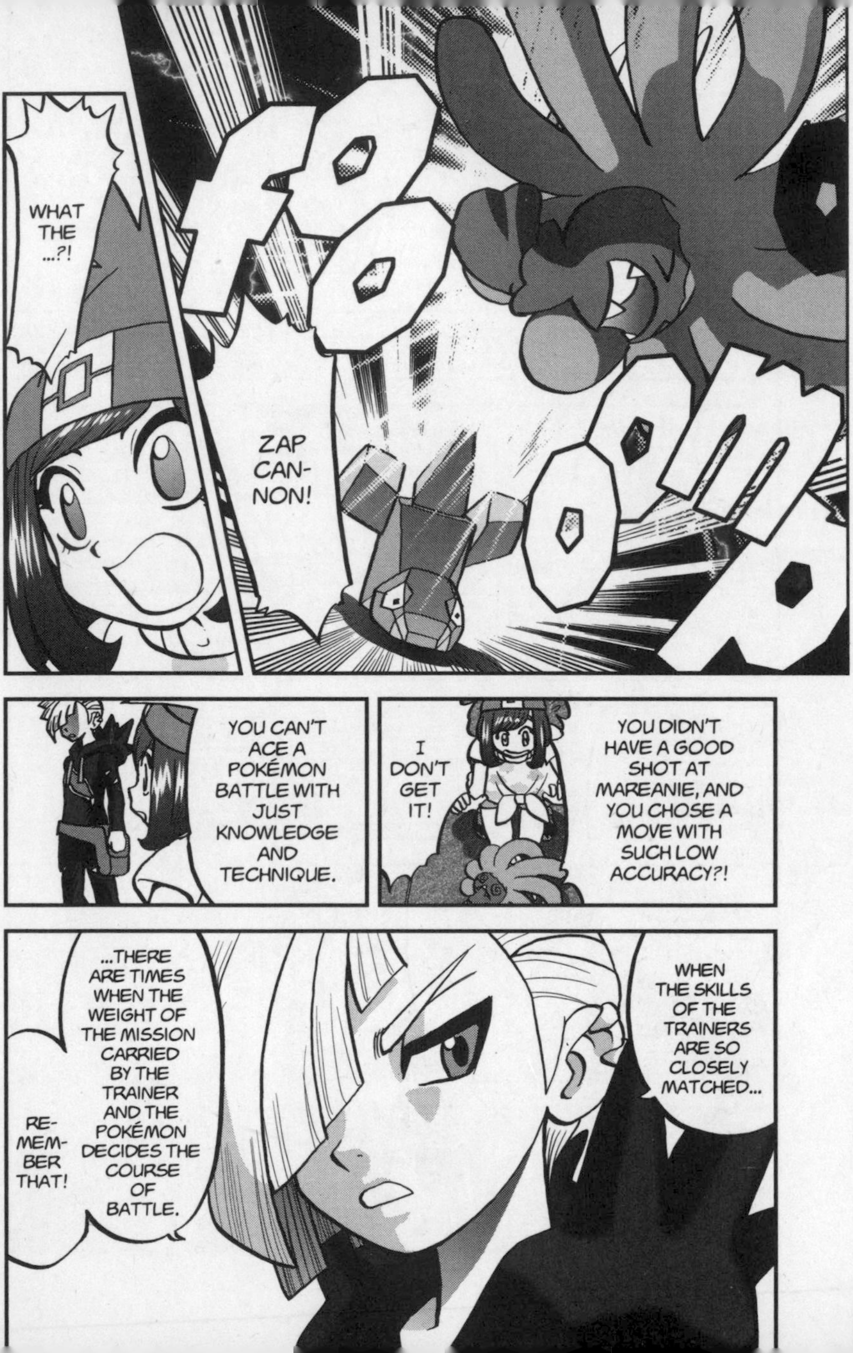
ZAP CANNON!
WHAT THE ...?!
YOU DIDN'T HAVE A GOOD SHOT AT MAREANIE, AND YOU CHOSE A MOVE WITH SUCH LOW ACCURACY?!
I DON'T GET IT!
YOU CAN'T ACE A POKÉMON BATTLE WITH JUST KNOWLEDGE AND TECHNIQUE.
WHEN THE SKILLS OF THE TRAINERS ARE SO CLOSELY MATCHED...
...THERE ARE TIMES WHEN THE WEIGHT OF THE MISSION CARRIED BY THE TRAINER AND THE POKÉMON DECIDES THE COURSE OF BATTLE.
REMEMBER THAT!

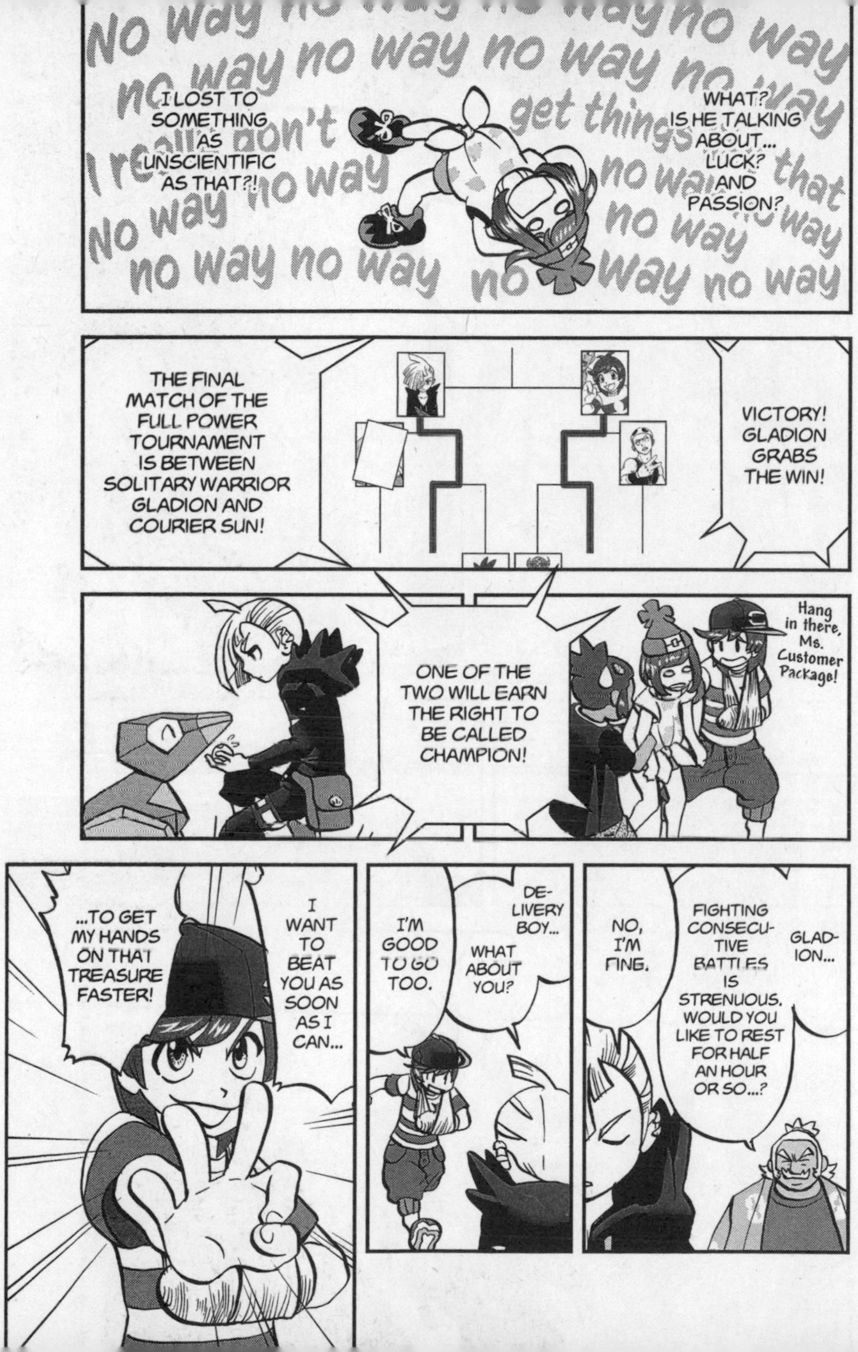
WHAT? IS HE TALKING ABOUT... LUCK? AND PASSION?
I LOST TO SOMETHING AS UNSCIENTIFIC AS THAT?!
VICTORY! GLADION GRABS THE WIN!
THE FINAL MATCH OF THE FULL POWER TOURNAMENT IS BETWEEN SOLITARY WARRIOR GLADION AND COURIER SUN!
Hang in there, Ms. Customer Package!
ONE OF THE TWO WILL EARN THE RIGHT TO BE CALLED CHAMPION!
GLADION...
FIGHTING CONSECUTIVE BATTLES IS STRENUOUS. WOULD YOU LIKE TO REST FOR HALF AN HOUR OR SO...?
NO, I'M FINE.
DELIVERY BOY... WHAT ABOUT YOU?
I'M GOOD TO GO TOO.
I WANT TO BEAT YOU AS SOON AS I CAN...
...TO GET MY HANDS ON THAT TREASURE FASTER!

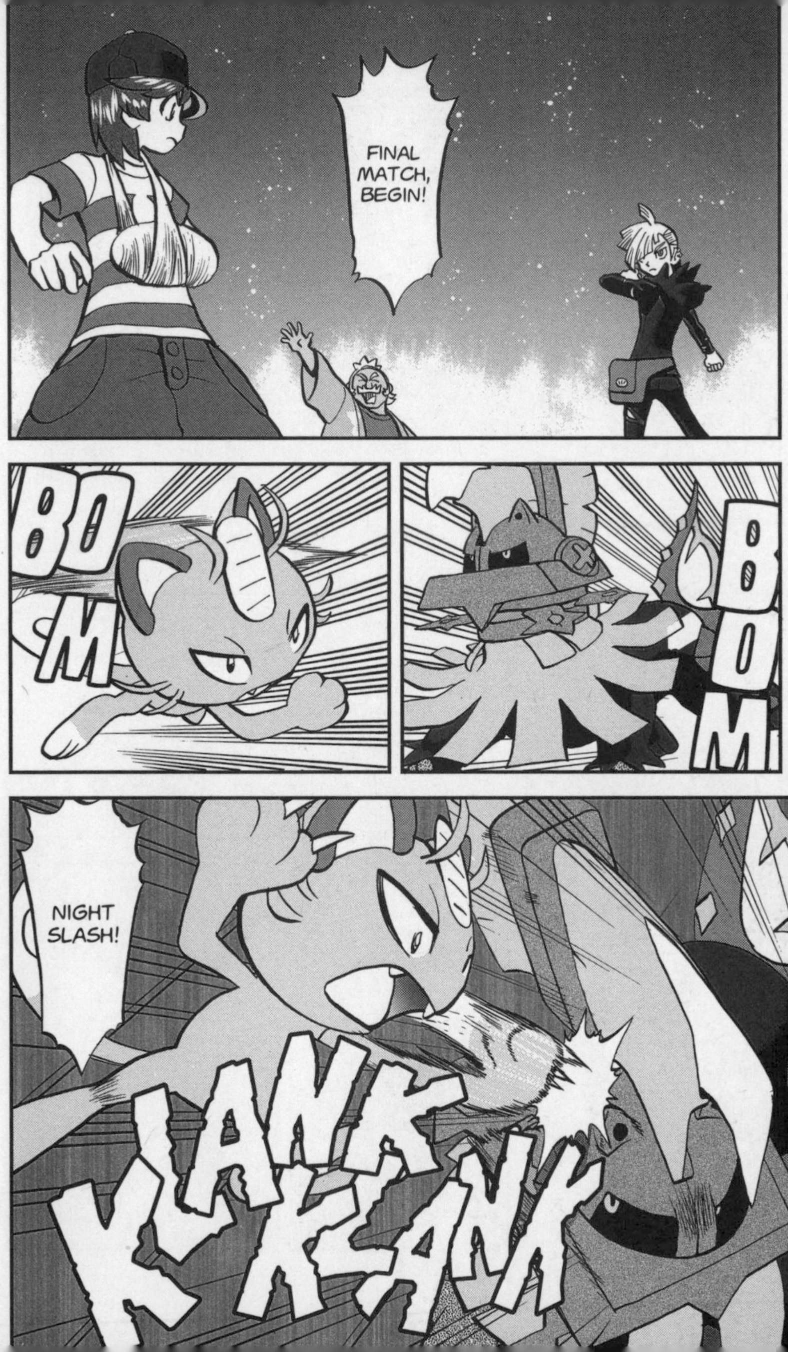
FINAL MATCH, BEGIN!
BOOM
BO
M
NIGHT SLASH!
KLANK KLANK

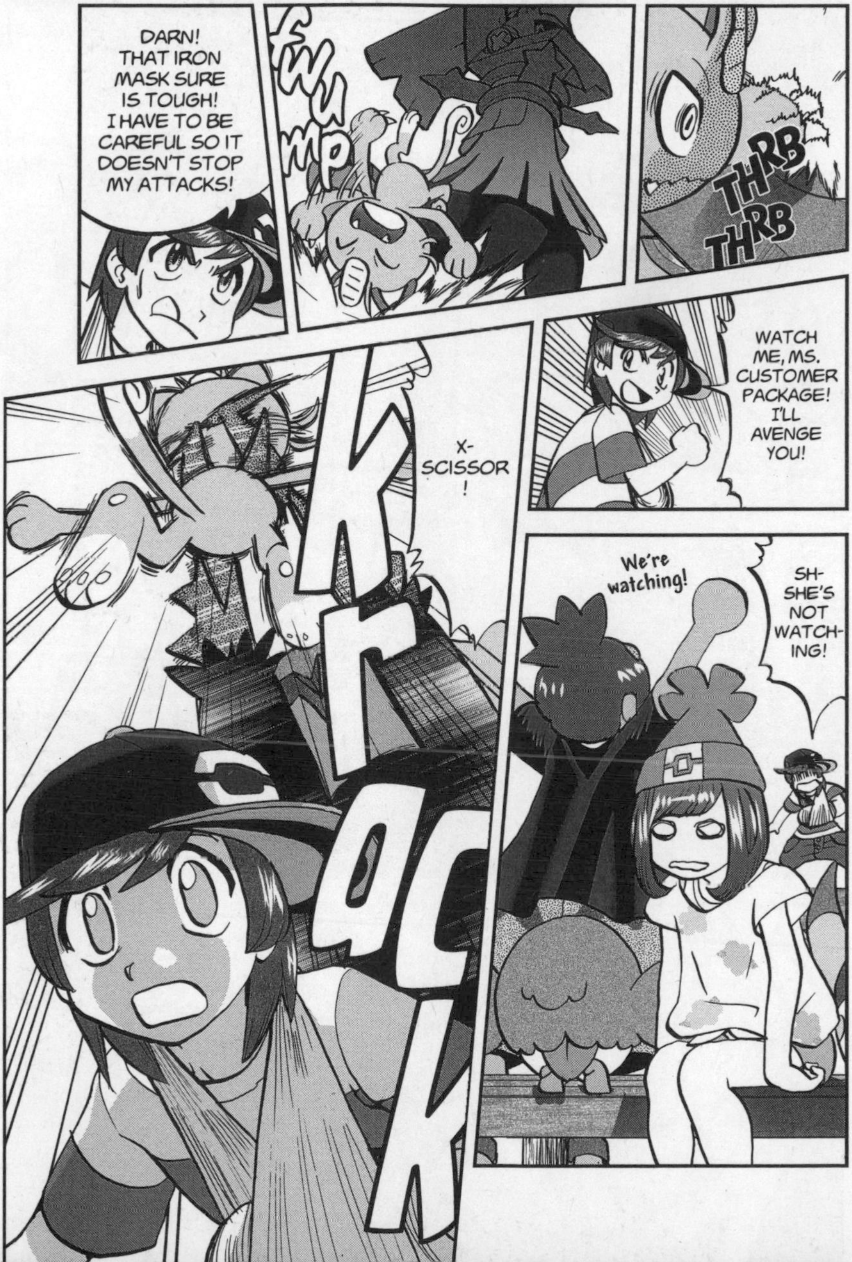
THRB THRB
fwump
DARN! THAT IRON MASK SURE IS TOUGH! I HAVE TO BE CAREFUL SO IT DOESN'T STOP MY ATTACKS!
WATCH ME, MS. CUSTOMER PACKAGE! I'LL AVENGE YOU!
SH-SHE'S NOT WATCHING!
We're watching!
X-SCISSOR!
KRACK

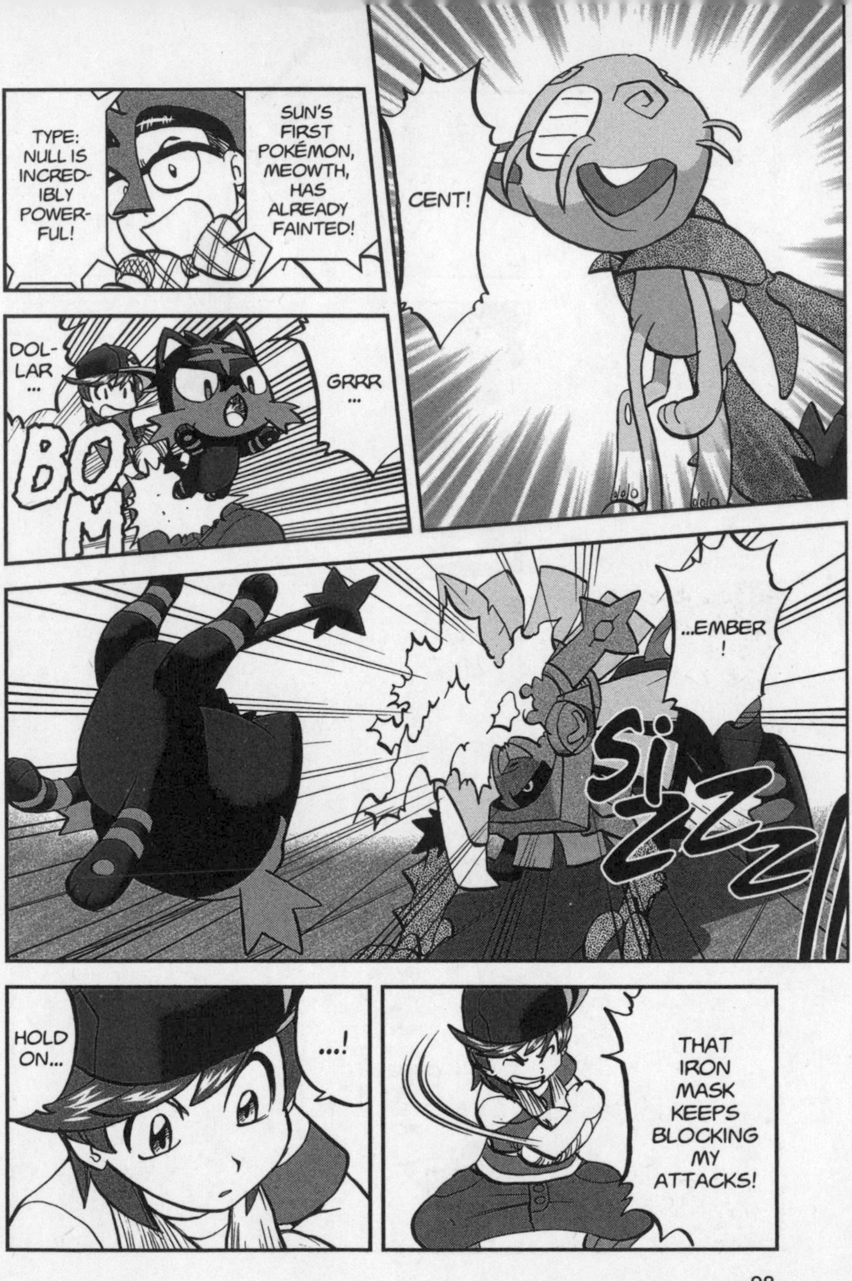
CENT!
SUN'S FIRST POKÉMON, MEOWTH, HAS ALREADY FAINTED!
TYPE: NULL IS INCRED-IBLY POWER-FUL!
GRRR ...
DOL-LAR ...
BOOM
...EMBER !
SIZZZ
THAT IRON MASK KEEPS BLOCKING MY ATTACKS!
...!
HOLD ON...

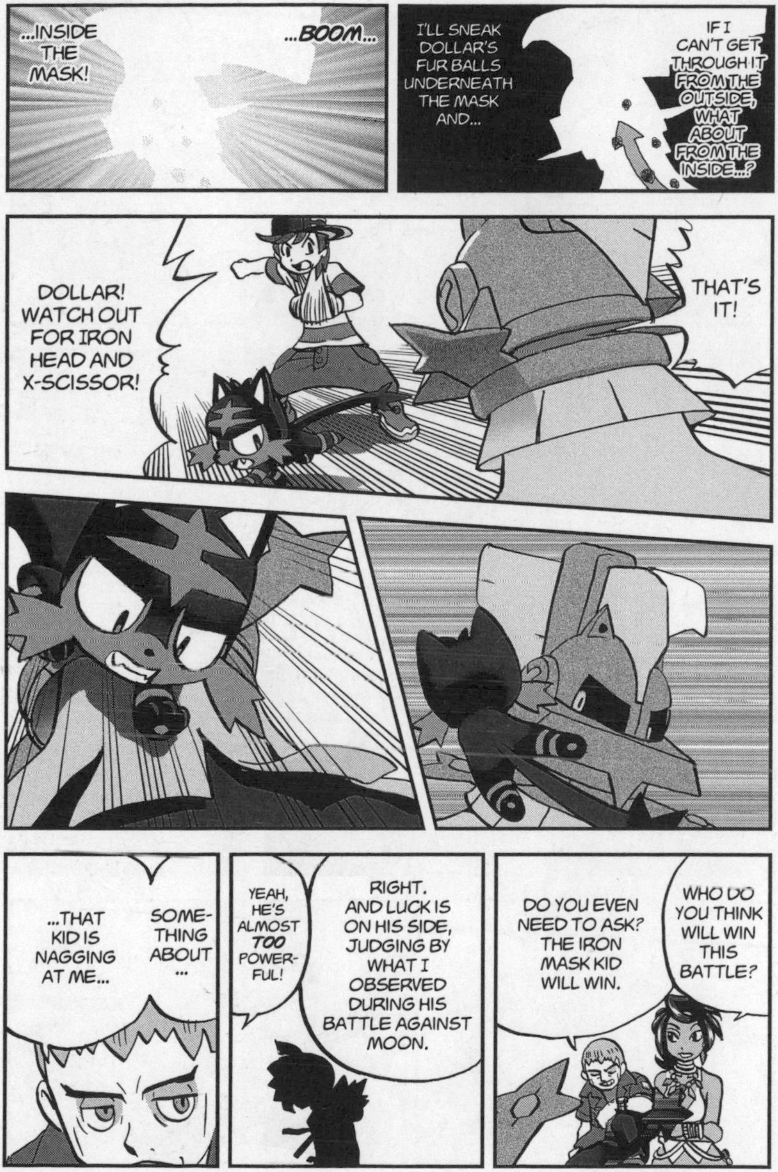
IF I CAN'T GET THROUGH IT FROM THE OUTSIDE, WHAT ABOUT FROM THE INSIDE...?
I'LL SNEAK DOLLAR'S FUR BALLS UNDERNEATH THE MASK AND...
...*BOOM*...
...INSIDE THE MASK!
THAT'S IT!
DOLLAR! WATCH OUT FOR IRON HEAD AND X-SCISSOR!
WHO DO YOU THINK WILL WIN THIS BATTLE?
DO YOU EVEN NEED TO ASK? THE IRON MASK KID WILL WIN.
RIGHT. AND LUCK IS ON HIS SIDE, JUDGING BY WHAT I OBSERVED DURING HIS BATTLE AGAINST MOON.
YEAH, HE'S ALMOST *TOO* POWER-FUL!
SOME-THING ABOUT ...
...THAT KID IS NAGGING AT ME...

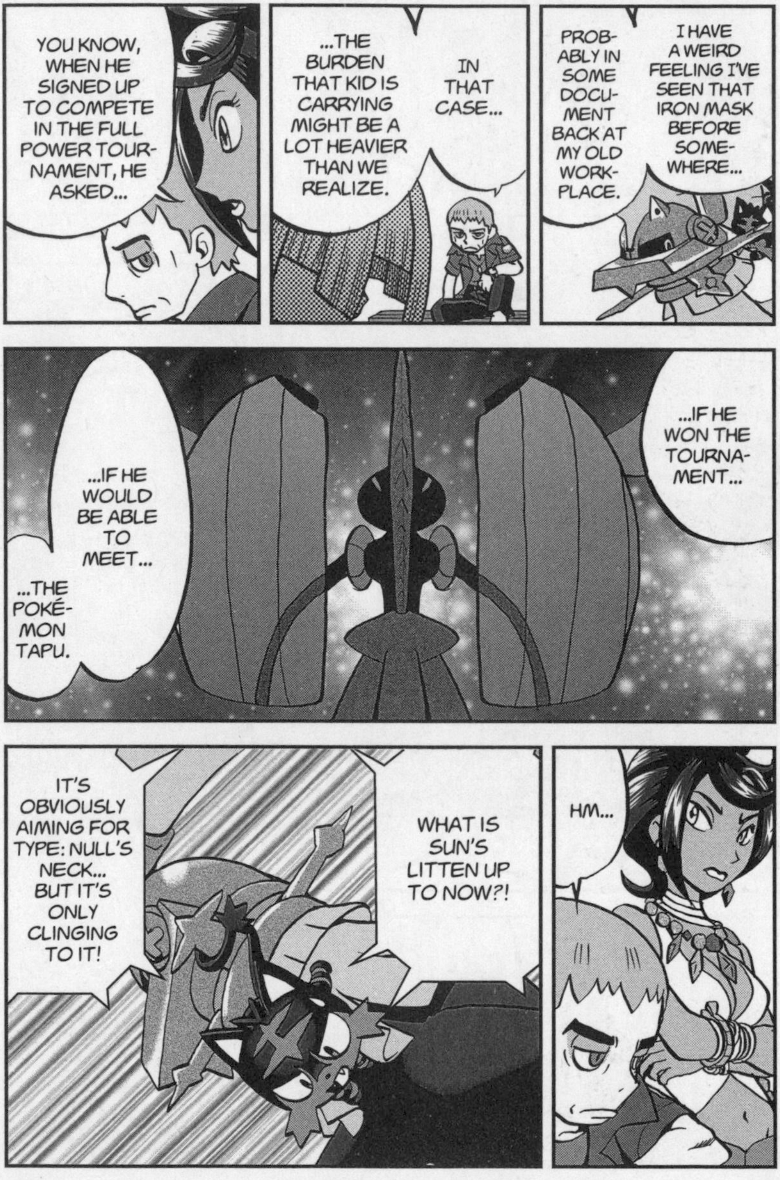
I HAVE A WEIRD FEELING I'VE SEEN THAT IRON MASK BEFORE SOMEWHERE...
PROBABLY IN SOME DOCUMENT BACK AT MY OLD WORKPLACE.
IN THAT CASE...
...THE BURDEN THAT KID IS CARRYING MIGHT BE A LOT HEAVIER THAN WE REALIZE.
YOU KNOW, WHEN HE SIGNED UP TO COMPETE IN THE FULL POWER TOURNAMENT, HE ASKED...
...IF HE WON THE TOURNAMENT...
...IF HE WOULD BE ABLE TO MEET...
...THE POKÉMON TAPU.
HM...
WHAT IS SUN'S LITTEN UP TO NOW?!
IT'S OBVIOUSLY AIMING FOR TYPE: NULL'S NECK... BUT IT'S ONLY CLINGING TO IT!

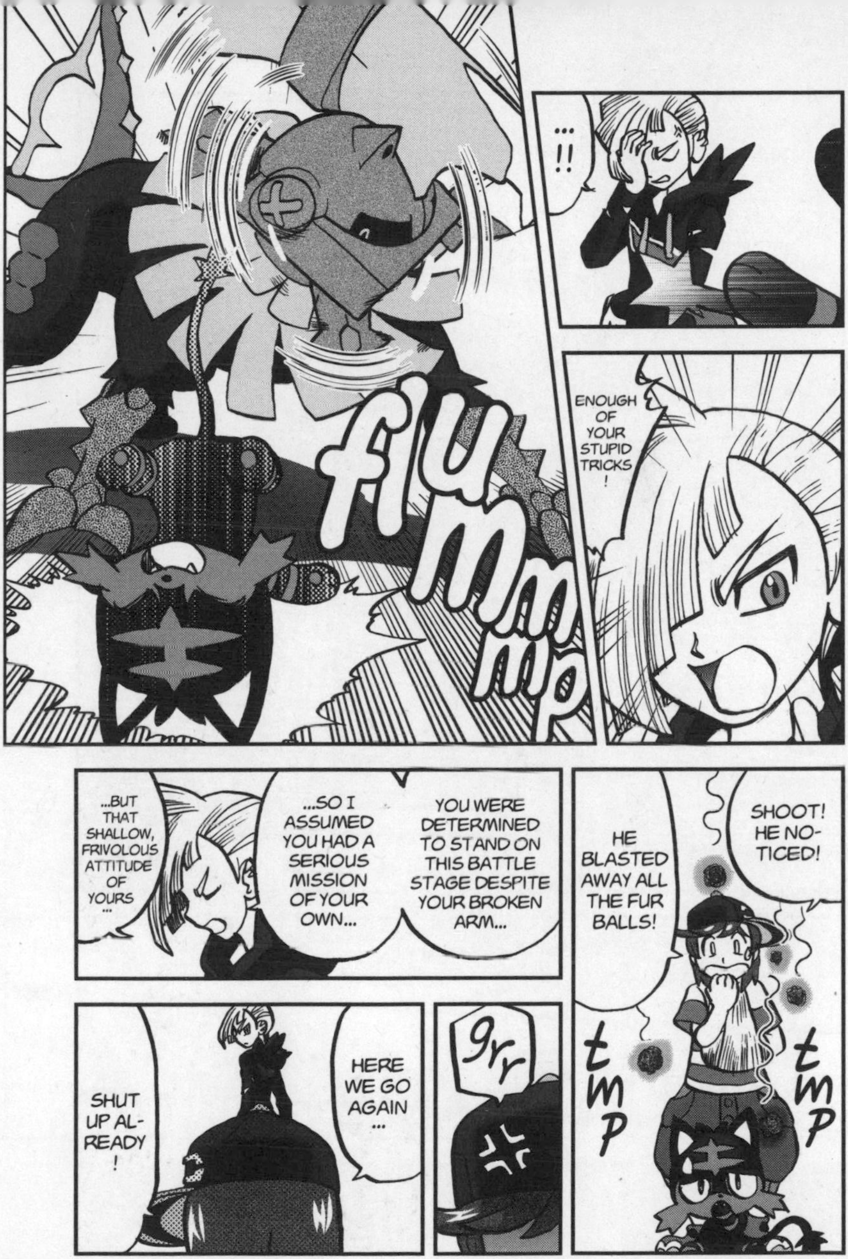
…!!
ENOUGH OF YOUR STUPID TRICKS!
flummp
SHOOT! HE NO-TICED!
HE BLASTED AWAY ALL THE FUR BALLS!
tmp
tmp
YOU WERE DETERMINED TO STAND ON THIS BATTLE STAGE DESPITE YOUR BROKEN ARM...
...SO I ASSUMED YOU HAD A SERIOUS MISSION OF YOUR OWN...
...BUT THAT SHALLOW, FRIVOLOUS ATTITUDE OF YOURS...
grr
HERE WE GO AGAIN...
SHUT UP AL-READY!

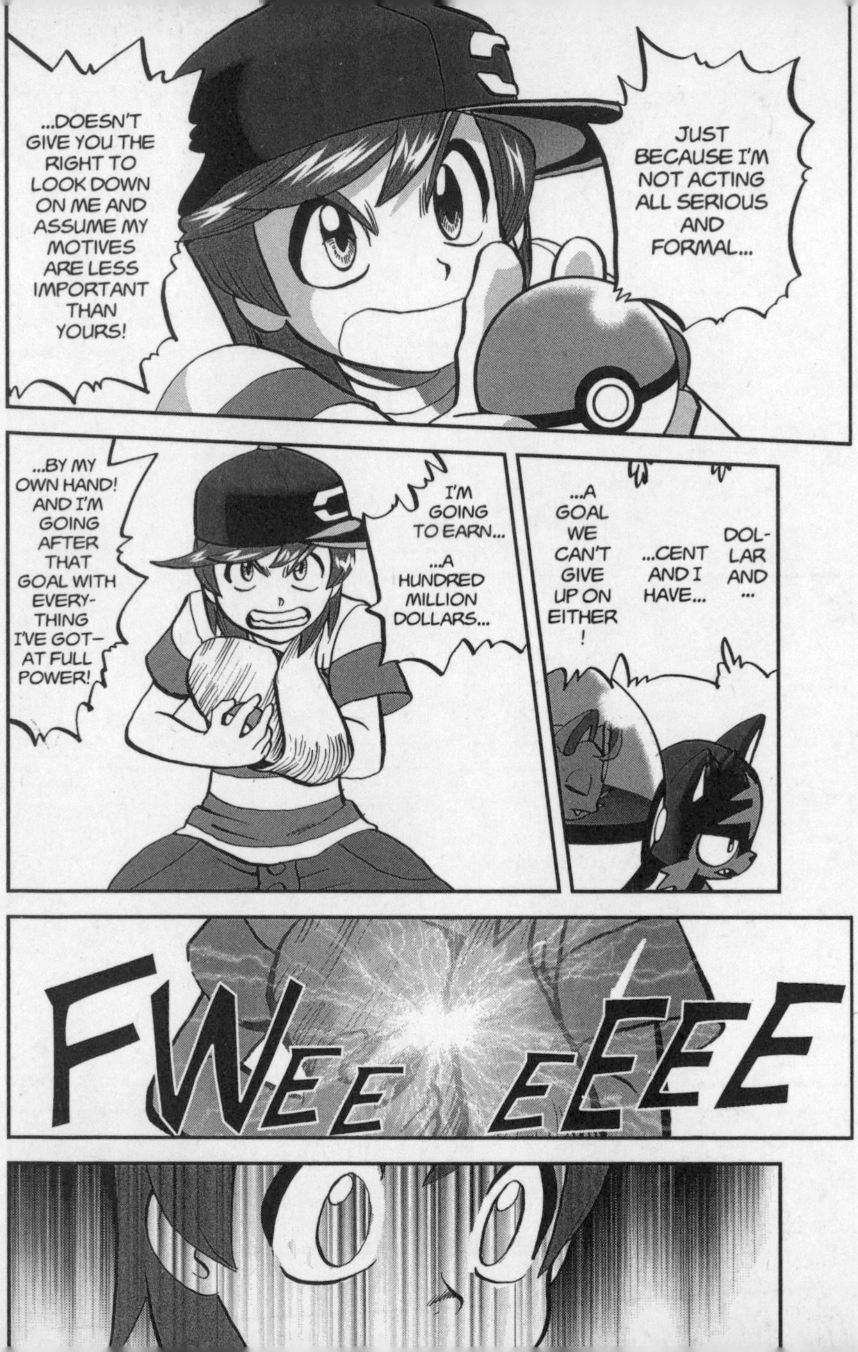
JUST BECAUSE I'M NOT ACTING ALL SERIOUS AND FORMAL...
...DOESN'T GIVE YOU THE RIGHT TO LOOK DOWN ON ME AND ASSUME MY MOTIVES ARE LESS IMPORTANT THAN YOURS!
DOL-LAR AND ...
...CENT AND I HAVE...
...A GOAL WE CAN'T GIVE UP ON EITHER!
I'M GOING TO EARN...
...A HUNDRED MILLION DOLLARS...
...BY MY OWN HAND! AND I'M GOING AFTER THAT GOAL WITH EVERY-THING I'VE GOT—AT FULL POWER!
FWEE EEEE

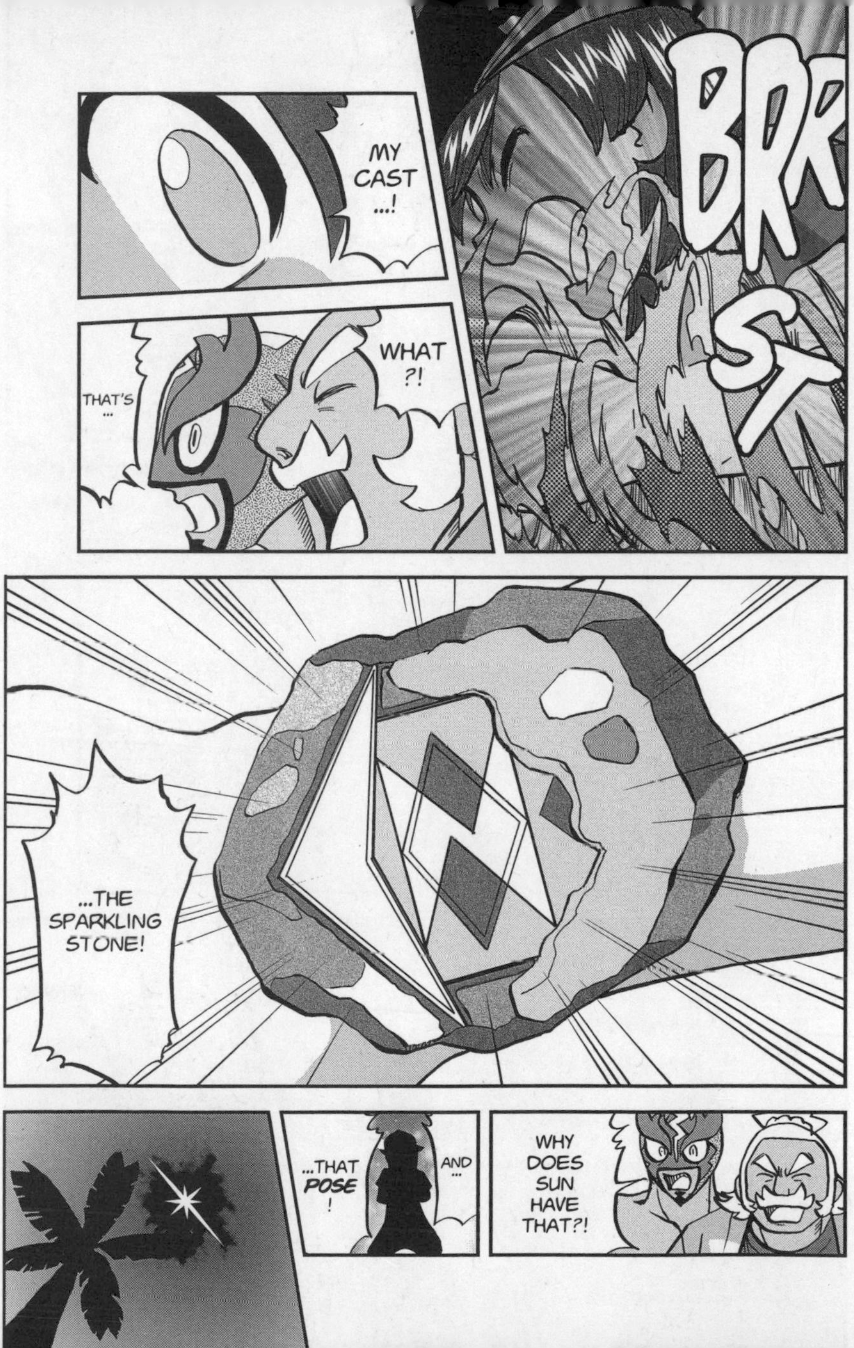
BRRST
MY CAST ...!
WHAT?!
THAT'S ...
...THE SPARKLING STONE!
WHY DOES SUN HAVE THAT?!
AND ...
...THAT *POSE*!

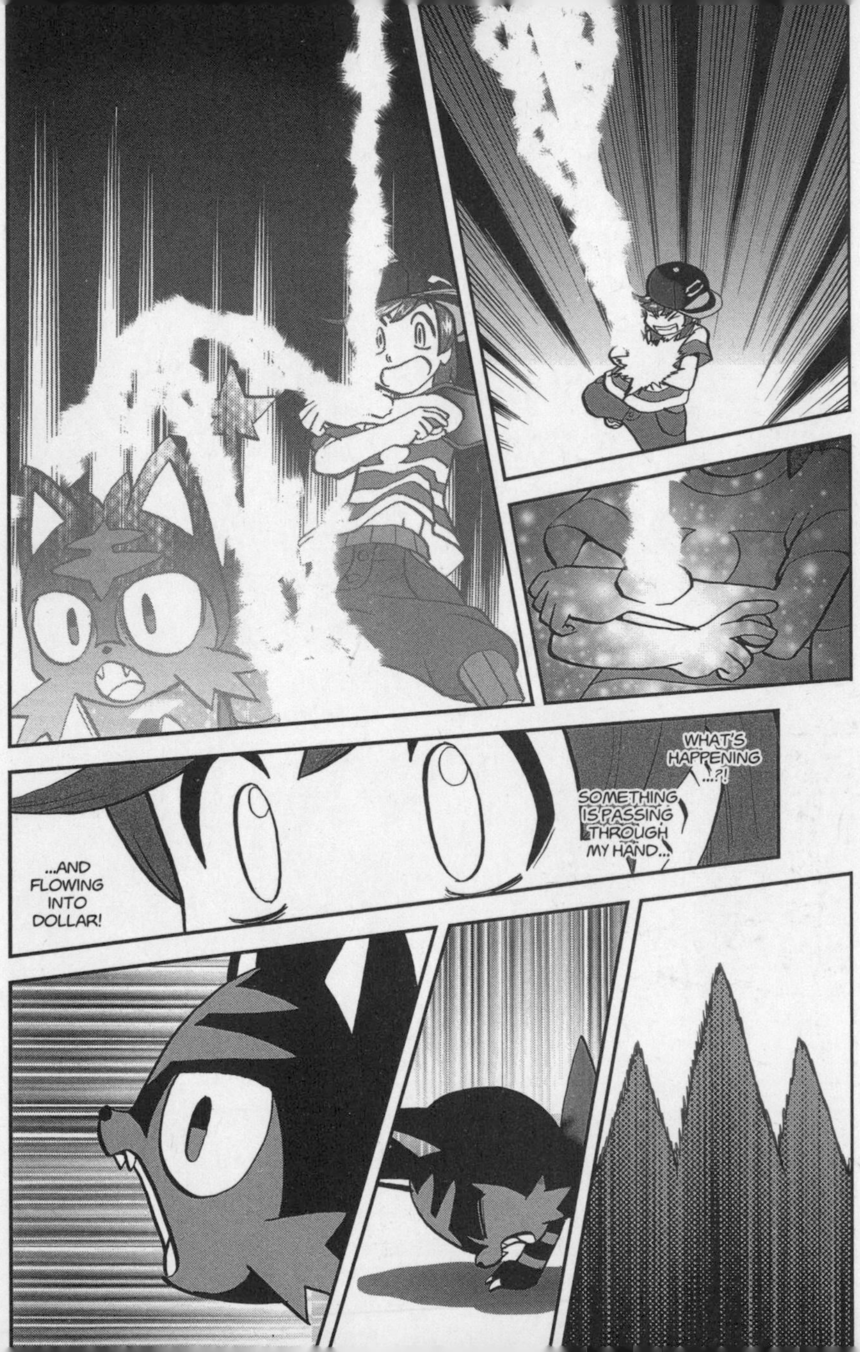
WHAT'S HAPPENING ...?!
SOMETHING IS PASSING THROUGH MY HAND...
...AND FLOWING INTO DOLLAR!

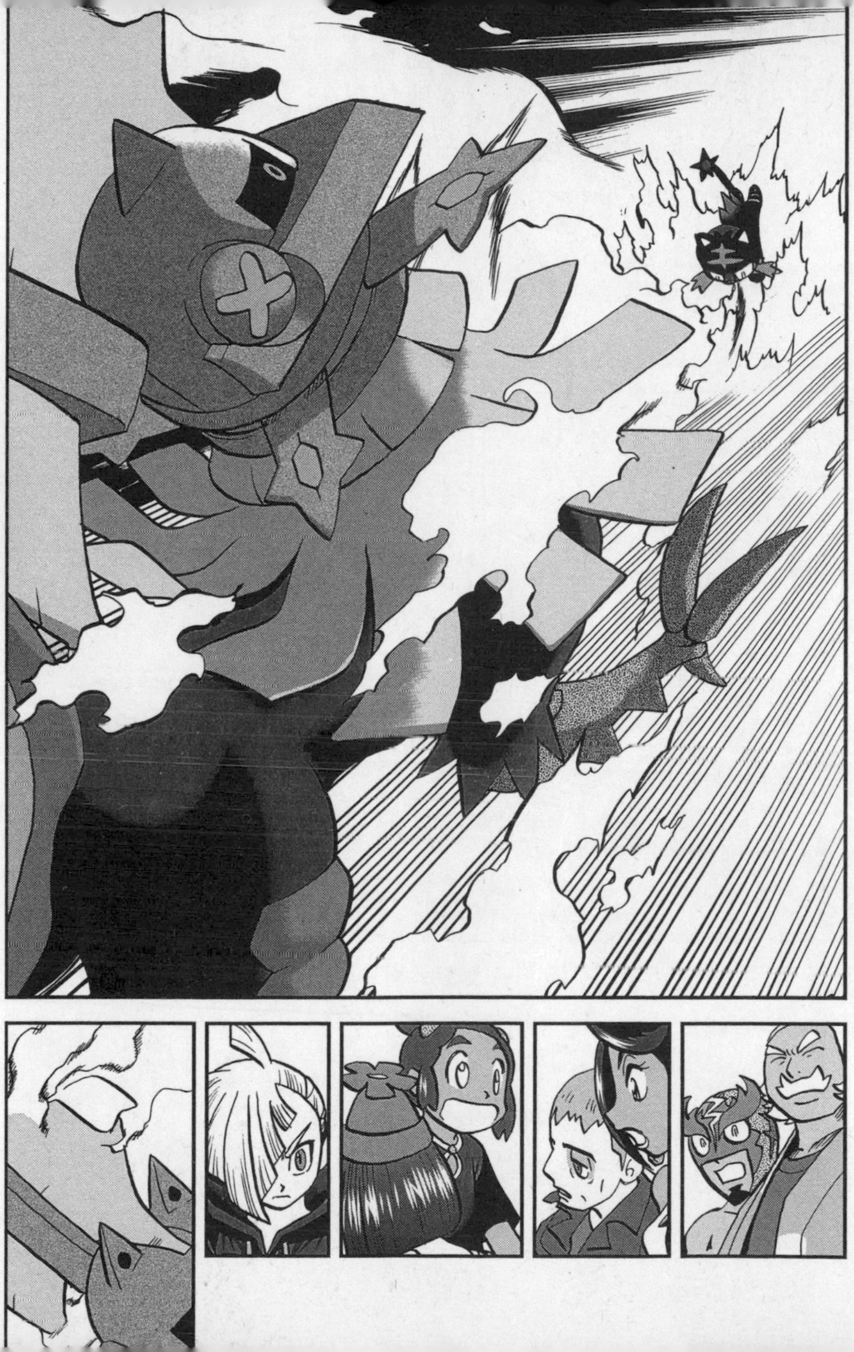

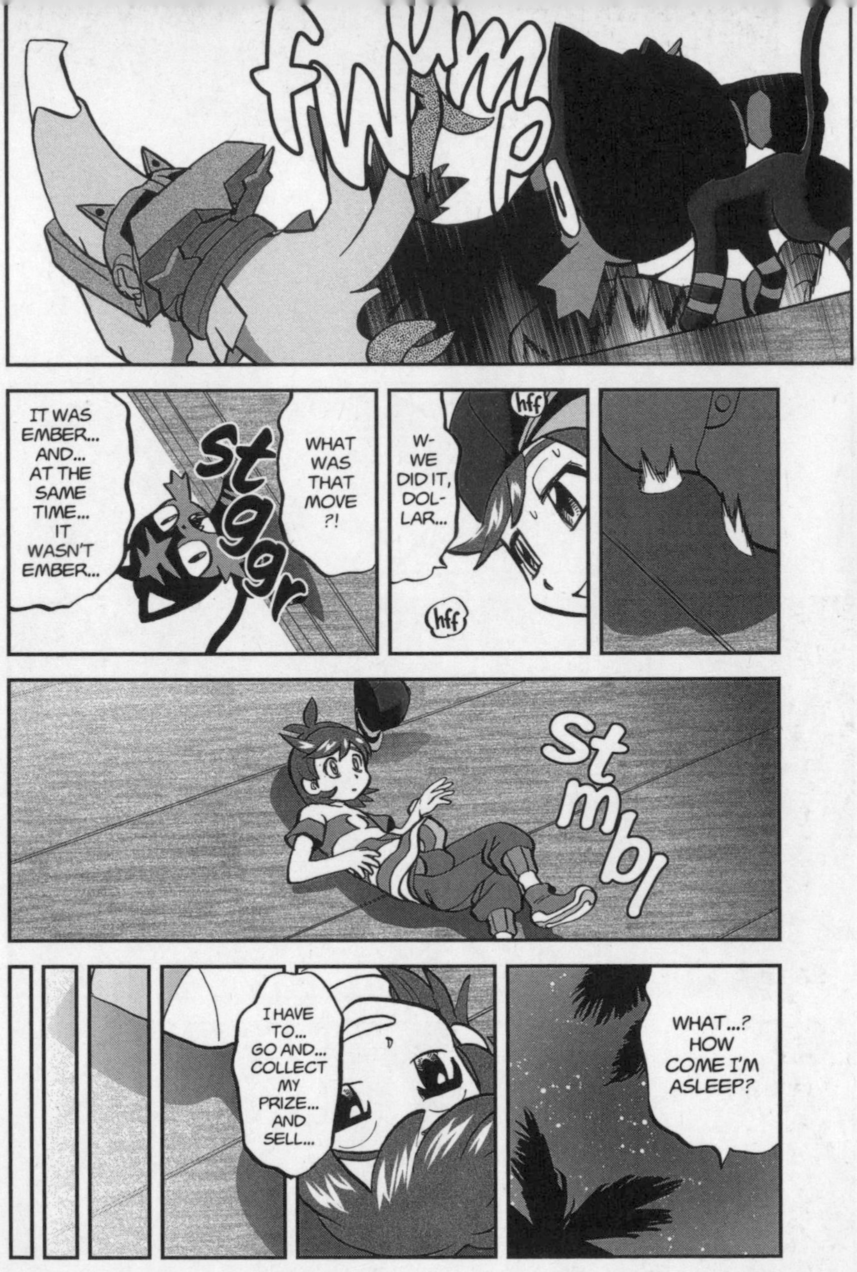
hff
W-WE DID IT, DOL-LAR...
hff
WHAT WAS THAT MOVE?!
IT WAS EMBER... AND... AT THE SAME TIME... IT WASN'T EMBER...
stggr
stmbl
WHAT...? HOW COME I'M ASLEEP?
I HAVE TO... GO AND... COLLECT MY PRIZE... AND SELL...

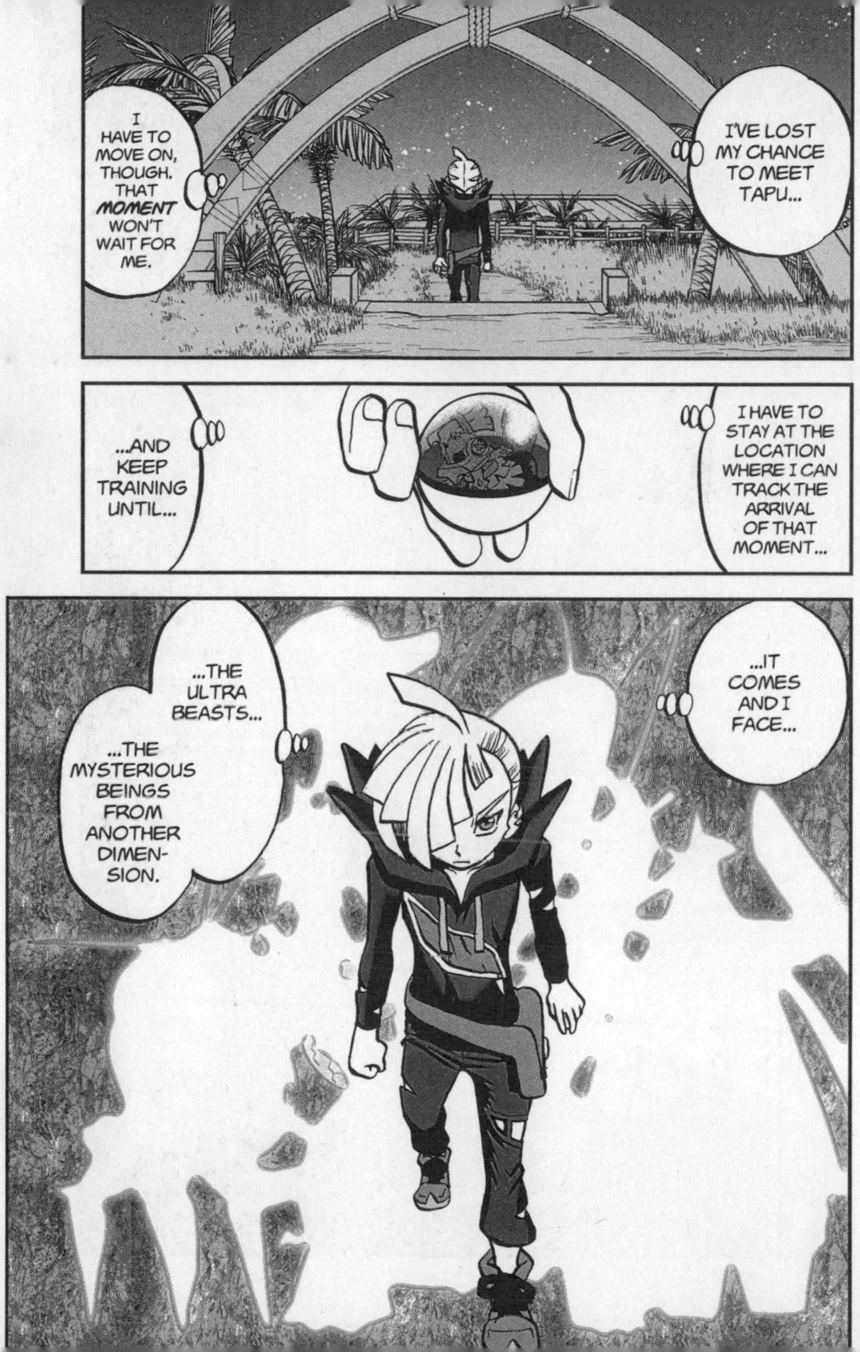
I'VE LOST MY CHANCE TO MEET TAPU...
I HAVE TO MOVE ON, THOUGH. THAT MOMENT WON'T WAIT FOR ME.
I HAVE TO STAY AT THE LOCATION WHERE I CAN TRACK THE ARRIVAL OF THAT MOMENT...
...AND KEEP TRAINING UNTIL...
...IT COMES AND I FACE...
...THE ULTRA BEASTS...
...THE MYSTERIOUS BEINGS FROM ANOTHER DIMEN-SION.

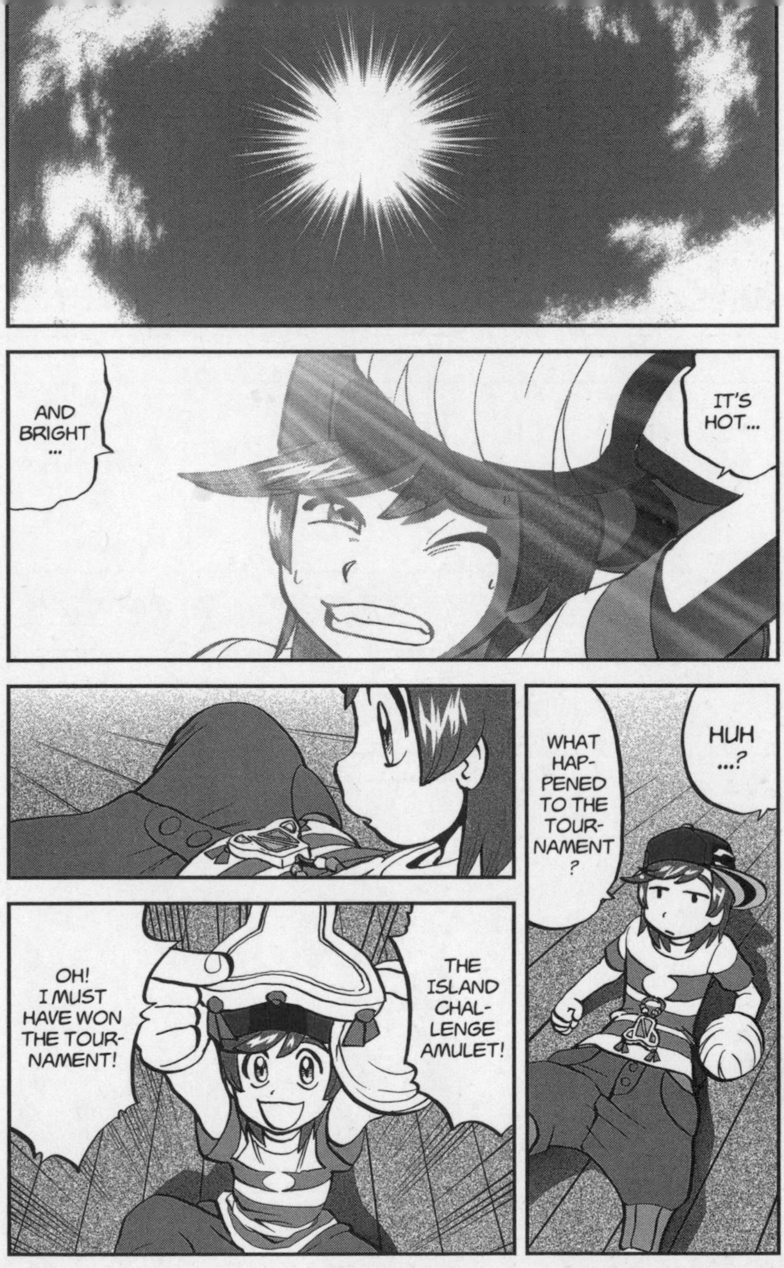
IT'S HOT...
AND BRIGHT...
HUH...?
WHAT HAPPENED TO THE TOURNAMENT?
THE ISLAND CHALLENGE AMULET!
OH! I MUST HAVE WON THE TOURNAMENT!

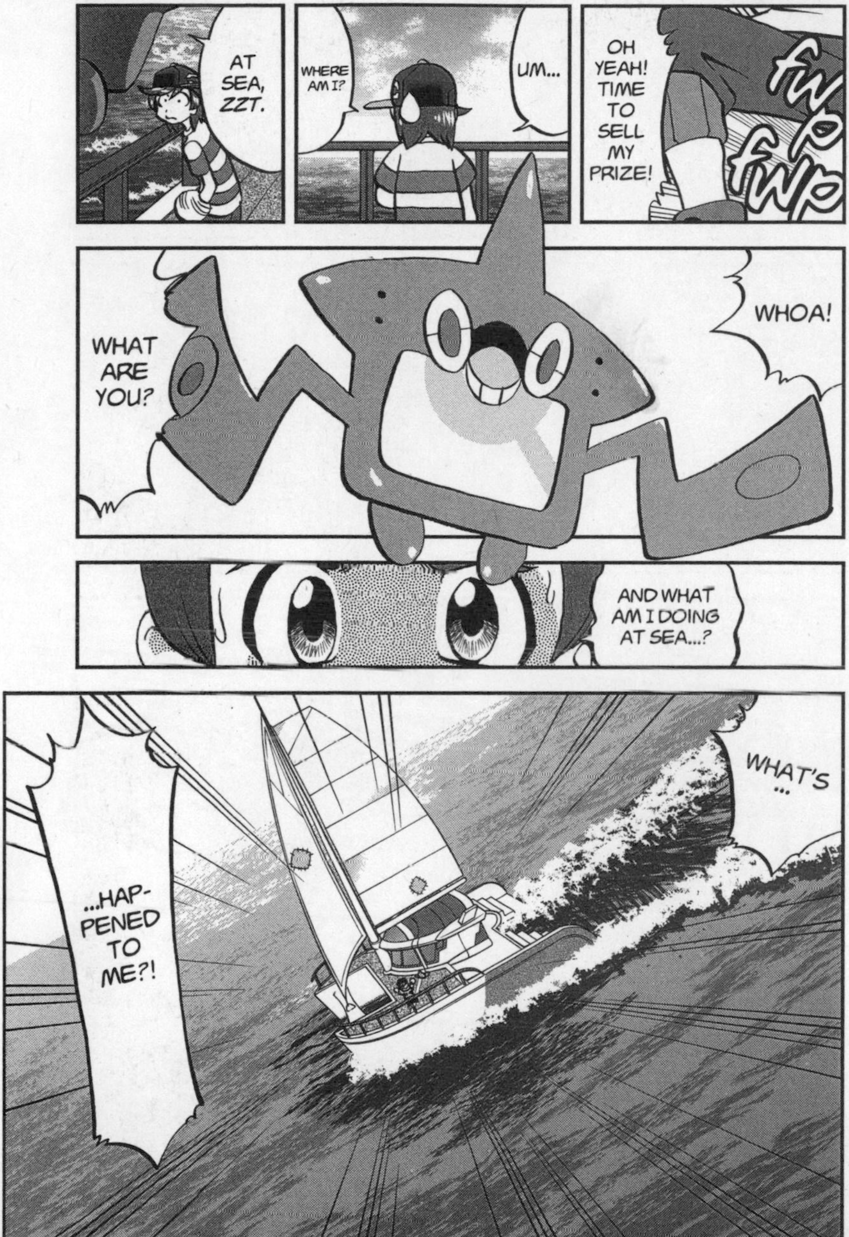
fwp fwp
OH YEAH! TIME TO SELL MY PRIZE!
UM...
WHERE AM I?
AT SEA, ZZT.
WHOA!
WHAT ARE YOU?
AND WHAT AM I DOING AT SEA...?
WHAT'S...
...HAP-PENED TO ME?!

Delivery Slip
SENDING ADDRESS
HAU'OLI CITY OUTSKIRTS
PROFESSOR KUKUI
NAME
RESEARCH LABORATORY
BEACH
Time of Delivery:
EARLY EVENING TODAY
8:00–10:00
10:00–12:00
12:00–14:00
14:00–16:00
16:00–18:00
18:00–20:00
ITEMS
GIRL, ROTOM
Breakable
Perishable
Fragile
Hazardous

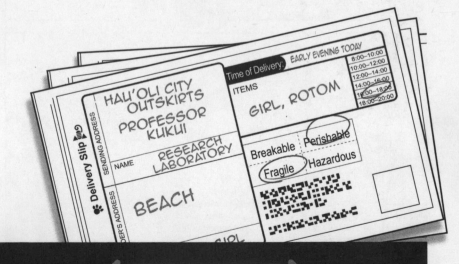

TO BE CONTINUED...

Coming Next Volume

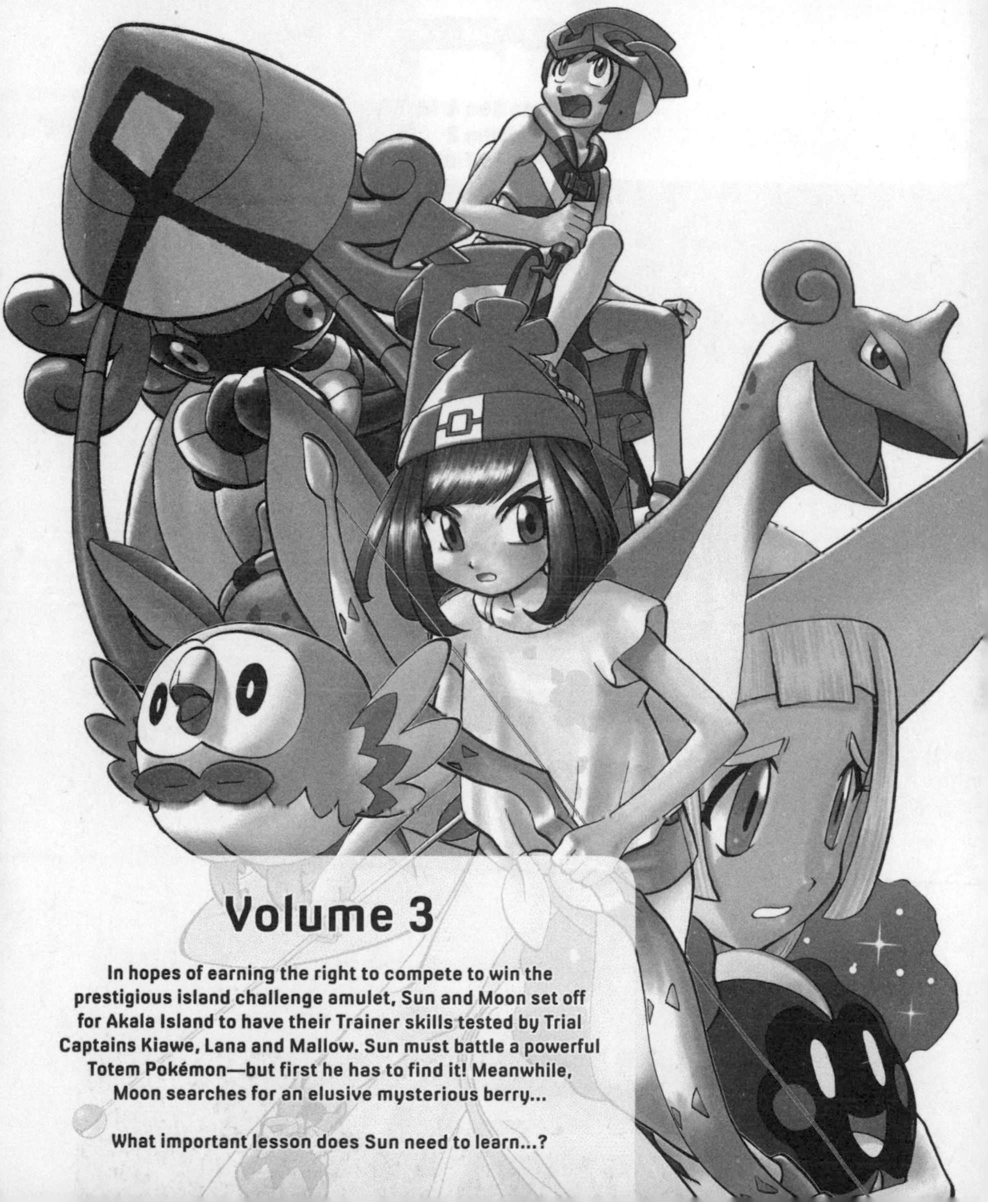

Volume 3

In hopes of earning the right to compete to win the prestigious island challenge amulet, Sun and Moon set off for Akala Island to have their Trainer skills tested by Trial Captains Kiawe, Lana and Mallow. Sun must battle a powerful Totem Pokémon—but first he has to find it! Meanwhile, Moon searches for an elusive mysterious berry...

What important lesson does Sun need to learn...?

...oon

...n

Story by HIDENORI KUSAKA
Art by SATOSHI YAMAMOTO

©2018 The Pokémon Company International.
©1995–2017 Nintendo / Creatures Inc. / GAME FREAK inc.
TM, ®, and character names are trademarks of Nintendo.
POCKET MONSTERS SPECIAL SUN • MOON Vol. 1
by Hidenori KUSAKA, Satoshi YAMAMOTO
© 2017 Hidenori KUSAKA, Satoshi YAMAMOTO
All rights reserved.
Original Japanese edition published by SHOGAKUKAN.
English translation rights in the United States of America, Canada, the United Kingdom,
Ireland, Australia and New Zealand arranged with SHOGAKUKAN.

English Adaptation—Bryant Turnage
Translation—Tetsuichiro Miyaki
Touch-Up & Lettering—Susan Daigle-Leach
Design—Alice Lewis
Editor—Annette Roman

Printed in the U.S.A.

Published by
VIZ Media, LLC
P.O. Box 77010
San Francisco, CA 94107

10 9 8 7 6 5 4 3 2 1
First printing, September 2018

viz.com

Begin your Pokémon Adventure here in the Kanto region!

POKÉMON
ADVENTURES
RED & BLUE BOX SET

Story by HIDENORI KUSAKA   Art by MATO

Includes **POKÉMON ADVENTURES** Vols. 1-7 and a collectible poster!

All your favorite Pokémon game characters jump out of the screen into the pages of this action-packed manga!

Red doesn't just want to train Pokémon, he wants to be their friend too. Bulbasaur and Poliwhirl seem game. But independent Pikachu won't be so easy to win over!

And watch out for Team Rocket, Red... They only want to be your enemy!

Start the adventure today!

VIZ media
www.viz.com

PERFECT SQUARE

RATED A ALL AGES
ratings.viz.com

Start the adventures in Kalos with Pokémon X•Y, Vol. 1!

STORY BY
Hidenori Kusaka

ART BY
Satoshi Yamamoto

As the new champion of the Pokémon Battle Junior Tournament in the Kalos region, X is hailed as a child prodigy. But when the media attention proves to be too much for him, he holes up in his room to hide from everyone—including his best friends. Then, his hometown of Vaniville Town is attacked by the two Legendary Pokémon Xerneas and Yveltal and a mysterious organization named Team Flare!

What will it take to get X to come out of hiding...?!

Only $4.99 US! ($5.99 in Canada)

***Available at your local comic
book shop or bookstore!***

ISBN: 978-1-4215-7980-1
Diamond Order Code: OCT141609

www.PerfectSquare.com   www.viz.com

Pokémon ADVENTURES™ HEARTGOLD & SOULSILVER

Story by HIDENORI KUSAKA
Art by SATOSHI YAMAMOTO

In this **two-volume** thriller, troublemaker Gold and feisty Silver must team up again to find their old enemy Lance and the Legendary Pokémon Arceus!

Available now!

www.viz.com

PERFECT SQUARE

The adventure continues in the Johto region!

POKÉMON™ ADVENTURES
GOLD & SILVER BOX SET

Includes POKÉMON ADVENTURES Vols. 8-14 and a collectible poster!

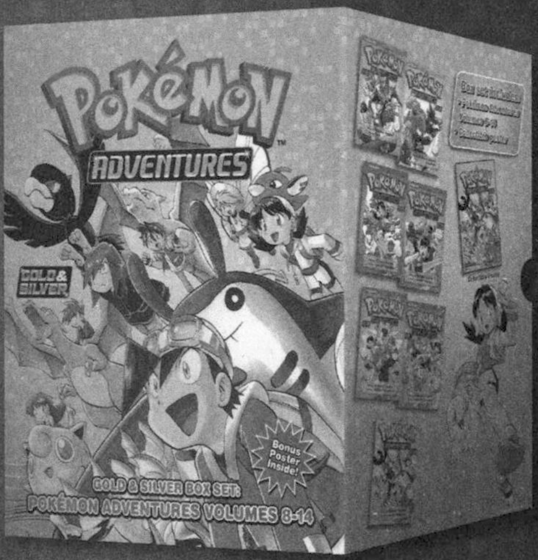

POKÉMON
ADVENTURES
GOLD & SILVER
Bonus Poster Inside!
GOLD & SILVER BOX SET:
POKÉMON ADVENTURES VOLUMES 8-14

Story by
HIDENORI KUSAKA

Art by
MATO,
SATOSHI YAMAMOTO

More exciting Pokémon adventures starring Gold and his rival Silver! First someone steals Gold's backpack full of Poké Balls (and Pokémon!). Then someone steals Prof. Elm's Totodile. Can Gold catch the thief—or thieves?!

Keep an eye on Team Rocket, Gold... Could they be behind this crime wave?

POCKET COMICS

STORY & ART BY SANTA HARUKAZE

BLACK & WHITE

LEGENDARY POKÉMON

X•Y

A Pokémon pocket-sized book chock-full of four-panel gags, Pokémon trivia and fun quizzes based on the characters you know and love!

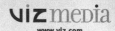

www.viz.com

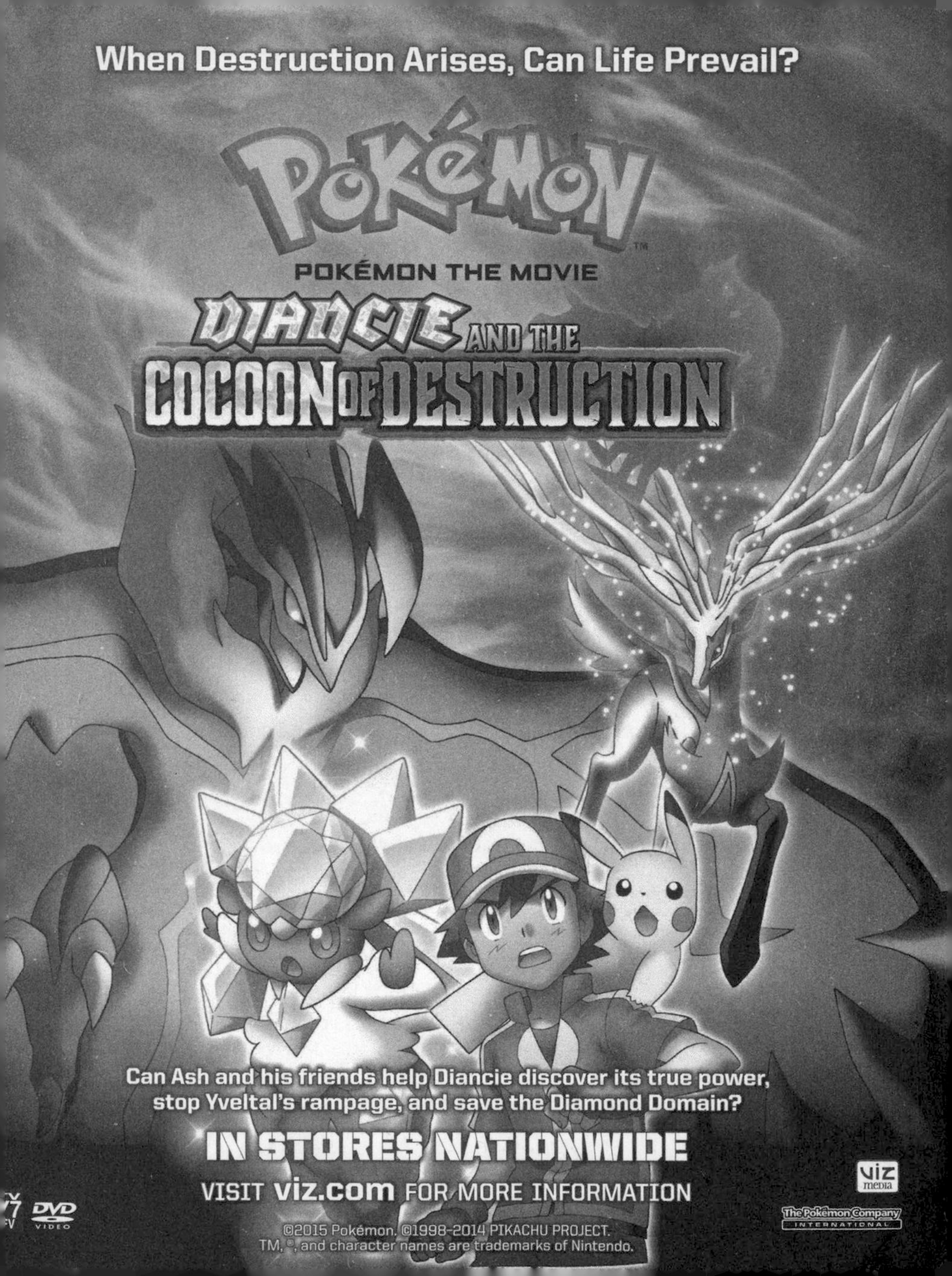

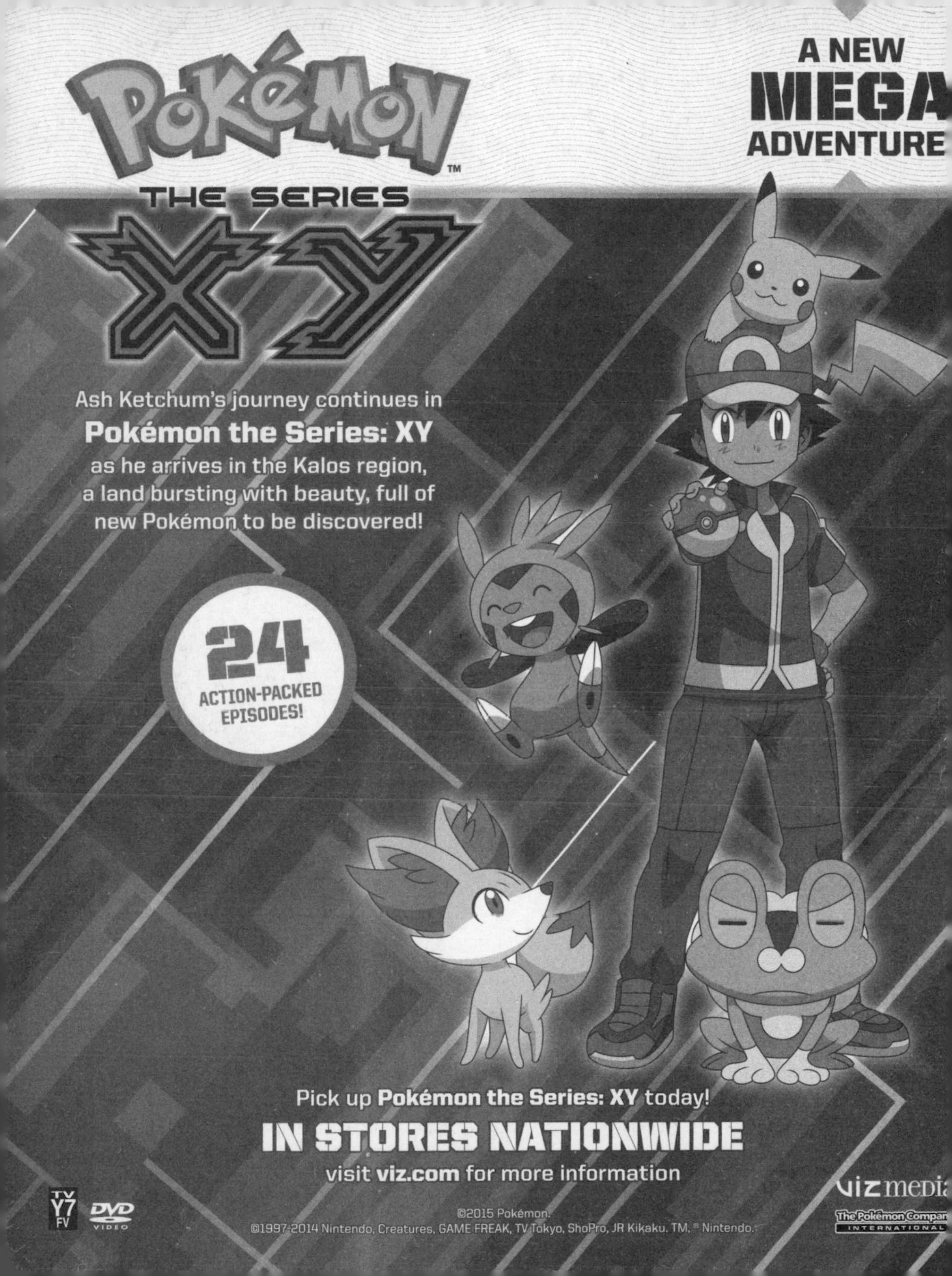
Pokémon™
THE SERIES
XY
A NEW
MEGA
ADVENTURE
Ash Ketchum's journey continues in
Pokémon the Series: XY
as he arrives in the Kalos region,
a land bursting with beauty, full of
new Pokémon to be discovered!
24
ACTION-PACKED
EPISODES!
Pick up Pokémon the Series: XY today!
IN STORES NATIONWIDE
visit viz.com for more information
TV Y7 FV
DVD VIDEO
©2015 Pokémon.
©1997-2014 Nintendo, Creatures, GAME FREAK, TV Tokyo, ShoPro, JR Kikaku. TM, ® Nintendo.
VIZ media
The Pokémon Company INTERNATIONAL

THIS IS THE END OF THIS GRAPHIC NOVEL!

To properly enjoy this VIZ Media graphic novel, please turn it around and begin reading from right to left.

This book has been printed in the original Japanese format in order to preserve the orientation of the original artwork. Have fun with it!

READ THIS WAY!

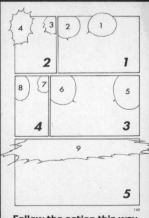

Follow the action this way.